Falling Star

By the same author

Wives and Mothers
The Long Way Home
Oranges and Lemons
This Year, Next Year
The Lost Daughters
Thursday's Child
Eve's Daughter
King's Walk
Pride of Peacocks
All That I Am
The Happy Highways
Summer Snow
Wishes and Dreams
The Wise Child
You'll Never Know. . .
Should I Forget You

Falling Star

Jeanne Whitmee

ROBERT HALE · LONDON

© Jeanne Whitmee 2010
First published in Great Britain 2010

ISBN 978-0-7090-9027-4

Robert Hale Limited
Clerkenwell House
Clerkenwell Green
London EC1R 0HT

www.halebooks.com

2 4 6 8 10 9 7 5 3 1

Typeset in 10/14pt Palatino
by Derek Doyle & Associates, Shaw Heath
Printed in Great Britain by the MPG Books Group, Bodmin and King's Lynn

CHAPTER ONE

'Are you really saying that this will be the very last time you'll be coming to Wycombe Heath?'

Sylvia looked so crestfallen that Juliet almost laughed. 'I only meant I wouldn't be staying here at the cottage,' she said. 'We'll still keep in touch, and I'll write. I promise. And of course I'll be back for Aunty Marion's wedding.'

'Of course, the wedding.' Sylvia looked relieved. 'I was forgetting.'

The girls were sitting in their favourite place, under the apple trees at the end of the garden where the ground sloped steeply away from the cottage to join the rolling heath beyond. Juliet shaded her eyes from the late August afternoon sunlight and drank in the view.

'I'm going to miss staying at the cottage and all this, 'specially at this time of year. Purple heather as far as you can see with just a thin ribbon of sparkling sea on the horizon.' She looked up at the cloudless sky. 'And the skylarks singing their hearts out – up and up till they're just a tiny speck.' She looked at her friend. 'Do you think it's true that they fly right up out of the atmosphere?'

Sylvia pulled out a stalk of grass and sucked moodily at the juicy stem. 'I'd have thought they'd have more sense,' she said. 'So where will you live when your Aunt Marion gets married and goes off to Canada?'

Juliet sighed. 'In London I suppose. Dad and Olivia have taken a flat in Edgware. It'll be a far cry from all this.'

'And the cottage will be sold?'

'I expect so. Granny left it to Aunty Marion so it's hers to do as she likes with.'

Sylvia sighed and threw away her stalk of grass. 'Well, I think it's a rotten shame,' she said. 'We were all so happy. I've looked forward so much to seeing you every holiday when you came home from school and I imagined you'd live here permanently once you'd left and the war was over. I imagined us going off to work together on the bus every morning and having so much fun at weekends. Oh, why do things have to end like this?'

'I know.' Juliet slipped an arm around her friend's shoulders and gave her a brief squeeze. 'It's what I always hoped for too, but I can't grudge Aunty Marion her chance of happiness, can I? She's had years of looking after people, first Granny and then me. It's lovely that she's met a nice man and is going to have an exciting new life in Canada.'

Marion Hunt, Juliet's aunt had been widowed at the age of twenty-three after only two years of marriage when her young husband died in a motor-bike accident. Since then she'd returned to nursing, the profession she trained for, later moving in with her widowed mother and helping to bring up her brother's only child. Juliet adored her. Marion had created a secure environment for her motherless niece and Juliet was trying hard not to think of what life would be like without her.

'What's he like, the fabulous Wing Commander Elliot Hamlin?' Sylvia asked.

'Tall and handsome, 'specially in his air force uniform. Just your type,' Juliet laughed. 'He's a lot like that new film star you're so potty about – what's his name?'

'Stewart Granger?' Sylvia looked at her with round eyes. 'You've got to be kidding. Go on, is he really?'

'Yes, honestly – a bit older of course. You'll see when you meet him at the wedding.'

'Wow! I can hardly wait. But if he's as gorgeous as that why isn't he already married?'

'He was,' Juliet told her. 'His situation is a bit like Aunty Marion's; his wife died when they'd only been married a few years. Till he met Marion he never looked at anyone else.'

'And they met at the VE celebrations last May?'

'That's right,' Juliet told her. 'At the big dance at the town hall. Aunty Marion was helping with the refreshments. He told her it was love at first sight. He hung around the refreshment bar all evening.' She laughed. 'She says she couldn't imagine how he could find room for so many Spam sandwiches!'

'Oh – how romantic.' Sylvia sighed and threw herself onto her back in the long grass. 'And now that the war is properly over all the Canadians will be going home, I suppose.'

'Yes, that's why they're getting married next month, so that she can go with him.'

Sylvia sighed. 'A whirlwind romance! I bet nothing that exciting ever happens to me.'

'You never know. It might.' Juliet contemplated her friend for a few moments. 'You know, sometimes I wonder if you know how lucky you are, Sylvie,' she said.

The other girl opened one eye. '*Me* – lucky?'

'Yes. You've got a mum and dad who love you and a nice home where you all live together. You've never had to go away to school and you've never been parted from your family for months on end like me. You have no idea how much I envy you that normal life.'

Sylvia grunted 'Huh! Can't see why. Normal's boring. And you forgot the horrible little brother.'

'No I didn't. I've always wanted a brother or sister.'

'Well, you can have mine. Believe me you'd soon change your mind.'

'My mother walked out on me when I was little,' Juliet said. 'I hardly ever saw Dad as a kid. He was always away on tour somewhere or other. Granny and Aunty Marion are the only family I've ever known. I really missed them when Dad insisted on sending me away to school. And now Granny's gone and Aunty Marion is going off to live on the other side of the world.'

'But you'll be going to live with your dad. Isn't that what you always wanted?'

'You're forgetting Olivia, his horrible girlfriend,' Juliet reminded her 'She's always resented me.'

'At least your dad hasn't actually married her.'

'He can't,' Juliet told her. 'He and my mother never actually divorced. At least she can't be my wicked stepmother. Anyway, once they get more work they'll be off on tour again. Then I'll have to fend for myself.'

'Won't you go with them like you did when they were in ENSA?'

Juliet shook her head. 'I had enough of trailing after them during the war,' she said. 'It might've sounded like fun but it wasn't. Living in draughty billets or hostels in all sorts of far away places; trying to think of things to fill the time while they were working. I couldn't wait to get back here to Wycombe most of the time. Now that I've left school I'll have to find a job.'

'It's funny, you've never said what you want to do. I suppose I've always taken it for granted that you'll follow your dad's footsteps and go into the theatre.'

'The theatre – *me*?' Juliet blew out her cheeks. 'Not on your life! I've seen enough of that life. I've always loved writing and people and I was good at English at school. I want to be a journalist. I might try some of the London newspapers – see if they'll take me on as a trainee.'

Sylvia looked at her friend wistfully. 'I think you're so brave, Ju.' She pulled at the wiry grass. 'The trouble with having a normal middle-class upbringing is that it stifles ambition, but you – you're so adventurous. You stayed on at school in the sixth and did that secretarial training. Look at me; left school after School Cert' to work in a boring solicitor's office, thumping a typewriter all day. I'd never dare do what you're planning. I mean, where are you going to live once your dad has gone off on tour?'

Juliet shrugged. 'There are plenty of hostels for single girls in London. I'll find something.'

'There, see what I mean? I'd never get up the nerve to break away and do things like that. I'd be haring off home to Mum and it's all because of the tight little world I've grown up in.'

Juliet smiled wryly. 'Don't knock it.'

Sylvia looked at her watch. 'Speaking of which, look at the time. Mum will have tea on the table and I'll be in the dog house if I'm late.' She scrambled to her feet and brushed the loose grass seeds from her skirt. 'Hide-bound by convention, that's me.'

'Never!' Juliet laughed and got to her feet. Together the girls walked up the steps of the terraced garden and along the side of the cottage to the front gate where Juliet let her friend out to walk the few yards to the house where she lived, just as she had done hundreds of times before, ever since they first met and played together as children.

Sylvia looked at her. 'You will remember to write, won't you? We won't just let our friendship slide?'

'Of course we won't.'

Sylvia brightened. 'Bye then. Have a good journey tomorrow. See you at the wedding.'

Walking back up the front path Juliet thought about what her friend had said earlier. Although there was hardly any difference in their ages she was aware that the kind of start she'd had in life had made her grow up quickly. She had been brought up first by her grandmother and then by her aunt until the war broke out when she was sent to a boarding school on the Isle of Wight. The holidays were spent with her actor father, Marcus King, wherever he happened to be performing with ENSA, the remainder here at Heathlands Cottage with Aunt Marion. Sylvia on the other hand had grown up in the comfort and security of her own home, attending the local day school. The furthest she had travelled was into Warnecliffe on the bus to attend the girls' high school after she turned eleven. Since she was seventeen she'd been working as a typist and taking a secretarial course at night school, hoping to become a secretary one day.

'In a couple of years she'll marry some nice local lad and start a family,' Juliet told herself as she let herself in through the back door.

'Who will?' Aunt Marion looked up from laying the table for supper.

Juliet smiled, suddenly aware that she had spoken out loud. 'Sylvia. Sorry, I was talking to myself.' She took two cups and saucers from the dresser and set them out on the gingham cloth; another of the routine things which reminded her painfully that this visit to Heathlands Cottage would probably be her last.

She watched her aunt busily slicing and buttering bread. Marion looked much younger than her thirty-five years. She was still slender and wore her shoulder length fair hair tied back in a casual girlish style. At this time of year her fair complexion was always touched with a golden glow from a summer spent caring for her beloved garden. And it hadn't escaped Julia's notice that since Wing Commander Hamlin had arrived to transform Marion's life her violet blue eyes had developed an extra sparkle.

Feeling her niece's gaze on her Marion looked up. 'Are you all right darling?' she asked. 'You're looking, and sounding, a bit wistful.'

'I can't believe I'll be leaving the cottage tomorrow for the very last time.' Juliet swallowed hard at the lump in her throat. 'Coming here – staying with you, it's been such a big part of my life. Something I've always looked forward to.' She bit her lip. 'Oh, I'm sorry. I don't mean to spoil it for you. I'm really happy for you and I like Elliot very much. It's just that I'm going to miss you terribly.'

'You'll be back for the wedding,' Marion reminded her. 'At least, you'd better be, considering you're to be my only bridesmaid. And, of course, you'll be coming over for a visit once we're settled.'

'That'd be lovely and I'm really looking forward to being your bridesmaid.' Juliet looked around the homely kitchen. 'I just can't imagine anyone else living here though. It's been our home for as long as I can remember.'

Marion smiled and reached out to touch her hand. 'I know it has love.' She pushed the bowl of salad towards her niece. 'Come on, eat up. I thought we'd go for a walk on the heath afterwards. I've got something rather special I want to talk to you about before you leave tomorrow.'

Juliet helped herself to salad. 'Something special – what is it?'

Marion smiled. 'Wait and see. I thought it might be nice to call in on the Lees as it's your last evening and see how Imelda's new baby is.'

The Lees were an extended gypsy family who lived in a settlement on the heath. Their colourful caravans and the little group of tethered piebald ponies could be seen from the garden at Heathlands. They had been a permanent part of the view for as long at Juliet could remember. In summer they would take off for weeks at a time, to Lincolnshire and Norfolk for the soft fruit picking, later to Kent for the hop gathering and apple season, but they always returned to their permanent campsite at Wycombe Heath.

Although they were true Romany some of the village people were wary of them but Marion had always respected them. When one of the Lee children had been ill with bronchitis and Celina, his mother had refused to allow him to be taken to hospital she had managed to persuade Celina to take advantage of her nursing experience to help nurse him back to health. Ever since then she had been welcomed at the gypsy encampment as a trusted friend.

'Imelda had her baby then?' Juliet asked.

Marion smiled. 'Yes. She's three months old now; a lovely little girl with the biggest brown eyes you ever saw. Danny is besotted with his new daughter. They're going to call her Clover.'

'Did you assist at the birth?'

'Oh no.' Marion shook her head. 'They have their own ways. I'd never intrude unless I was asked.'

They washed up the tea things together in silence then fetched cardigans against the cool evening air and walked down the garden and though the gate onto the heath, walking single file along the narrow gritty pathway towards the cluster of brightly coloured caravans. As they approached Marion handed Juliet a shiny new sixpenny piece. 'That's for you to give the baby,' she said. 'Put it somewhere safe.'

'What's this "something special" you want to talk to me about?' Juliet asked, pausing to pick herself a sprig of heather.

'Later.'

'No, now!' Juliet took a stubborn stance, her feet apart and her hands on her hips. 'I won't take another step until you tell me.'

Marion laughed. 'Patience never was your strong suit. All right, it's this. When I go to Canada with Elliot I want you to have the cottage.'

Juliet stared at her aunt, her cheeks pink with surprise. 'What – Heathlands – *me*?'

Marion nodded. 'It's the only home you've ever known and it's only right that you should have it. I know it's what your granny would have wanted. I'll have it signed over legally to you before I go. I'm not sure about your age and whether you'll be allowed to hold the deeds yet. You might have to wait till you're twenty-one before the Land Registry will agree, but that's only a couple of years away. It'll all be done properly before we leave so don't fret.'

Stunned, Juliet stared at her. 'But . . . it's yours,' she argued. 'It must be worth a lot of money.'

'I've talked to Elliot about it and he agrees wholeheartedly with me,' Marion assured her. 'Elliot is a lawyer. There's a job waiting for him at home in Toronto – in his father's practice. He's only waiting for Elliot to come home and take over so that he can retire. We shan't need the money, so don't worry on that score.' Marion reached out and hugged her niece. 'It's yours, darling. Please accept it. It's the one way I can leave you with a clear conscience.'

Juliet swallowed hard. 'Oh, Aunty Marion, I don't know what to say – and you don't have to have a *conscience* about leaving. I think it's wonderful that you're marrying Elliot.'

Marion laughed. 'Right. That's settled then.'

Imelda Lee sat on the steps of her spotless caravan, her dark-eyed baby gurgling happily in her lap, whilst her two-year-old son played at the bottom of the steps. She smiled and stood up when she saw Marion and Juliet approaching.

'You'll take a sup of tea, Mrs Hunt?'

'No, thank you, Imelda, we've just had tea,' Marion said. 'I wanted Juliet to see Clover.'

The gypsy girl stepped down and laid the baby in Juliet's arms. 'Here, you hold her,' she said. 'Good practice for when you have your own.'

Juliet knew that the girl was a year younger than she was herself and yet already had two children. Her husband, Danny, wasn't even old enough to be called up for National Service yet. The tiny child felt warm and wriggly in her arms and the huge dark eyes looked up into hers solemnly, then the little face crumpled and the baby began to cry. Juliet looked up at Imelda.

'Oh dear, she doesn't like me,' she said.

'You have to put the sixpence into her hand,' Marion prompted in a whisper. 'It's traditional – for luck.'

Juliet fumbled in her pocket for the sixpence and put it into the little hand. The tiny fingers closed around it in a tight grip. Imelda and Marion laughed.

'She already knows to hold on tight to money,' Marion said. 'She'll make a good housewife.'

'We might have to move on soon,' Imelda remarked, her brown eyes clouding.

Marion looked up in concern. 'But you've been here for so long, who is saying you have to go?'

'No one,' Imelda shook her head. 'But because we've been here so long the council think we should give up our vardas and live in houses like the other village folk,' she explained. 'They've even offered to build them and rent them to us.'

'But that's not what you want?'

Imelda shook her head. 'We like it here,' she said. 'Danny and me, we was both born here on this heath, but we couldn't live in no bricks and mortar houses. We need to be able to go where the work is. I fear we'll have to move on.'

'I'm moving on too,' Marion told her.

Imelda's eyes widened. 'Where're you goin', Mrs Hunt?'

'I'm to be married to a Canadian airman. I'll be going home with him to Canada. I'd have liked to picture all of you still here,' Marion said wistfully.

'Me an' all.' Imelda took her baby daughter back and sat down again, unbuttoning the front of her dress to feed her baby. 'Me and Danny and all of us. It's real sad.'

As they walked back across the heath, the sky pink and golden with the setting sun Juliet said suddenly, 'How can the local council be so mean, and so ignorant? Don't they know that gypsies can't be shut up in houses? I wish there was something we could do to help.' She paused. 'Dad's a bit like a gypsy, isn't he? The same roving life, no nine-to-five job or real stability – moving from place to place.' She looked at her aunt. 'Do you think he'll ever want to change – stay in one place and do something different?'

Marion smiled wryly at her niece. 'I wouldn't take any bets on it, my love.'

In bed that night Juliet thought long and hard about Marion's suggestion that she should take over the cottage. True, it would be hers outright, but she would still have the running of it and now that she thought about it she wondered how she would manage without an income. It would be wonderful to own the only home she had ever known – a really grown-up thing, to be a home owner. But it would bring big responsibilities with it. She had inherited a small legacy from her grandmother, but the money was in trust for her until she reached the age of twenty-one. She would have to find a way to earn some money – and quickly. She wondered hopefully if Dad could be persuaded to come and share it with her, maybe give up the stage and get some other kind of work. But she quickly dismissed the idea as a non-starter. Olivia would never agree to what she would see as being 'buried in the sticks' and since they had been together Dad always did what Olivia wanted. Then there was her dream of training to be a journalist. She couldn't live here and work in London. As she finally fell asleep the idea of being a property owner suddenly seemed rather daunting.

The following morning at breakfast she voiced these worries to Marion.

'I did think of all that when I first had the idea,' her aunt said. 'I didn't make the decision lightly. Warnecliff is only four miles away and it's on a regular bus route. Before the war it was one of the country's most popular seaside resorts and now, with the beach defences being cleared, the hotels gearing up for a new start, the town will definitely come to life again by next summer. There are three bedrooms here at Heathlands Cottage. If you don't want to live here yourself, or you get a job in London you could easily let it, either permanently or as holiday accommodation. It would help pay for your overheads and provide you with a regular income.'

Early next morning Marion and Juliet caught the bus to Warnecliff Station. As the London train steamed into the platform Marion hugged her niece.

'Ring and let me know when you get there,' she said. 'And don't forget to try and get Marcus to come to the wedding. I know it's only to be a quiet affair but I would like my only brother to give me away.'

'I'm sure he'll come if he can,' Juliet said. Inwardly, she told herself it would all depend on whether he had the chance of an audition on that day, but she didn't say so.

'Olivia, too, of course,' Marion added, as Juliet climbed onto the train. 'Make sure she knows she's welcome too.'

'I will.' Juliet waved from the window as the train moved out. She pictured Olivia's beautiful, bitchy face and the grimace it would assume when she received her invitation to Marion's wedding. Juliet doubted very much whether she would attend. Someone else would be the centre of attention for the day and that would not suit Olivia at all. Anyway, it would be far too low-key for her. The trouble was that if Olivia turned the invitation down Marcus probably wouldn't come either. Juliet sighed, wondering why her father, who was older than

Olivia by twelve years, allowed himself to be led by the nose by such a demanding woman. Could it be that he was afraid of her? Or did having a beautiful younger woman on his arm make him feel younger? Juliet felt she had a lot to learn about men, especially her own father.

CHAPTER TWO

Juliet hadn't been expecting luxury but when she arrived at the address Marcus had sent her and looked up at the grimy windows her spirits plummeted.

She had taken the tube to Edgware and followed Marcus's directions. The flat was over a greengrocer's shop located in a busy street of shops. Entry was by way of a peeling door at the side of the shop which led to a dusty staircase. Juliet climbed the stairs and rang the bell. After a moment or two her father answered the door. He was still in his dressing-gown.

'*Juliet!*' He held out his arms. 'Darling! I wasn't expecting you till this afternoon.' He hugged her and she winced as his unshaven jaw grated her cheek.

'Dad! I did tell you I'd be here this morning.'

'Did you? Well, you know what I'm like – head like a sieve.' He held his daughter at arms' length and smiled at her. 'Important thing is, you're here. It's terrific to see you. You look wonderful; so *well*! All that Dorset sea air and sunshine, I expect. How's Marion?'

'She's blooming; looking forward to the wedding.'

'No doubt. No doubt. Come through to the kitchen, angel, and I'll make you some coffee. Sorry Libby's not here. She had to rush off to an audition.'

The window of the cramped little kitchen looked out onto a landscape of rooftops and chimney pots. Marcus busied himself pushing aside what looked like several days of washing up to ease the kettle under the tap. Once a strikingly handsome man he was now in

15

his mid-forties and Juliet noticed with a pull at her heart strings that his once abundant fair wavy hair was now thinning and more grey than blond. There was even a tell-tale balding patch at the crown. His blue eyes were puffy and bloodshot and, together with the stubble on his face, gave him an overall raddled appearance.

'Dad, are you OK?' she asked.

He turned. '*Me*? A-one, darling, as always. Just not looking my loveliest this morning. Bit of a do down at the local last night – too many ginger beers if you get my meaning.' He sat down at the table and fumbled in his dressing-gown pocket for cigarettes and lighter. As he lit one he caught Juliet's look of disapproval. 'Just this once poppet,' he said with a rueful grin. 'It's a bit nerve-racking, this "resting" business. You know I never touch the damned things once I'm working. Think more of the old larynx.'

Marcus had a rich, velvety voice, cultivated by his training at the Old Vic and his early Shakespearean experience.

'I should hope so,' Juliet remarked. 'Anything in the offing for you?'

Marcus drew hard on his cigarette and blew out a cloud of smoke. 'Not a bloody sausage, darling.' He eyed her speculatively. 'Actually Libby and I are thinking of starting up our own company.'

'That sounds exciting.'

'Mmm.' Marcus pulled down the corners of his mouth and flicked his cigarette ash onto the floor. 'There's this little theatre up in the Midlands – an industrial town called Rushfield. It's owned by a syndicate of local big-wigs and they want to sell it as a going concern. It's a real little gold mine for someone with the cash. Unfortunately banks don't lend the likes of us money for that kind of venture. They seem to think it's too dicey.'

'Oh, hard luck.'

'Yes.' He paused, looking at Juliet. 'Still, never know, maybe there'll be some film work soon. Libby knows this chap at Pinewood.' He patted his stomach. 'Just need to lose the odd pound or two and let a good hairdresser loose on the old thatch.' Again he flicked his ash onto the floor.

'Dad! Don't do that,' Juliet said. 'And just look at the state of this place. Are you supposed to be tidying up this morning?'

Marcus looked surprised. 'Not really. Libby's not what you'd call the domestic type and you know me, darling. We wash up when we run out of plates. Seems to work.'

The kettle boiled and Juliet got up to make coffee. She opened the window to let out the smoke, but the odour of rotting vegetables rising up from the back yard of the greengrocers made her close it again quickly. 'I'll have a tidy round for you when we've drunk this if you like,' she said, looking pointedly at her father as she passed him the mug of coffee. 'While you have a bath and shave.'

By the time Marcus emerged from the bathroom looking refreshed, Juliet had washed up and put away the mountain of dishes and washed the dingy linoleum on the floor. Marcus stopped in the doorway, throwing up his hands theatrically.

'My God! Have I stepped into a parallel universe? Darling, you've worked wonders.' He stared at the floor. 'Heavens. I never realized there was actually a pattern on this lino.'

'I'm not surprised.' Juliet rolled down her sleeves. 'I've only done what you're supposed to do every day.' Inwardly she labelled Olivia a lazy slut. 'I'm just surprised you haven't gone down with food poisoning.'

She was pleased to see that her father looked much better for his bath and shave. It was clear that he was losing his matinee-idol looks but he was still a good looking man. He'd been right when he said he needed to lose weight. His stomach muscles, once so taut and firm now hung over the waistband of his trousers. Juliet prodded them.

'I bet you've been living on fish and chips,' she said. 'And I'd hazard a guess that you don't have enough green vegetables, or fruit.'

He groaned, putting a hand to his head dramatically. 'Lord save me from preaching women,' he said. 'It's clear to see that you've been brought up by my mother and sister. Anyway, it's all very well on carrot-crunching-cloud-nine Dorset. Up here those things are at a premium.'

'Don't believe you. You're living over a greengrocer's shop for heaven's sake! It's a good job I didn't have to rely on you to teach me about dietary requirements and domestic hygiene.' She looked round. 'Dad, where do I sleep? I'd like to unpack and freshen up.'

'Ah . . .' Marcus sighed. 'Darling, I'm so sorry but there's only one bedroom here so it'll have to be the couch.'

17

Juliet's heart sank. 'Oh – I see.'

'It's not for long. I mean we're on the lookout for a better place. Trouble is we're a bit financially embarrassed at the moment. You know . . .'

'Broke, you mean?'

Marcus spread his hands. 'Couldn't have put it better myself.' He assumed the hang-dog expression she knew so well. 'I wasn't going to broach the subject this soon, but I suppose you wouldn't like to make an investment in your old dad, would you, sweetie? It's a downright tragedy that we can't afford that theatre in Rushfield. Libby and I are just what it needs. I guarantee we'd make a sure fire success of it. They already play to full houses most nights of the week. You wouldn't be out of pocket. In fact you'd probably make a huge killing.'

'Dad! What makes you think I've got that kind of money?'

His eyebrows rose. 'What about what your grandmother left you?'

'It's in trust, Dad – till I'm twenty-one. I'm in London to look for work myself,' Juliet said. 'I only left school in July, remember?'

He rolled his eyes. 'Nice to have had the opportunity to stay on at school till your age.'

Juliet bit back the remark that it was only thanks to her grandmother that she'd been able to benefit from a good formal education. 'What about what Granny left you?' she ventured.

Marcus sighed and spread his hands. 'All gone I'm afraid.'

'*All* of it?'

'An actor has to keep up appearances,' Marcus said defensively. 'And I haven't worked since we left ENSA, neither has Libby. We have to be here in London at the heart of things and living up here isn't cheap.'

'Mmm.' Juliet looked around her. 'I can imagine.'

He frowned. 'It's all right for you, looking down your nose at where we're living. There's Marion with a delightful cottage near the sea to cash in on when she's already got a wealthy Canadian fiancé in tow. All I got was a few measly hundred.'

Juliet knew exactly how much her father had inherited and she guessed that Olivia had been more than happy to help him spend it. She wondered apprehensively what they would say when they knew that the cottage was to be hers. She moistened her lips. 'Dad . . .' she began.

The flat door banged shut and Marcus ran a hand through his hair. 'That'll be Libby. Better put the kettle on again.'

The kitchen door opened and Olivia stood framed in the doorway. She was undeniably attractive with her raven black hair and golden eyes, but her luscious scarlet lips could turn from smiling and flirting coquettishly to twisting into a cold sneer at the drop of a hat. She looked unsmilingly at Juliet.

'You've arrived then.'

'Doesn't she look well?' Marcus gushed. 'And just look what she's done to the kitchen.'

Olivia looked around her. 'The kitchen? What has she done to the kitchen?'

'Washed up and cleaned the floor. It smells so fresh and clean. Isn't she a clever sausage?'

Olivia took off the silver fox fur she was wearing and threw it carelessly over the back of a chair. 'Did anyone ask you to skivvy for us?' she asked, raising one perfectly arched eyebrow.

'No. I just thought—'

'If you think our flat isn't clean enough, darling, you can always find somewhere else to stay. There isn't really room here anyway. I'm sure you're going to be fiendishly uncomfortable on that lumpy sofa.'

'Of course she won't!' Marcus forced a laugh and quickly passed her a mug of coffee. 'How did it go, sweetheart?' he asked. 'Any luck?'

'They're letting me know,' Olivia said, sipping the coffee. 'Is there any hot water? I feel like a long hot soak.'

Marcus looked sheepish. 'Oh, I think I might have used it all.'

Olivia sighed deeply and got up abruptly from the table. 'I might have known. I seem to come last around here.' She glared at Juliet. 'I'm going to lie down. I've got a thumping headache.' She picked up her fur and whisked out of the kitchen leaving Juliet and her father looking at each other helplessly.

'It was me who suggested you had a bath,' Juliet said guiltily.

'And I was late rousing myself,' Marcus returned. 'Not your fault. I always seem to be in the wrong nowadays.' He sat down at the table looking depressed. 'I'm sorry I asked you about the money, sweetheart. It was rotten of me. It's all this waiting for work to come up,' he said. 'It's tearing our nerves to shreds.'

'What can I do to help?' Juliet asked. 'I know, I'll go out and find something nice for lunch and I'll come back and cook it. Maybe I can find a nice fish shop – something that's off-ration. Can you peel some potatoes and lay the table?'

Marcus brightened. 'I thought you said we shouldn't have too much fish and chips.'

'But these won't be fried,' Juliet told him.

She managed to get three whole plaice and she bought fresh vegetables and fruit at the shop below the flat. When Olivia emerged wearing an expensive-looking negligée the table was laid and the food was cooked, the plaice steamed with a tasty sauce, the potatoes creamed and the runner beans thinly sliced. In the centre of the table stood a bowl of shiny red apples and a little posy of dahlias in a tiny vase that Juliet had found in the cupboard under the sink. Olivia sniffed, her elegant nose wrinkling.

'Oh my God, *fish*! If there's one thing I can't *stand* it's the smell of fish. It'll hang about for days.'

'But you like the taste of it, my love, don't you?' Marcus said, already seated at the table, knife and fork at the ready. 'Ju has done us proud so sit down and tuck in. It'll do your headache the world of good.'

In spite of herself Olivia managed to do justice to Juliet's meal and even peeled and ate an apple afterwards.

'I hope you'll both be able to come to Marion's wedding,' Juliet said. 'She wants you to give her away, Dad. It's on 4 October at St Marks.'

'I'll be there, you bet,' Marcus said.

'Well, you can count me out,' Olivia said, taking a cigarette from the little mother-of-pearl case she carried them in. 'I hope to be working.'

'You don't know that yet,' Marcus pointed out.

'One of us has to be available,' she said pointedly. She lit her cigarette and turned her chair round, crossing her long legs. 'I'm pretty sure I'll get the part I auditioned for, but apart from that, I was offered some BBC drama work this morning.'

Marcus's eyes lit up. 'Darling! Why didn't you say?'

Olivia shrugged. 'It's just rep' stuff but the pay isn't bad. It'll do to fill in, but as I said, I'll have to be available.'

Juliet felt a guilty little leap of relief. 'You'll come though, won't you, Dad?'

But he was staring at Olivia. 'Any chance there'd be something for me?'

'Dad, you can't miss Aunty Marion's wedding,' Juliet said. 'You will come, won't you? After all, it's only one day and she's going to Canada almost immediately afterwards.'

He frowned. 'I don't know. It won't be the same without Libby.'

Olivia tapped ash into her saucer irritably. 'I'm sorry, but one of us has to earn some money!' She glared at him. 'And I wish you wouldn't call me that stupid name. It makes me sound like a tinned peach or something.'

'Ah, but such a *gorgeous* peach,' Marcus simpered, in a way that made Juliet cringe.

Olivia looked as though she might be about to say something cutting and Juliet jumped up from the table. 'Shall I put the kettle on for coffee?'

Olivia made a face at Marcus behind her back and asked pointedly, 'How long are you planning to stay, Juliet? As you'll have noticed we are a bit pushed for space.'

'I'm hoping to find a job,' Juliet told her. 'When – *if* I do, I'll get a room in a hostel.'

'Obviously that would be best,' Olivia said.

'What if you can't find a job, darling?' Marcus asked. 'Where are you going to live then?'

Juliet put milk on to heat in a saucepan and sat down. 'I'll probably go back to Dorset.'

'But as you've just said, Marion will be off to Canada after the wedding.' Marcus pointed out.

Juliet took a deep breath. There was no putting it off. 'Actually I've got something to tell you, Dad,' she said, trying to make her voice light. 'Aunty Marion is going to sign Heathlands Cottage over to me when she leaves.'

'You mean she'll let you live there till it's sold?'

'No. It's to be mine. She says it's what Granny would have wanted because it's the only home I've ever had.'

Marcus looked taken aback but he recovered quickly. 'I see – so I suppose you're planning to sell it?'

She shook her head. 'It won't be mine legally till I'm twenty-one, so

I can't. If I don't need to live there I thought I might rent it out.'

'What a good idea.' Marcus's Adam's apple bobbed up and down as he swallowed hard. He took a swift sideways glance at Olivia. 'I think it's really lovely of Marion, darling. You deserve it.'

'*You deserve it!*' Olivia mimicked, her voice shrill with fury. Dropping her cigarette stub into the dregs of her coffee cup with an angry hiss, she glared at him. 'You *idiot!*' she spat. 'That property is rightfully yours. As the eldest child it should have passed to you long ago when your whining sister got it. And now that she's thrown herself at some rich Canadian she's playing Lady Bountiful and handing it over to the little princess here!' She glared at Juliet. 'I've never heard of anything so bloody iniquitous.' She got up and swept out of the room slamming the door behind her. Juliet looked apologetically at her father.

'Oh, Dad.'

He shook his head. 'Don't worry, sweetheart, leave her to me. She'll soon calm down.' He got up and followed Olivia, closing the door firmly behind him. Juliet began to clear the table and wash up, feeling terrible. What a first day this was turning out to be. From the living room next door Olivia's raised voice carried clearly through the thin wall.

'We could have sold it,' she said. 'Property is making loads of cash at the moment. We could have bought that theatre in Rushfield and started our own company. It would have been the answer to all our problems. It should be yours. It's so unfair. So *bloody unfair*. I hope you're not going to be spineless enough to let it go at that.'

'There's nothing I can do. I can't take away my own daughter's inheritance.'

'Your *what*? Well, all I can say is, you'd better. You'd just better. If not, don't expect me to hang around.'

'Look, Libby, Juliet has never had a proper home. Marion nursed Mother through a long illness and she practically brought Juliet up.'

'Huh! Spoilt her rotten, you mean. Paying for her expensive education – molly-coddling her! What's a girl of her age going to do with a cottage anyway? Will she want to live at the back of beyond? You bet your sweet life she won't. She'll sell it as soon as she's twenty-one. You won't see a penny of it!'

'I owe the child, Libby,' Marcus said. 'She wouldn't have had much of a childhood if it hadn't been for Marion. I've got so much to be grateful to her for.'

'Yes, and she's rubbing your nose in it now. What kind of man are you, Marcus? Look at you – you're overweight; drinking too much; showing your age more with every day. Frankly I'm beginning to wonder why I'm still with you! What producer is going to want you for anything but bit parts? If you don't make a stand on this one last thing then I warn you – you can count me *out*!'

Juliet couldn't bear to stand there listening to her father being humiliated any longer. Tears choking her, she took her coat and ran out of the flat. Maybe by the time she returned they'd have stopped rowing.

CHAPTER THREE

When Juliet returned to the flat her father was alone. He sat in the living room, a glass of Scotch in his hand. It was clearly not his first. As she came in he looked up blearily.

' 'Lo darling. Where've you been?'

'Oh, round and about, looking at the shops. I thought you and Olivia needed some time to talk.'

He smiled wryly. 'That's more than she thought,' he said, taking a drink from his glass and wincing as the fiery liquid hit his throat. 'She took off soon after you did.'

Juliet dropped onto the sofa beside him. 'I'm sorry Dad – about Heathlands Cottage, I mean. I didn't realize she'd be so upset.'

Marcus put an arm around her shoulders and pulled her close to his side. 'It's not your fault, sweetheart. You deserve to have it and I couldn't approve more of Marion's generosity. I just wish she'd warned me she was going to do it. I could have eased the idea into Libby's head more gradually.'

'But why do you have to, Dad?' Juliet glanced up at her father sideways. 'You're not afraid of her, are you?' A thought suddenly struck her. 'You don't owe her money, do you?'

He laughed. 'You're joking. Far from it! You asked earlier about the money your grandmother left me. It was actually Libby who spent it.'

'You let her spend the money that Granny left you?' Juliet was shocked. 'All of it? What did she spend it on?'

Marcus shrugged. 'How would I know?' He spread his hands. 'Illegal clothing coupons; stuff to wear – being seen here and there. You know – keeping up appearances.'

Juliet was appalled. 'Why are you still with her, Dad? She treats you like dirt.'

Marcus looked down at his daughter. His eyes were bloodshot and there was sadness and depression etched in every line of his face. 'I love her, I suppose. I need a beautiful woman on my arm to boost my confidence. Your old dad isn't getting any younger love. I get the feeling more and more lately that Libby won't stay with me much longer.' He sighed. 'Where will I be then?'

'Better off by far!' Juliet told him hotly. 'You don't need anyone to boost your confidence, Dad, least of all her.' She snatched the whisky glass from his hand. 'You don't need this either. It's sheer poison!'

'I know – and I will give it up, Ju, I promise. The minute there's the merest sniff of a decent part in the offing. Don't you see, I need Libby beside me to help boost my ego.' He looked at Juliet with slightly unfocused eyes. 'She's very well connected, you know. She comes from a very good family; stately homes and all that.'

Juliet was sceptical. 'Really? If that's the case why is she spending all your money?'

He lifted his shoulders. 'You know what these aristocratic types are like when it comes to the stage. That's why she's got so much to prove. She wants her family to approve of her – wants to make them proud.' His hand reached for the glass again but Juliet gently edged it out of his reach. 'That's why I'm so afraid I'm going to lose her. What good is an old has-been like me to a beautiful woman like her?'

Juliet nudged him. 'Dad, wake up! You're not a has-been and you're not old by a long way. You just need taking in hand. Stop drinking, watch your diet and take more exercise. Take a long hard look at yourself in the mirror.'

He shook his head. 'Oh I don't know. It's probably too late.'

'It's nothing of the kind. Olivia was right in one thing she said: no producer is going to give you a leading part while you're in such poor shape. And you don't want to give up acting, do you? What else would you do – take up plumbing, or sweep the streets?'

'*What?*' The expression of comic disbelief on his face almost made her laugh. 'My God! I couldn't do either of those things. It'd mean getting up before ten!'

They laughed together and Juliet hugged him. 'That's more like my dad,' she said, kissing his cheek. 'Look, why don't you stay on with me at the cottage after the wedding. I'll help you get back into shape and the rest will do you good.'

He looked at her quizzically. 'Libby too?'

Her heart sank. 'I thought you said—'

'I can't let her go, Ju. I need her.' Marcus sighed. 'I've got to hang onto her for as long as she can put up with me.'

Juliet sighed. 'OK, Olivia too, but I doubt if she'll want to come.' She looked at him. 'And that means neither will you – doesn't it?'

He gave her his wry smile again and bent to kiss the top of her head. 'You're a good girl, Ju, and a wonderful daughter to care so much about your selfish old dad. But you know me. Something'll turn up, and if it doesn't I'm afraid you'll just have to let me go to hell my own way.'

Juliet thought a lot about what her father had let slip that afternoon. She realized that he had probably said more than he meant to. If he hadn't been slightly fuddled by the whisky he'd have been more discreet. What worried her most was the fact that Olivia had spent most of Marcus's legacy. And now she had the cheek to object that he wasn't getting Heathlands Cottage as well. The woman was nothing more than a leech. She was encouraging Marcus to drink and let his career slide and then mocking him for it. She was using him as a meal ticket and the moment her own career took off or the money ran out – whichever came first, she'd ditch him and walk away without a backward glance. Why couldn't Marcus see it? Could he really be so besotted? He was literally bribing her to stay with him. And as for that cock and bull story about the aristocratic family background, Juliet didn't believe a word of it. When Olivia lost her temper her cultivated accent slipped. She'd been known to use some far from ladylike language too.

Juliet spent the days that followed walking Fleet Street in search of a job. Every day her hopes sank a little lower. Most of the editors on the national dailies were too busy to see her. Of those who did the more agreeable seemed slightly amused by her audacity whilst the irritable ones, who were definitely in the majority, sent her away with a cutting remark. She met only one who showed her any kindness. He was the editor of a minor London evening paper whose office was in Southampton Street.

'So, you want to be a journalist?' The man swivelled his chair round to face her. 'What makes you think you have it in you to make a good one?'

Juliet swallowed. 'Well, I'm interested in people and I like writing. I think I'm quite good at it too,' she added.

The man's lips twitched but he bit back his smile. 'I'm sure you are,' he said gravely. 'But what experience do you have?'

'I used to edit my school newspaper.'

'Good for you. How long ago was that?'

Juliet looked down at the hands clasped tightly in her lap. 'I left in July. I've got matric,' she added quickly. 'And I've done shorthand and typing – passed the exam.'

'That'll be useful. Congratulations. Have you thought about studying journalism at college?'

'Yes, but I'd rather learn on the job.'

'I admire your enthusiasm, especially since that was how I started.' He leaned forward. 'Suppose I sent you to interview a woman whose child had been killed in a tragic accident. How would you handle the interview?'

Juliet licked her lips. 'Well, sympathetically I hope.'

'That approach doesn't always work. It might just make the woman crumble. What if she told you to go away and not bother her – if she was angry or resentful about the intrusion on her grief?'

Juliet hesitated. 'I suppose I might leave it and go back the next day.'

'And come back to me with no copy for the evening edition?' He shook his head and she felt her colour rising.

'I see what you mean,' she said quickly. 'I'd have to harden my heart and – and insist.'

'I hope none of my reporters have hard hearts.' He smiled. 'You'd have to know how to be firm and persistent,' he told her. 'Your first duty would always be to the editor who pays your wages.'

'Of course. I'm sure I'd soon get the hang of it.'

'It takes a lot of determination, not to say strength of character to put your foot in the door and keep it there. If you don't fancy college, my advice to you would be to find yourself a job on a local paper, somewhere in the provinces. It'll mean making the tea and running errands to begin with; putting up with the editor's filthy temper when he's hung over, or he's had a row with his wife; being ordered about by the senior reporters, but if you're keen enough you'll stick it out. You'll learn your craft from the bottom up and that seems to be the way you want it.'

Juliet's heart sank. 'Yes, I see.'

He raised an eyebrow. 'Am I right in assuming that you've trudged the length of Fleet Street before coming to me?'

She blushed and nodded. 'You're saying that I'm aiming too high?'

'Just a bit.'

She stood up, trying hard to retain her dignity. 'Thank you for seeing me. I won't take up any more of your time. Thanks for the advice.'

'Don't be despondent. I'm sure you'll do well. You've got the spark. I can see that.' He stood up and held out his hand. 'Come and see me again in five years' time.'

She took his hand. 'Thanks. I will.'

'I mean it. I can see that you're not a girl to be discouraged. That's good.'

It was only two o'clock when Juliet left the office, but she knew she'd had enough for the day. Looking for work in London was clearly a non-starter. Maybe considering her youth and inexperience it had always been an unrealistic idea. The editor she'd just seen had been kind. He'd taken the time and trouble to advise and encourage her. It seemed a good note on which to end the day – and probably her search. The sofa at the flat was lumpy and too short. She hadn't had a decent night's sleep since her arrival. And right from the first Olivia had made it more than clear that her presence was an inconvenience.

As she left the newspaper office building she thought about Wycombe Heath and felt a sudden rush of homesickness. It was only a couple of weeks now till the wedding. She might as well go home and help Aunty Marion with the arrangements.

Knowing that there'd be no food at the flat she shopped for an evening meal in Covent Garden and then caught the tube to Edgware. Marcus had said he'd be out all day today. His agent had rung yesterday to say that auditions were taking place for the supporting cast of a new film to be shot at Pinewood Studios. The previous evening Juliet had trimmed his hair and helped him press his best suit. He'd pointed out that auditioning wasn't like being interviewed for an office job but Juliet had insisted.

'You don't want people thinking you don't care what you look like, do you, Dad?'

She'd turned in time to see Olivia's derisive smirk and chosen to ignore it. If only Marcus could get even a small part, it would be such a boost to his flagging confidence.

At the top of the stairs she let herself in with the spare key Marcus had given her. She was about to go into the living room when she realized that she wasn't alone in the flat. She heard Olivia's voice speaking quietly but urgently.

'*Get out* before I throw you out!'

The voice that replied was male, but he spoke too quietly for Juliet to hear his actual words. Realizing that she should make her presence known she reopened the front door and slammed it hard then walked into the kitchen, humming a tune as she went. Once inside, she closed the door.

She was making tea when Olivia came in. She looked a little shifty but gave Juliet a forced smile. 'Hello. Had a good day?'

Juliet nodded. 'No job offers, but one editor gave me some good advice. I think I'll go back to Warnecliff tomorrow and help Aunty Marion with the final wedding arrangements.'

Olivia could hardly conceal her relief. 'Well, perhaps that would be best – for you, I mean.'

'I'm hoping Dad will be coming down for the wedding,' Juliet said. 'You, too, of course.' She eyed the older woman warily. 'Actually I was hoping he'd stay on for a while and let me help him get back into shape. He's been neglecting himself, I think.'

Olivia bridled, clearly taking Juliet's remark as criticism of her. 'I do keep nagging him, but he's not a child. What Marcus does is his own affair. After all, he should be old enough to know what's good for him by now.'

'You'd have thought so, yes,' Juliet said levelly. 'But by the look of things he clearly doesn't.'

Olivia's nostril flared. 'Are you implying—?'

Her sentence was interrupted by the door slamming. A moment later Marcus stood framed in the kitchen doorway. He'd obviously been drinking. 'Hel-*lo*,' he said, leaning on the door jamb. 'My two favourite girls. What a lovely homecoming. Ah!' He reached out his hand and assumed his 'Shakespearean' voice. 'Is that a pot of tea I see before me – the handle towards my hand?'

Juliet silently poured him a cup and drew out a chair for him while Olivia stared at him with distaste. 'If you ask me, it's coffee you need – very *black* coffee!'

'Are you all right, Dad?' Juliet asked quietly.

'Better than all right,' Marcus exclaimed, with a wave of his hand. 'You are looking at a member of the supporting cast of the new David Lean production, as yet to be titled.'

'You got a part!' Juliet bent to kiss him.

'Not exactly what you'd call a *part*, darling.' Marcus took a deep draught of his tea. 'I play a drunk. I stagger out of a pub doorway and…' He held up one finger. 'Wait for this – I actually have A LINE. I say '*Pardon me, madam. I'm ever so slightly ine-ineb-bria-t-ted*.'

Olivia gave a short laugh. 'Huh! Type casting!' she said scathingly. 'A couple of days' work at the most and the result will probably end up on the cutting room floor.'

Suddenly stone-cold sober, Marcus looked up at her. 'At least I'll be earning some bloody money,' he said. 'What about you? Have you landed anything lately? If you hadn't spent all the available cash we had we'd have been able to put a deposit on that theatre in Rushfield.'

Juliet left the kitchen hurriedly and started gathering her things together. The situation here was impossible, but there was nothing she could do about it. The sooner she left the better. All she hoped was that she could persuade Marcus to join her at Wycombe Heath, at least for a short break.

The train for Warnecliff left Waterloo at 12.50 which meant that Juliet had most of the morning to wait around. Marcus had an appointment with his agent at ten, to sign his contract and Olivia left the flat early, announcing that she would be out all day, though not revealing where she was going. As Marcus left he was in a good mood.

'Take care of yourself, darling, and give my love to Marion,' he said. 'Tell her I'll get down there for the wedding if I possibly can.'

Juliet stood on tiptoe to kiss him. 'You will try, won't you, Dad? It means a lot to her to have you give her away.'

Marcus gave her a wry grin. 'I doubt that, my love. Between you and me, I don't think my little sister has a very high opinion of me. All the same, I would like to be there if I can.'

'Good luck with the film.'

He sighed. 'No more than a cough and a spit, but better than nothing I daresay.'

'It's a foot in the door. You never know what it might lead to.' She looked at him. 'Since Olivier's film of *Henry V* there'll probably be more Shakespeare films in the offing. Why not ask your agent to put your name forward? You have the experience.'

'I'm afraid my Shakespeare days are over, my darling.'

'Over! You can't be serious. You've always said you'd play King Lear when you were old enough. And Falstaff and all those other parts for older actors.'

He ruffled her hair. 'After five years of playing froth and bubble with ENSA it just isn't in me any more.' Before she could deny it he looked at his watch. 'Got to dash now.' He kissed her forehead. 'Take care poppet. Have a good journey. Drop me a postcard to say you're OK. Bye, love.' And he was gone, clattering down the uncarpeted stairs and leaving the silent vacuum she always felt when her father made his exit.

She was just putting the last of her things into her case when the doorbell rang. Dad hadn't mentioned that he was expecting anyone. She opened the door to find a man waiting outside. Tall and slim, his dark hair was touched with silver at the temples. He was good looking in a slightly rakish way.

'Well, *well*. Hello there.' he said. 'And who have I the pleasure of meeting?' He smiled disarmingly, his dark-brown eyes crinkling attractively at the corners.

Julia hesitated, taking in the well-cut suit and the trilby hat he carried. 'I'm Juliet King,' she said. 'Who were you hoping to see?'

'Well, well – Marcus's daughter, eh?' he said, ignoring her question. 'What a pleasant surprise.' He extended a hand. 'Well, aren't you going to ask me in?'

Juliet touched his fingertips lightly and said, 'If you're looking for my father, I'm sorry, but he isn't here at the moment and I have a train to catch. I was just about to leave.'

'Ah, now that *is* a shame.' The man made no move to leave. 'Marcus's girl, eh? Who'd have thought it? What an unexpected pleasure.'

Juliet was beginning to feel distinctly uncomfortable. 'If you'd like to give me your name I could leave a note,' she said. 'Or maybe you could call back later.'

'Oh, don't worry.' He smiled, displaying perfect white teeth. 'I'm so sorry, I should have introduced myself. Very remiss. I'm Adam Kent.' When Juliet looked bemused he added, 'Olive – sorry, *Olivia*'s brother.'

Juliet was taken aback. 'Oh! I didn't know she had a brother.'

He assumed an expression of desolation. 'Alas, the story of my life. Ignored – disowned. Tossed onto the scrapheap of obscurity.'

'Is she expecting you?' she asked.

He shrugged. 'Possibly not. I called yesterday. We had a slight – er – shall we say, *contretemps*.' He smiled his disarming smile again. 'You know what brothers and sisters are like.'

'Not really. I'm an only child.' Juliet looked at her watch. 'Look, I'm sorry but I really do have to go now. Can I leave a message for her?'

He shook his head. 'Don't worry. I'll try again some time.' He put on his hat and gave it a little tap as he smiled at her. 'It's been lovely meeting you. I do hope you're here next time I call – *Juliet*.'

31

CHAPTER FOUR

When Juliet telephoned her aunt from Waterloo to tell her she was on her way home Marion seemed concerned that her niece was returning sooner than expected.

'Is everything all right, darling?'

'Of course. I just thought you could probably do with some help with the wedding preparations.'

'Marcus all right?'

'Fine.'

'Good. Well I'll look forward to seeing you in time for tea then.'

Marion always knew when she was hiding something and Juliet was afraid she'd have the truth out of her almost before she'd had time to take her coat off. However, when she arrived Marion didn't mention her brother. She had a meal ready and insisted that Juliet sat down to eat as soon as she arrived.

'I collected my dress yesterday,' she said, as Juliet pushed her empty plate away with a satisfied sigh. 'Yours as well, so we'll have a dress rehearsal when you've had a little time to relax.' She eyed her niece surreptitiously, as she poured her a cup of tea. 'So, how is that dear brother of mine – not to mention the lovely Olivia?'

Juliet smiled. 'I wondered how long it would take you to contain your curiosity,' she said. 'Actually I'm worried about Dad. He's let himself go.'

'In what way?'

'He's having difficulty finding work and it's taking its toll. He's put on weight; stopped caring about his appearance . . .' She stopped short of mentioning the drinking problem, but it wasn't easy to fool Marion who cocked an eyebrow in Juliet's direction.

'And?'

'Well, like I said. I don't think he eats properly.'

'But I'm guessing that he drinks more than adequately. Right?'

Juliet sighed. 'It's only because he's depressed about not working. He got a tiny part in a film a couple of days ago. Only one line, but at least it's something. I'm hoping he'll make the most of it.'

'And Olivia?'

'No change there.' Juliet bit her tongue. She longed to pour out to her aunt all her concerns about Olivia, but she had made up her mind not to say anything at this time.

On the train she'd gone over her meeting with the man who said he was Olivia's brother. It seemed more than likely that he had been the unseen visitor who was at the flat yesterday. What had he wanted and why had Olivia been so angry? The odd thing was that there was something vaguely familiar about him, though Juliet was fairly certain that they had never met before. Why had Olivia never mentioned him before? Was he demanding money from her?

Marion's wedding dress was of rose-pink georgette. The skirt was floor length and it had long sleeves with tiny pearl buttons. It suited her blonde hair and golden skin to perfection. With it she was to wear a shady picture hat of white straw with one pink rose nestling in the white ribbon at the back. As they stood before the mirror in Marion's bedroom Juliet clapped her hands.

'Oh! It's perfect. You look beautiful! What flowers are you having?'

'Pink roses to match the one on the hat.' Marion opened the wardrobe. 'But you must try yours on now.' She opened the wardrobe and drew out Juliet's dress which was of watered silk in pale pink. 'It should fit you perfectly after the fittings you've had, but if it needs any alterations there's still plenty of time.'

Marion had saved up her clothing coupons to get material for the dresses and a friend had made them for her. Juliet slipped into the dress and Marion fastened it for her. It fitted perfectly.

'It's lovely,' Juliet breathed, as she looked at her reflection in the mirror.

'You are to have a posy of deep-pink roses,' Marion told her and I've ordered a band for your hair with rosebuds of the same colour.'

Juliet clapped her hands delightedly. 'It's going to be the wedding of the year here in Wycombe Heath.' She bit her lip, her enthusiasm dampened for a moment as she remembered that Marcus might not be there to share it with them 'Marion, if Dad can't make it. . . ?'

'Don't worry. A friend of Elliot's is going to step in for us,' Marion told her. She smiled wistfully. 'I know how unpredictable my brother is so we've been careful to cover every eventuality.'

As they stood side by side in front of the mirror, Marion slipped an arm around her waist and said quietly. 'When it's your turn I will come home to be with you, you know.' She smiled and Juliet laughed shakily.

'Me – getting married? That's a long way off.'

'You never know,' Marion said. 'Love can strike at any time. Look at me.'

Juliet was silent for a moment then she asked, 'Aunty Marion, what happened between Dad and my mother? Why did she walk out on me? Dad never talks about her and Granny never told me.'

Marion sat down on the edge of the bed and drew her niece down beside her.

'I'm telling you the truth, darling, when I say that I just don't know. Marcus never told me. I don't know if he told Mother, but she never said anything to me. I was only in my teens at the time. All he said was that Christine had decided to leave. It was a shock. We all loved her, Marcus included. She wasn't connected to the theatre herself, but we thought that was a good thing; that she'd help to keep his feet on the ground. Thinking about it now I feel she must have been lonely. Marcus was at the height of his career at the time. He hardly ever went home and when he did it was only for a fleeting visit. It couldn't have been much of a life for a young woman, alone for weeks at a time with only a baby for company. But apart from that, what went wrong between them is a mystery.' She picked up Juliet's hand and held it tightly between both of hers. 'What I do know is that she loved you very much,' she said. 'I've never seen a more devoted mother.'

'And yet she could walk away and leave me. Was there another man, do you think?'

Marion shook her head. 'I've no idea, darling. It's difficult for me to believe that she didn't fight for you, or that she didn't mean to come back for you.'

'So, do you think she might be dead?'

Marion sighed. 'Who knows? Something must have happened; something really desperate. Marcus simply refused to talk about it, but personally, I think he should tell you the truth now that you're grown up. He owes it to you. I can't tell him what to do about it but perhaps you should ask him. After all, you have a right to know the truth.'

*

On the Thursday before the wedding Juliet rang her father. There had been no word from him as to whether he'd be down for the wedding or not. To Juliet's dismay Olivia answered.

'Oh, Olivia. Is Dad there?'

'No, he isn't.'

'I just wondered if he – if you will be coming to the wedding. It's on Saturday.'

'Wedding? Oh, *that* wedding,' Olivia said dismissively. 'No. I'm sorry, but we shan't be able to make it.'

'Are you sure?'

'What do you mean – are we *sure*? Of course we're sure. It's out of the question. We're both far too busy.'

'I thought Dad would have rung to let us know. It's not like him.'

'Sometimes, Juliet, I wonder if you have the least idea *what* your father is like.' Olivia's caustic tone and the spiteful remark stung Juliet.

'Right,' she said. 'Oh, by the way, your brother called just as I was about to leave the other morning. Mr Kent, I think he said his name was. He didn't leave a message except to say that you and he had had what he called a *contretemps*.' She replaced the receiver quietly, her cheeks burning. Marion, who had overheard the last part of the one-sided conversation, raised an eyebrow.

'Was that Olivia?'

Juliet turned. 'Yes. I was a bit naughty I'm afraid, but she has a habit of putting my back up.'

'Something about her brother?'

'Yes. This man turned up just as I was leaving to catch my train. I'm pretty sure he was there the day before. Olivia was talking to someone when I came in, but she clearly wasn't very pleased to see him and she soon got rid of him.'

'What did you say his name was?'

'Kent. Adam Kent.'

'What was he like?'

Juliet pursed her lips. 'Quite good looking – but a bit oily if you know what I mean. I wouldn't trust him as far as I could throw him. And he kept referring to her as *Olive*.'

Marion laughed. 'I'm sure that would have pleased her.'

'Dad is under the impression that Olivia comes from a very upper-class family.'

Marion smiled. 'Poor Marcus. He's always been a little on the gullible side.'

Juliet frowned. 'The thing is, Aunty Marion. I wasn't going to mention this and – oh dear, I suppose really I shouldn't.'

'Oh go on, you can't stop now!'

'Well, it's just that apparently Olivia has spent all of the money that Granny left Dad. He had plans to buy a little theatre in the Midlands and run it as a repertory theatre but most of it has gone.'

Marion looked shocked. 'It was quite a substantial amount. What on earth can she have done with it?'

'Dad says he doesn't know. But now I'm wondering if this brother had anything to do with it.' She looked thoughtful. 'You know, it's odd, but there was something vaguely familiar about that man. I can't put a finger on it, but I'm sure I've seen him somewhere before.'

Juliet was more upset than she would admit over Olivia's curt dismissal of Marion's wedding. Why hadn't her father telephoned to say he couldn't come? There had been no word from him, no card or present for Marion – nothing. It wasn't like him.

She found sleep difficult that night and when she did fall into a restless slumber it was to be haunted by dreams. She was in a dark corridor, feeling her way along the wall until she found a door. In the dream she was very small and had to stand on tiptoe to reach the handle. She turned it and pushed the door open a crack. Inside the room it was dark, but she was aware of a feeling of danger – that someone was there standing in the shadows. Fear rose in her throat and she tried to run away but a hand descended on her shoulder and stopped her. She heard herself calling I want Mummy but the person who held her in an iron grip just laughed. *Too bad, Juliet. Mummy's not coming. Mummy's gone away!*

She wakened with a start to find the blankets on the floor and the bed in disarray. She lay for several minutes, waiting for her heartbeat to slow and the horror of the dream to abate. Whose hand had held her so tightly in the dream? Whose was the voice she had heard so clearly? It had all been so vivid. But by the time she wakened next morning the memory of the dream had faded.

The morning of Marion's wedding day dawned bright and clear, a perfect blue and gold autumn day with barely a cloud in the sky. Juliet was awake early and she decided to take Marion her breakfast in bed as befitted a bride-to-be. She put the kettle on and laid the tray. Deciding to see if there were any roses left in the garden she opened the back door and found a bunch of wild flowers and a small package on the doorstep. They were addressed to Marion and she put them on her breakfast tray. Inside the package Marion found a delicate, cobweb-like lace handkerchief and a note.

From Celina. To bring you luck and happiness on your wedding day. The flowers had been gathered by Imelda. Marion was touched.

'Celina makes the lace herself,' she told Juliet. 'It would cost a fortune in the shops, yet she sells it for practically nothing.'

'She doesn't forget the kindness you did her,' Juliet said. 'You saved her child's life.'

They dressed together in an atmosphere of nervous excitement. The flowers had arrived early that morning and everything was ready. As there had been no word from Marcus, Elliot had put his emergency plan into action, assuring Marion that his friend Bob would be waiting at the church to give her away.

Finally they stood in the living room waiting for the car that would take them to the church. Marion fingered her bouquet nervously.

'Are you sure I look all right?'

Juliet smiled. 'You look wonderful,' she said. 'Radiant. Just wait till Elliot sees you.' But seeing the tiny shadow of sadness in her aunt's eyes she added quietly. 'I'm sure Dad would have been here if he could. He's probably filming.'

Marion nodded. 'I know. I know.'

But both were thinking that he could surely have sent a telegram – could at least have telephoned.

Juliet was standing by the window and was the first to see the car arrive. 'This is it,' she said excitedly. 'The car is here. Are you ready?' She went to her aunt and kissed her cheek. 'Good luck, Aunty Marion. You deserve it. And thank you for all you've done for me over the years.'

Tears filled Marion's eyes. 'Stop it,' she said. 'You'll start me off and ruin my make up.' She hugged Juliet. 'Just one thing: from now on I think you'd better call me just plain Marion. Aunty is so ageing!'

They both laughed a little shakily. 'All right, *just plain Marion*,' Juliet said. 'But we'd better go now or your bridegroom will think he's been jilted.'

They were about to get into the car when a taxi screeched to a stop behind it and a figure in a dark suit leaped out waving his arms frantically.

'*Wait*!' he called. He thrust some cash at the driver through the taxi window then ran over to where his sister stood, shaking slightly with shock. 'Sorry, Marion. Thank God I'm in time. I almost didn't make it. I'll explain on the way.'

Juliet was staring at her father. His dark grey suit was respectable enough but the red and blue plaid tie he wore with it was totally inappropriate. '*Dad*! Where did you get that awful tie?'

Marcus fingered the tie doubtfully. 'It was all I had – nothing any quieter. Won't it do then?'

Marion laughed and gave him a push. 'Just get in the car,' she said. 'We're lucky to have him at all, Juliet. Tie or no tie.'

Elliot's friend, Bob was waiting in the church porch and was more than happy to be relieved of his emergency duty. He quickly agreed to exchange ties with Marcus, taking off his pearl grey one and accepting Marcus's gaudy replacement, which he hastily pushed into his pocket. The verger gave the signal to the organist, Marion took her brother's arm, smiling up at him, and Juliet took up her position behind them. Her heart swelled with pride. Her father had made it after all. Now Marion's day would be truly perfect.

The reception was held at The Seaward Heights, a hotel in Warnecliff. It was quite a small gathering consisting of friends and nursing colleagues of Marion's and Elliot's fellow officers. A photographer was there to mark the occasion and Elliot had also notified the local press. Just before the newly-weds were about to cut the cake a flushed and rather dishevelled young man arrived armed with a notebook and camera. Juliet spotted him standing in the doorway and went across.

'Can I help you?'

He cleared his throat. 'I'm Nigel Foreman from the *Warnecliff Clarion*,' he told her. 'Here to jot down a few notes about the happy couple for the paper.'

Juliet looked at the small box camera he carried. 'Are you taking your own photographs?' she asked.

He blushed. 'All our photographers were busy.' He shrugged. 'It's Saturday – you know – football and stuff. Sorry I'm a bit late but this is my third wedding this afternoon,' he confided.

'I see, well, you'd better hurry up if you want to get one of them cutting the cake. They're just about to do it.'

'Right.' He looked at her. 'Are you the bride's sister?'

'No, niece.'

'Do you think you could give me the low down on them afterwards?'

'Low down?'

'Yes. You know, how they met – where they're going to live – that sort of stuff.'

'Oh, I see. Yes, all right.'

The cake cutting over, plates were passed round and glasses were filled for the speeches. Marcus's was a resounding success. He delivered it in his velvety actor's voice with perfect timing for the jokes. The young reporter looked at Juliet.

'He's very good, isn't he? Is he a relative?'

'He's my father,' Juliet told him. 'The bride's brother. He's an actor.'

'No kidding!' Nigel looked impressed. 'Should I know him? What did you say his name was?'

'Marcus King,' Juliet said. 'He did a lot of Shakespeare with the Old Vic before the war but he's been busy with ENSA since 1939. He's making a film at the moment. We were lucky he could get here today.'

'Do you think he'd give me an interview?' Nigel asked eagerly.

Juliet looked doubtful. 'I know he wouldn't want to take the interest away from Marion and Elliot.'

'I promise I'll be discreet,' Nigel said. 'Now, about the happy couple?'

She answered all his questions as best she could and he took another couple of photographs. Juliet was circulating with the last of the cake later when he caught her up again.

'I'm just off.'

'OK. Thanks for coming.' He hesitated, looking awkward and she asked, 'Is there something else?'

'Well. . . .' He coloured. 'I wondered if you were doing anything later? I'm finished at six.' He looked at her, his head on one side. 'I thought, a drink perhaps – once the happy couple are on their way?' When she hesitated he said quickly. 'But perhaps you have a train to catch. Are you going back to London with your father?'

'No. I live here now – sort of.' She smiled. 'How nice of you to ask me. Yes, a drink would be lovely. I'll have to go home and change first though.'

He beamed. 'Good. That's super. Shall we say eight o'clock? Where can I pick you up?'

Juliet gave him the address. As he left, Sylvia sidled up to her. 'At last I've found you on your own for a minute! I thought the wedding was lovely. Your aunt looked beautiful.' She looked her friend up and down. 'You don't look so bad yourself. That pink really suits your dark hair. That newspaper bloke seemed really taken with you.'

Juliet laughed. 'He's asked me to have a drink with him later.'

Sylvia's eyes opened wide. 'Wow, a date! He's a fast mover!'

Juliet took her arm and drew her aside. 'I've been hoping for a word with you. I've got some good news. Aunty Marion has signed the cottage over to me. It looks as though I'll be living down here from now on.'

Sylvia's eyes lit up. 'Ju! That's amazing! But I thought you were going to get a job in London.'

'That didn't quite come off,' Juliet admitted.

'Will you make changes?' Sylvia asked. 'To the cottage, I mean.'

Juliet shook her head. 'Why would I want to change anything? Heathlands Cottage is the only home I have ever known.'

Sylvia shrugged. 'Not even to update the kitchen? I thought you might want to put your own stamp on it – make it yours.'

Juliet considered for a moment. 'Well, thinking about it, I might move into the biggest bedroom,' she said slowly. 'And maybe move the furniture round a bit.' She looked at her friend. 'I'm still not sure whether I can afford to live there though. At the moment I've got no money coming in. I still have to find a job.'

'Oh you'll find something,' Sylvia assured her airily.

Juliet shook her head 'We'll get together soon and I'll fill you in on all the news.'

Marcus joined them. He smiled at Sylvia. 'Hello there. Nice to see you – er – Cynthia.'

Juliet frowned at him. 'Dad, this is Sylvia.'

He shook his head. 'Of course it is. Silly of me. You know how useless I am with names.'

'That's all right, Mr King.' Sylvia grinned at Juliet. 'See you later then, Ju. I can see Mum signalling to me. I think she's ready to leave.'

'Who *was* that?' Marcus asked when she was out of earshot.

'Dad! Only my oldest friend,' Juliet told him.'

'What have you done to that young reporter,' Marcus asked, cocking an eyebrow at his daughter. 'He looked positively euphoric when I passed him just now on his way out.'

'Me? Nothing. He asked me out for a drink, that's all.'

'And you said yes? No wonder he looked as though he'd just won the football pools.'

Juliet laughed. 'I thought your speech was super, Dad. You must have worked really hard on it.'

Marcus shook his head. 'Just scribbled a few notes on the train coming down.' He looked down at her. 'Went down quite well though, didn't it? If I do say so myself.'

'It was fabulous, Dad.' She linked her arm through his. 'Thanks for making the effort. It's made the day for Marion.'

He glanced across the room. 'I must say she's looking radiantly happy. I hope that bounder takes good care of her.'

'He will. And he's not a bounder, he's the best thing that's ever happened to her.' She looked at him. 'How did you manage to get away today, Dad? I know Olivia didn't want you to come. She was adamant on the phone.'

He sighed. 'It's a long story. Maybe it's best you don't know. Least said, soonest mended as they say.' He grinned. 'That young whippersnapper had the damned cheek to ask me for an interview,' he told her.

'Did you give him one?'

Marcus raised an eyebrow. 'Never let it be said that Marcus King turned down the offer of publicity,' he said. 'Even if it is only for a tuppenny ha'penny provincial rag like the *Clarion*.'

'Are you staying the night at the cottage with me, Dad?' Juliet asked.

Marcus shook his head. 'Better not.' He glanced at his watch. 'I'll catch the six o'clock train if I don't hang about. Libby'll be expecting me.'

A sudden hubbub on the far side of the room made them look up. Elliot and Marion were about to leave. Everyone followed them out onto the forecourt of the hotel where Elliot's car was waiting. Marion held up her bouquet and turned with her back to them, throwing it high into the air. To everyone's surprise it was Sylvia who caught it.

It seemed strange to Juliet, walking into the cottage alone; even stranger to think that it now belonged to her. She stood in the kitchen looking around the familiar room affectionately. There was the Aga, giving off its welcoming warmth to greet you the moment you walked in; the big table where they had always taken their meals, and Granny's prized set of Royal Doulton jugs hanging on the wall. On the far wall stood the dresser with the willow pattern plates and, facing it, the window that looked out onto the front garden. She reflected how the sun streamed in through the yellow net curtains in the mornings. 'As if I'd ever want to change a thing in here,' she told herself. When she was a little girl Granny had had a canary. She used to hang his cage in the window every morning. Basking in the sunshine, he'd sing his heart out while they had breakfast. It was one of the homely little things she'd looked forward to all term when she was away at school.

Nigel arrived on time in the battered pre-war Austin Seven provided by the *Clarion*. He took her to The Wheelhouse, a small pub on the outskirts of Warnecliff. They found a table in a quiet corner and Nigel studied Juliet while she sipped her orange juice. She was a great-looking girl, but she looked surprisingly different dressed in ordinary clothes. Older maybe – a little more sophisticated with her dark curls cut in a fashionable short style and her tall, slender figure in a cream skirt and jacket.

'So you're going to be a resident of Wycombe Heath now then?' he asked.

'I'm still not sure what my plans are at the moment,' she told him.

'But the cottage at Wycombe is yours.'

'It belonged to my grandparents, and then to my aunt.'

He waited a second but she didn't elaborate. 'I see, so now you're living there?'

'For the time being, yes.'

'I daresay you'll miss your aunt.'

'Yes, I will.'

'You've still got your father though.'

Juliet looked at him. He was a newspaper reporter. Only a junior one, it was true, but already he knew how to wheedle a story out of people. She turned to look at him.

'My grandparents are both dead and I-I lost my mother when I was little. My aunt and grandmother practically brought me up,' she told him. 'There's nothing in the least interesting about it. Dad was away a lot with his career. I went to a boarding-school on the Isle of Wight and spent the holidays here.' She raised an eyebrow at him. 'And that's more or less all there is to know about me. I'm not much of a scoop, I'm afraid.'

He blushed. 'Oh my God! You didn't think – I mean, I wasn't trying to. . . .' He shook his head. 'I guess it gets to be a habit. I only wanted to get to know you a bit better. Did I sound as though I was interrogating you?'

Juliet couldn't help laughing at his crestfallen expression. 'It's all right. Why should I imagine you'd want to interview me anyway? I'm a nobody. I've never been anywhere or done anything.'

'Don't put yourself down,' Nigel said. 'Are you planning to get work down here?' He bit his lip. 'Oh there I go again – sorry.'

She laughed. 'No, *I'm* sorry for being so suspicious. Yes, I am looking for work. In fact I'd go so far as to say that if I don't get a job I won't be able to afford to stay on at the cottage.'

'What's your line?'

She smiled ruefully. 'I haven't got one as yet. I only left school last summer. What I'd really like is to be a journalist, but I'd rather learn on the job than go to college. I've had enough of that kind of environment When I was staying with Dad in London recently I tried all the national dailies but even those who agreed to see me didn't take me seriously.'

It was his turn to smile. 'Frankly, I'm not surprised. I think the nationals expect you to have a bit more experience under your belt before they'll give you a go.' He looked at her thoughtfully. 'Actually there's going to be a vacancy shortly at the *Clarion*.'

Juliet's heart leapt. 'Is there really?'

'Yes, Unfortunately His Majesty will be calling on me shortly to serve my country. I've already had a deferment to finish my training.'

'Oh, that's a shame.'

'Can't avoid it, more's the pity. Why don't you come in and have a word with our editor?'

'Do you think I dare? I'm a bit apprehensive after the put-downs I had in London.'

'You shouldn't be. Ring on Monday morning and ask to speak to him. Tell him you're looking for a job and you've heard there might be one going. He likes to give the impression that he's fierce and unapproachable, but don't take any notice of that. His bark is worse than his bite. His name is Mr Bates. Gerry.' He smiled. 'I'll let you into a secret, he's got a soft spot for pretty girls so be prepared to bat your eyelashes at him and I'll bet you a pound to a penny that the job'll be yours.' He glanced at the bar where the landlady was serving food. 'Are you hungry? I don't know about you but I could eat a horse.'

They ate pork pie and pickles and Nigel introduced Juliet to lager, which she drank but wasn't really sure that she liked. But she enjoyed Nigel's company and by the time he dropped her off outside the cottage later she had agreed to see him again later the following week. 'Just so that you can tell me how you get on with our esteemed editor,' as he put it.

Following Nigel's suggestion she telephoned the *Clarion* first thing on Monday morning and asked to speak to the editor. When his loud, gruff voice boomed into her ear she almost dropped the receiver.

'Bates here,' he barked. 'Who are you and what do you want?'

'I'm – er – Juliet King,' she told him. Clearly he wanted her to come straight to the point. 'I'm looking for work and I heard that there might be a vacancy for a trainee reporter at the *Clarion* soon.'

'The hell you did!' he growled. 'And who told you that?'

Juliet was taken aback. Anxious not to land Nigel in trouble she said the first thing that came into her head – a phrase she'd read somewhere in the papers. 'I'm afraid I can't reveal my source.'

There was a great shout of laughter at the other end of the line, ending in a fit of coughing that almost deafened her. She was beginning to be alarmed when he suddenly composed himself. 'What did you say your name was?'

'Juliet King.'

'Well, Juliet King, you'd better come in and see me. Your *source* was correct, we do have a vacancy coming up for a trainee, but you'll have to convince me that you're up to the job. I warn you, I don't suffer fools gladly.'

'Oh I'm sure you don't and I will – convince you, I mean.'

'Good! Come and see me this afternoon then,' he barked. 'About three o'clock. And don't be late. I can't abide unpunctuality.'

He hung up abruptly, leaving her staring at a buzzing receiver. Well, he'd agreed to interview her. It was a start, even if he did sound like a bear with a sore head.

Juliet presented herself at the *Clarion* office at exactly five to three that afternoon. She'd thought very carefully about what to wear, finally choosing a navy-blue coat and flat-heeled shoes. The only flash of colour was a scarlet scarf tucked into the neck of her coat. The girl on the reception desk eyed her surreptitiously. There were no other female reporters on the *Clarion*. Gerry Bates liked to be known for his intolerance of all things feminine, although most of the girls in the office knew that the twinkle in his eye said something different. At three o'clock precisely the telephone rang on the reception desk and the girl looked up at Juliet.

'Mr Bates will see you now,' she said. 'It's through that door and down the corridor; second on the left.'

Gerry Bates looked up as she knocked on the door and came in. He was a heavily built man in his fifties. He wore a shapeless brown tweed suit and a pipe was firmly clamped between his teeth.

'Sit down, Miss King,' he said without removing it. He looked at her as she sat down on the chair opposite, taking in the slim figure and small piquant features at a glance. Removing the pipe he smiled at her.

'So, you want to be a journalist.'

'Yes.'

'And what makes you think you have what it takes?' He leaned back and puffed on his pipe, regarding her through a cloud of exhaled smoke.

'I like people and writing and I think I'm good at sniffing out a story,' she told him. She considered telling him she had edited the school newspaper then decided against it and closed her mouth.

'And you don't *reveal your sources*,' he added gravely. 'That's very good. I enjoyed that.' He frowned. 'I hope you realize, Miss King, that what we do here at the *Clarion* is hardly world-class stuff. We deal in small town things – births, marriages and deaths, the goings-on of the local council. We report on church fêtes, dog and baby shows and who won this year's prize marrow competition. We photograph couples who've made the long haul to their golden wedding and those whose little angels have won a scholarship to the grammar school.' He replaced the pipe between his teeth. 'It's hardly earth-shattering stuff. Do you think it's exciting enough for you?'

Juliet wasn't sure whether he was laughing at her or not. 'I just want to learn the job from someone who knows what they're doing,' she said.

His eyebrows twitched. 'Really? I'm not sure we've got anyone here like that,' he said. Suddenly he took the pipe from his mouth and tapped it hard on an ashtray, making her jump. 'If I take you on I hope you realize that you'll spend most of the first year making tea and coffee and running errands.' He leaned across the desk and fixed her with a steely eye. 'Given to fainting or hysterics, are you?'

'Certainly not!'

'Temperamental mood swings?'

'Not at all!'

'Good! This is no place for young women prone to the vapours. You'd be the only female in the reporters' room and I can tell you now that won't be popular. Watching their language and remembering to wash will go against the grain. But I like your style and I'm willing to give you a chance. I've warned you – it won't be a doddle, but if you still want to try it and you're prepared to stand your ground with that bunch of jackals, shall we see how it goes till – shall we say Christmas?'

Juliet nodded eagerly. 'Oh yes, please,' she said. 'When can I start?'

CHAPTER FIVE

Juliet's first month at the *Clarion* was disappointing. She'd been warned that in her initial weeks she'd be little more than a dogsbody; running errands and doing the jobs that nobody else wanted. Most of her time was spent making tea and coffee and putting up with the snide remarks of the male reporters, some of whom were newly out of the services and seemed to resent a young woman taking a valuable job when many of their demobbed comrades were still unemployed. The one benefit was that she grew to know Warnecliff better than she ever had before. In the school holidays excursions into town were mainly to visit the beach, the botanical gardens or the shops in the town centre. Now she was gradually finding her way round the back streets and suburbs as she went about gathering details for obituaries and details for local WI meetings.

Warnecliff was busy gearing up for next year's summer season. Most of the beach defences had now been cleared away and the gardens were being redesigned and the Victorian ironwork that the town was famous for was being painted pristine white. The large hotels, previously requisitioned by the Canadians who had been stationed on the South Coast were being refurbished and staffed ready for next summer's hoped-for influx of holidaymakers and there was an air of anticipation about the town.

Juliet had received several letters from Marion who seemed to be settling into her new Canadian life well. She sent snapshots of the nice house that she and Elliot had bought in the suburbs of Toronto and said that he had settled into his old job as though he had never been away from it. In each letter she reminded Juliet that she would always be welcome to come over for a visit.

Nigel, now Private Foreman 19083508, was stationed only twenty miles away and managed to get home almost every weekend. When he was home he usually telephoned Juliet and took her out, keen to hear about her progress at the *Clarion*. Although she had inherited the use of his old 'company' car she was still unable to drive it, managing to run all the errands she was sent on with Marion's old bicycle. Nigel promised that he would give her some lessons if she could get permission from Gerry Bates to use the old Austin.

'Once the spring gets here and the evenings are lighter I'll be able to take you out,' he told her. 'And I'll be due for some proper leave in the New Year.'

As they entered the run-up to Christmas it was Nigel who suggested that she approach Gerry Bates about her first proper assignment.

'If you don't jog his memory about how long you've been acting as slave for that bunch of deadbeats in the reporters' room you'll never get to do anything,' he warned. 'Knowing him, he's probably forgotten how long you've been there.' His face brightened as an idea occurred to him. 'Hey, tell you what, why don't you ask if you can go and interview the producer at the Theatre Royal about the pantomime. I hear they're putting on a super show this year 'specially written for the company, music and all. Tell him who your dad is and how you know a bit about the theatre. It'll be an exclusive and the theatre will be glad of the free publicity.'

Juliet's heart leapt at the idea but she shook her head. 'Mr Bates won't let me do anything that important,' she told him.

He shook his head at her. 'That doesn't sound like the Juliet King I've come to know,' he admonished. 'Don't be such a pessimist. It's time to show him what you can do. You have the edge over the others, having an actor father.'

Nigel nagged her into agreeing to beard Gerry Bates in his den on Monday morning.

'You have to keep reminding him that you're there,' he told her. 'Show him you've got the confidence.'

'I'm not sure . . .' she began.

He put a finger over her lips. 'That's enough of that. Of course you can do it.'

By the time they parted he had extracted a solemn promise from her that she would speak to Gerry Bates first thing on Monday morning and so it was that at nine o'clock she stood outside the editor's door steeling herself to appear more confident than she felt.

She tapped on the door and, at his bark of '*Come*', she took a deep breath and walked in.

'May I have a word with you, Mr Bates?' she asked.

He looked up at her, frowning bemusedly as he removed the ubiquitous pipe from between his teeth. For a moment she got the distinct impression that he had forgotten who she was, then his expression relaxed and he said, 'Ah, Miss King. And how are we progressing at the *Clarion*? Everything all right, is it – enjoying your training?'

At the word 'training' Juliet saw red. Her nerves forgotten she flushed an angry scarlet. 'My *training*?' she questioned. 'So far I've done little more than make drinks and write up trivial details for the obituary column. I haven't really learned anything. I'm here to ask if you can give me an assignment that has something to do with journalism.'

His jaw dropped. 'An *assignment*, is it? I might remind you, Miss King, that I did warn you that your early days would be spent attending to menial tasks.'

'My *early* days, yes, but I've been here almost two months now,' she reminded him. 'I think the reporters are beginning to see me more as a tea lady than a trainee.'

Gerry Bates' lips twitched and he hastily bit down hard on his pipe and frowned as ferociously as he knew how. 'Do they now?' He leaned back in his chair. 'So, am I to take it that you have something in mind that you're burning to do?'

Juliet swallowed hard and took a deep breath. 'Right, well . . .' It looked as though he was at least prepared to listen to her. 'I believe that the Theatre Royal is preparing to begin rehearsals for their Christmas show,' she said. 'And, as I come from a theatrical background, I wondered if I might be allowed to interview the producer about the forthcoming production. I've heard it is to be something innovative.'

His eyebrows rose. 'Innovative, eh?' He leaned forward to peer at her. 'You say you've heard. May I ask. . . ?' He shook his head. 'No. I mustn't ask, must I? You're a lady who never reveals her sources.' He looked up at her. 'A theatrical background, did you say?'

'Yes, my father is an actor – Marcus King.'

'Really?' He looked unimpressed. 'Can't say I've ever heard of him. Now, if you were to have said his name was Ralph Richardson. . . .'

Although his face was perfectly straight she knew that he was laughing at her. She blushed warmly. 'Mr Bates, may I have the assignment, or is someone else doing it?'

He smiled. 'As it happens no one else has spotted the opportunity, so full marks for that. But I must point out, Miss King – *Juliet*, that in journalism you will have to develop a thick skin. It's the first and probably the most important lesson to be learnt in this business. And it is the reason that you've spent the past few weeks picking up the dross and putting up with the banter of the reporters' room where I daresay they've been less than gentle with you. You're going to have to earn your spurs as far as they're concerned – give as good as you get. If you're going to take offence at every put-down you're handed, you'll be a nervous wreck before your first year is up.'

'I can take it,' she assured him hastily. 'I'm not touchy.'

'Except when it comes to your father, eh?' He laid his pipe down on the overflowing ashtray on the desk. 'I only wish my own daughters were as loyal.' He smiled. 'All right, you can have your assignment. Go and interview this producer character and the best of luck with it.' As an excited smile lit her face he held up a warning finger. 'But it had better be good, mind, or it'll be back to the obituary column.'

Thinking it best to do a little research before she attempted to interview the Theatre Royal's producer, Juliet went in search of the theatre. She found it tucked away unobtrusively down a side street. Looking at the playbills displayed outside she saw that the current production was a Noel Coward play, *Private Lives*. Going inside she bought a ticket for the following evening's performance at the box office and then wandered round the foyer, looking at the photographs of the cast members. The producer's name was Max Goddard. She stood back, studying his photograph. He looked about thirty, she calculated, with dark compelling eyes and a wide mouth. There was a broad streak of silver in his thick dark hair that gave him a rather interesting appearance and she found herself looking forward to meeting him.

The Theatre Royal was a Victorian theatre, decorated with an abundance of gilt cherubs, masks and lutes in the theatrical tradition. The seats were upholstered in red plush. It was just the kind of theatre Juliet loved, with its warm, intimate atmosphere, and she settled back and opened her programme looking forward to the performance. Each of the principal cast members had a small biography and Juliet learned that Max was twenty-nine and that he had recently come out of the RAF where he had taken part in several documentary films, directing two of them.

Her expectations of the small provincial repertory company had not been great but as the first act of the play progressed she found herself enjoying it. The standard of acting was high and the performance polished. In the first interval she scribbled a few lines on the back of one of the *Clarion's* cards, requesting an interview about the coming Christmas production and asked an attendant to deliver it for her. The lights were just dimming for the second act when the attendant tapped her arm and passed her a note, which, frustratingly, she was unable to read until the lights went up again. The moment they did she scanned the note eagerly.

Dear Miss King
Thank you for your interest. Please join me for a drink in the theatre
greenroom after rehearsal at 12.30 tomorrow and we'll talk further.
Max Goddard

Juliet took a lot of time deciding what to wear for the interview with Max Goddard. She was well aware of the fact that she looked young and she didn't want him to think her inept and inexperienced. She chose a navy suit and crisp white blouse; twisting her hair up into a French pleat, hoping that the effect would make her look older.

She was glad to have seen a photograph of Max Goddard and read his brief biographical details. She would have felt at a disadvantage not knowing what he looked like as she arrived at the theatre greenroom. Sitting at the bar she ordered herself an orange juice and glanced around. There were only two other people in the place, both middle-aged women, probably members of the theatre's supporters' club, she told herself. Thank goodness she was the first to arrive. It would give her time to collect her thoughts and think about how to handle the interview.

She could hear the sounds of a rehearsal still going on in the distance, magnified every time the door at the back of the bar opened – a piano and a single voice singing. She did not recognize the song.

The barman, polishing glasses studied her thoughtfully. 'Here to see someone about a job?' he asked at last.

Juliet looked up. 'No. I'm with the *Clarion*,' she told him, a touch of pride in her voice. 'I'm here to interview Mr Goddard.'

He grinned. 'You don't say. Well, the best of luck.' He nodded towards the door. 'Sounds like they're about finished so he shouldn't be long. Want me to tell him someone's here to see him?'

She shook her head. 'It's all right. I have an appointment.'

He gave her a mock bow. 'Pardon me, I'm sure.'

Juliet blushed scarlet, but before she had time to think of a reply the door opened and a crowd of people flooded noisily into the greenroom – clearly the cast, thirsty for a drink after their rehearsal. She spotted Max immediately and saw at once that he was better-looking than his photograph. He was taller than she expected, casually dressed in slacks and a black roll neck sweater. In his photograph he had appeared quite stern and unsmiling but now he was laughing with a member of the cast which made him look much more approachable. He noticed her sitting alone at the bar and, with a dismissive word to his companion, he walked towards her.

'Miss King, I presume.' He smiled and held out his hand. 'I hope you haven't been waiting long.'

'Not at all. It's good of you to give me a little of your time.'

'Can I get you anything?'

'No, thank you.' She pointed to her half finished orange juice.

He pulled up a stool and ordered himself a beer, then turned to her. 'So, how can I help you?'

'Well, I was hoping I could help *you* actually,' Juliet told him. 'I hear that you're planning a rather different kind of pantomime and I wondered if the *Clarion* could give you some free publicity.'

If she'd expected him to jump at the offer she was to be disappointed. He looked doubtful. 'Well, that is extremely kind of you, but it rather depends what kind of publicity. I'd hate to give people the wrong idea and put off potential audiences. You see what we're planning is quite innovative. As a matter of fact, it's a bit of a gamble on my part. You see this is my first Christmas at the Royal and I have to compete with the Pier Theatre's lavish production, so I decided to try something completely different.'

'Yes, that's exactly why I'm interested,' Juliet told him. 'Why do you think people might be put off?'

He took a long pull at his drink. 'You see, Miss King, what we're putting on is not what most people think of as panto,' he said. 'More of a musical play.'

'It's Juliet – please.'

'Juliet.' He smiled his disarming smile. 'There'll be none of the conventional stuff.'

'No song sheets or slapstick, you mean? No "*Oh yes it is – Oh no it isn't*".'

'Exactly.'

'More sophisticated in other words?'

He looked doubtful. 'Mmm, I'd hesitate to use that word. I appreciate that children love all the traditional stuff. However, I think that what we have is just as enjoyable and entertaining for all that – plenty of laughs and fun. It's Dick Whittington, but with a difference. For instance, no cross dressing. Dick will be played by an actor – a very male actor.'

She smiled. 'And Sarah the cook?'

He nodded, 'By a very vociferous actress wearing lots of padding and gaudy costumes. And we've got the best cat you've ever seen.'

'Sounds intriguing.'

'Also the music; no current popular songs. Both the incidental music and the songs have been specially written by Harry Gregson, our musical director, who is very talented and, like me, just out of the services.'

'And the script?' She looked up at him, pencil poised above her notebook.

'Specially written again.'

'By?' Her eyes met his enquiringly.

He put his glass down looking slightly amused. 'Why do I get the feeling that you're already one step ahead of me?'

She laughed. 'By *you*. Am I right?'

'As it happens, yes.'

She looked thoughtful. 'So if there's to be no cross dressing what about costumes? I take it they're to be specially made?'

He nodded.

She grinned at him mischievously 'You're not going to tell me you're a dab hand with a needle as well?'

'We have a very inventive and talented wardrobe mistress,' he told her solemnly. 'I do hope you're not making fun of me, Juliet.'

'No! Of course not.' She blushed. 'Sorry. It's just that—'

'I know, it all sounds a bit ambitious and perhaps even a bit highfalutin to a young person like you. But we're all a hundred per cent behind this and we are determined to make it a success. I wouldn't be putting so much effort into it otherwise. And if *you* have any doubts at all on that score; if you're planning some kind of tongue-in-cheek article, I'd rather you forget all about it. I'd hate all our plans to be ruined before we've had a chance to prove ourselves.'

Dismayed, Juliet shook her head. 'Please, I'm sorry if I've given you the wrong impression. I think it sounds terrific – *truly*. I'm sure we can give you just the boost you want. In fact what about a *double-page spread*?'

The moment the words were out of her mouth she wanted to bite her tongue off. Gerry Bates would have forty fits. He'd never give her – the most junior reporter in the entire world – a double-page spread. What was she thinking about? Her heart sank as she looked at Max's astonished face.

'A double-page spread! Well, that really would be something.'

Juliet swallowed hard, her heart thumping. *In for a penny*. 'Of course I'd have to sit in on some rehearsals,' she said. 'And I'd like to interview your musical director, the principal cast members and the wardrobe mistress.'

'Of course.'

'And we'll need photographs of course.'

'Anything. When are you planning to run this?'

'When are you opening?'

'Boxing Day.'

'Then it had better be the week before Christmas,' she told him, flipping her notebook shut. 'But we'll put a piece in earlier to whet people's appetite.'

He walked out to the street with her and shook her hand. 'Thank you, Juliet. We're rehearsing on Sunday afternoons at the moment until the present production ends and then we're closed for rehearsals.

Perhaps you'd like to sit in next Sunday. We start around two o'clock.'

'Thanks. I'd love to.'

Walking away her head was in a whirl. What had she done? How was she going to convince Gerry Bates that it was a good idea? And what if he said no?

The following morning she stood in front of the editor's office door, her knees trembling with fear. She'd spent all the previous evening working out how she would handle the double-page spread about the Theatre Royal's Christmas production and she clutched her notebook to her as though it was some kind of talisman. The idea excited her so much. She could already picture the spread she would produce and in her mind she had already planned the text. But how would she sweet talk Gerry Bates into agreeing to it?

Something about the way he barked, '*Yeah! Whaddya want?*' to her knock told her that he wasn't in the best of moods. Licking her dry lips she took a deep breath and went in. He looked up without enthusiasm.

'Miss King.'

'I – er – thought I should report to you about my interview with Max Goddard yesterday,' she said.

The corner of his mouth twitched. 'Written your little piece already, have you? There's keenness for you. Give it here then.' He held out his hand.

'Well, no.' Juliet swallowed. 'As a matter of fact I thought – well, I was very impressed by what they are planning and I thought – well, actually I said – I *promised*—'

He looked up with a frown. 'Oh, for God's sake, girl, spit it out. What have you promised?'

'That – that the *Clarion* would give the story a double-page spread.' There, she'd said it. She lowered her eyes, hardly daring to look at him. When she did she saw that a hot purplish flush had flooded his cheeks and his eyes bulged as he stared incredulously at her.

'You've *what?*' he thundered.

'I've planned it all out,' she told him, holding out her notebook. 'Interviews with the principal cast members; the musical director and the wardrobe mistress – photographs. It's to be a very special Christmas show, specially written from the script to the music – all original work – including the costumes.'

'I don't care if they've dug up bloody William Shakespeare to write it,' he shouted. 'I always allow half of page eight for Christmas entertainment write-ups and that includes the WI Christmas Fair and the Mothers' Union Bring and Buy. The Theatre Royal panto will get a single column inch and a half like always and be bloody grateful for it. The centre double is always reserved for the Pier Theatre's production and that's because they buy a lot of advertising space. Now, if there's nothing else. . . .'

'Can I just show you how I mean to handle it? I spent all last night working it out.' She took a step towards his desk but the look in his bloodshot eyes stopped her in her tracks.

'Are you *deaf*, girl or just sodding stupid? You heard what I said and there's an end to the matter.' As she reached the door he barked, 'I'll take my coffee black this morning and you can make it as soon as you like, so get cracking and stick with what you're best at!'

His parting shot really stung and, as Juliet waiting for the kettle to boil in the kitchen, she swallowed hard at the lump in her throat. She'd known he wouldn't exactly be happy about it, but she'd felt confident that when he saw what she'd planned he'd come round. But he wouldn't even look at her notes or listen to her ideas. What was she to say to Max Goddard now? She was going to look such a complete idiot.

She was spooning instant coffee into Gerry's special mug, the one with LMS RAILWAY on it when a voice behind her said, 'Blow you out, did he?'

She turned to see Fred Simms, the *Clarion*'s elderly photographer standing behind her. He smiled apologetically. 'Sorry, but I was passing his door and I couldn't help overhearing. Gerry's tones are hardly what you'd call dulcet, are they? Specially when he's roused.'

She smiled ruefully. 'You can say that again. I suppose it was my fault. I interviewed the producer of the Theatre Royal yesterday and I promised him a double-page spread write-up for the panto.'

He blew out his cheeks and laughed. 'A double? Wow! That was stretching it a bit.'

'Mr Bates didn't tell me that all he was prepared to allow was a single column inch and a half,' she protested. 'I did ask him first if I could have the assignment and he agreed. An inch and a half is hardly an assignment, is it?'

'Sounds to me like you've chosen the wrong morning,' Fred said. 'I hear he was at a big Rotary Club do last night and I guess our Gerry is suffering from a monumental hangover.' He nodded towards the kettle. 'Make me one of those and tell me what you've got planned.'

Juliet smiled at him gratefully. 'I will, but I'd better take his lordship his coffee first or I'll be in worse trouble.' She handed him her notebook. 'Here, you can have a look at my notes while I'm gone if you like.' In the doorway she turned. 'Fred, I'd be grateful if you kept this to yourself. I'm hardly favourite in the reporters' room and when they get to hear about this. . . .'

He smiled. 'Don't worry,' he said. 'Me lips is sealed, as they say.'

Gerry merely grunted without looking up when she put the coffee on his desk. She withdrew without speaking. She'd had enough of him for one morning.

When she returned to the kitchen Fred was sitting at the table reading her notes. 'Looks like you've put a lot of thought into this,' he said.

'I have,' she agreed. 'I was up half the night working on it. I've even been invited to sit in on their rehearsals, starting this Sunday afternoon.'

Fred looked thoughtful. 'I must admit that it sounds as though this show is worth a bit more than being squeezed in between the WI and the Mothers' Union.'

'It is!' Juliet embarked on a detailed account of Max's plans for the show. 'And with your photos to back it up, Fred—'

'Whoa!' He laughed, holding up his hands. 'You still have to convince our esteemed editor, remember?'

'You think there's still a chance I might get him to change his mind?' She held her breath.

He closed the notebook and handed it to her. 'Look, I like your enthusiasm. Gerry and I go back a long way. Let me have a word with him – once his head has stopped pounding that is.' He reached across to pat her shoulder. 'Meantime, you go to your rehearsal. Sounds to me as though you'll enjoy it. Just keep your fingers crossed.'

CHAPTER SIX

When Juliet arrived home that evening she found a postcard from Nigel waiting for her on the mat.

> *Dear Juliet*
> *Sorry but I shan't be seeing you for a while. Got a sudden posting to Yorkshire. Rather puts the lid on your driving lessons, I'm afraid, but I'll make up for it as soon as I can. I'll write soon and let you have my address.*
>
> *Love Nigel*

Poor Nigel, she would miss his weekend visits and she was disappointed that she wouldn't be able to tell him about her interview with Max Goddard, or the run-in she'd had with Gerry Bates as a result. He was the only person she could share her highs and lows with, knowing as he did what life at the *Clarion* was like. Nigel would have put the whole episode into perspective for her and made her laugh. If he was in Yorkshire goodness only knew when she would see him again.

Along with the postcard there were two Christmas cards in the post. The sight of them, all frost and robins brought Juliet up sharply. She hadn't given a thought to Christmas; bought any cards or presents, neither had she made any plans for what she would do over the holiday, but she realized now that it was only three weeks away. Now that Marion had gone there would be no one to share it with. Sylvia's house was always bursting at the seams over the festive season with the Trent family's many relatives and, although she knew she was always welcome to join them, she hesitated about putting extra strain on poor uncomplaining Mrs Trent.

Her thoughts turned to Marcus and she wondered what he would be doing. The thought of spending Christmas with Olivia in the cramped Edgware flat did not appeal to her. On the other hand it would be nice to see her father over the holiday. On impulse she decided to give Marcus a ring.

She was relieved when he answered the phone himself. He sounded rather gloomy but cheered up at the sound of her voice.

'Juliet, darling! You must be telepathic. I was just thinking about you.'

'Hello, Dad. How are you?'

'Oh – all right, I suppose.'

'You've finished filming?'

'Finished that ages ago,' he told her. 'Three days' work – hardly what you'd call *filming*. Been kicking my heels around the flat ever since.'

'What about your agent? Hasn't he come up with anything for you?'

'What do you think? He seems to have forgotten my existence! Sometimes I wonder if I should approach someone new.'

She made no comment. They both knew full well that Marcus's track record since ENSA would hardly tempt a top theatrical agent. 'And Olivia?' she enquired.

'Oh, she's all right – did a bit of radio work and she's off this weekend to start rehearsing a panto up in Hull.'

'Does that mean you're going to be on your own for Christmas?'

He sighed. 'Looks a lot like it. Libby can't come home because they're rehearsing up to and including Christmas Eve and then opening Boxing Day. I suggested going up there, but she says she's got some cheap digs – just a tiny single, so there wouldn't really be room.'

Juliet could well imagine what Olivia had in mind and it wouldn't include Marcus, but she refrained from commenting. 'Look, Dad, if you're at a loose end why don't you come down here and spend the holiday with me?' she said. 'I'll be on my own too. I've got lots to tell you. I might be getting involved with the local theatre if I can persuade my editor to let me do a piece about their Christmas show.'

'Are you sure you want an old has-been like me cluttering up your new life?'

'Do I detect a note of self pity?' Juliet chuckled. 'Come off it, Dad. You're not an old has-been and you know it. Your career is just going through a rough patch.'

He grunted at the other end of the line. 'Some rough patch! Sometimes I think—'

'So what's Olivia's pantomime?' Juliet interrupted determined not to allow him to indulge in self pity. 'And what is she playing?'

'It's *Snow White*,' he told her. 'She's playing the wicked queen.'

Juliet had to bite her tongue to stop herself from laughing. *Typecasting* was the phrase that sprang to mind but she had more sense than to say it. 'What about it then, Dad? Is it a yes?'

'I'd love to come, my darling. When?'

'Beginning of Christmas week if you like.'

'Fine. What shall I bring?'

'Nothing. Just bring yourself,' she told him. 'And for heaven's sake try to cheer up! It's called the festive season, remember?'

In her lunch hour the following day Juliet slipped out to Brightwell's the town's largest department store to buy Christmas cards and presents. For Marcus she found a biography of Sir Henry Irving that she knew he would love. In the same department she found a pen and pencil set for Nigel, then, as she was passing the toy department she remembered the Lee children. She had promised Marion she would keep an eye on the gypsy family and so far she hadn't visited them since the wedding. She bought a colourful rattle for baby Clover and a wooden engine for her big brother, Billy. She bought hankies for Imelda and Celina and some tobacco for Danny.

Later at home she wrapped all the presents and sat down to write her cards. There weren't many, just the few schoolfriends she had stayed in touch with; her father and Sylvia and Marion and Elliot of course.

When she had finished she looked around her with a sigh. She still hadn't done a thing about the cottage. The main rooms could do with redecorating and when spring came around there would be the garden to think about. Her heart sank a little as she wondered how she would find the time. Owning a house was an even bigger responsibility than she had realized.

On Saturday afternoon she made her way down the garden and onto the heath, carrying her bag of presents. At the last minute she had remembered to add the photographs of Marion's wedding.

The door of Imelda and Danny's caravan was shut which was unusual and her tap was answered by Imelda who looked heavy-eyed.

'Baby's chesty,' she explained. 'Had us up all night she has.'

'I'm sorry to hear that. I brought you some Christmas presents,' Juliet said, holding out the bag. 'But I won't stop.'

'Oh no, come in and have a cup of tea,' Imelda said quickly. 'Danny's taken Billy and Celina's boy Tom to work with him on Cater's farm. He's doin' a bit of hedging. Celina's here. She'd like to see you. She come over to rub goose grease onto baby's chest and give her some of her special herbal medicine.' She held the door open for Juliet to step inside.

It was warm and cosy inside the caravan. It was spotlessly clean and decorated with brightly coloured paintings of flowers and birds in the Romany tradition, but Juliet wondered not for the first time how two adults and two children managed to live in such a tiny space. Celina sat nursing the baby whose chest wheezed gently in her sleep. She smiled at Juliet.

'Good to see you, missie. How's Miss Marion and how did the wedding go off?'

'Very well,' Juliet told her. 'I've brought the photographs to show you.' While Imelda made a pot of tea she fished the wallet of photographs out of her bag and sat down to show the two women, who nodded and smiled their approval at each one, admiring Marion's dress and remarking on how happy she looked.

'I told her she'd meet the man of her dreams, you know,' Celina said as she passed back the last photo. 'Did she ever tell you that?'

Juliet shook her head. 'No, she didn't.'

Celina smiled. 'She never did really believe I had the sight, but she never refused to let me read her palm or the tea leaves. Too polite, bless her. She deserves a good life with a man as'll take care of her, that one. A real lady, your aunt Marion.'

'I know. I miss her very much.' Juliet took the delicate china cup that Imelda handed her and sipped the strong hot brew.

'So what about you, missie?' Celina looked closely at her, her dark eyes twinkling. 'Is there a man in your life?'

Juliet laughed. 'Several, but no one special.'

'No one special?' Celina shook her head. 'That's a cryin' shame, a pretty young thing like you an' all.'

'The only special man in my life is my dad.'

'Ah!' Celina nodded wisely. 'And he gives you some worries, this dad of yours?'

'Now and again.'

Celina reached out. 'Give me your hand, my pretty.' When Juliet hesitated she smiled. 'Don't be shy. You don't have to believe what I tells you but you can listen, can't you? You never know, you might get a surprise.'

Juliet put her hand into Celina's brown, work roughened one and watched as she bent over it. 'Ah yes. Your dad's a lovely man – but weak-willed.' Juliet smiled to herself. She had already let that much slip anyway. Suddenly Celina said, 'You ain't seen your ma for a long time, have you?' She looked up intently, her dark eyes burning into Juliet's.

'My mother left my father and me when I was two years old,' Juliet said, her voice shaking a little. Celina shook her head.

'Oh no. The woman I see here never abandoned no child,' she said. 'She loved her babby – she still does. I reckon she had a wrong done 'er. I see her grievin' sore.'

Juliet swallowed, her heart beating fast. 'She's – still alive?'

Celina shrugged. 'Who's to say who's alive and who's dead?' she said. 'Sometimes those we love live on in our hearts.' She bent over Juliet's hand again. 'This dad o'yourn – he's unhappy, eh? Woman trouble? Takin' a little drink too many maybe?'

'I – er don't know . . .' Juliet shuddered and Imelda said quickly, 'Celina – let it be now. Maybe another day Miss Juliet'll come back and ask you to read her palm again.'

Celina let go of the hand she held. 'As you wish. I'm always here if you want me my pretty,' she said. 'I try to help folk and I don't never mean no harm, but sometimes the truth comes hard.'

Juliet finished her tea and handed the cup back to Imelda who shot Celina a warning look and asked brightly, 'How do you like livin' at Heathlands Cottage then?'

'I love it,' Juliet said. 'I worry a little about how I'll manage the garden once the spring comes though.'

'Don't you worry about that,' the girl told her. 'My Danny'll come and give you a hand – be glad to. I'll get him to walk across and see you as soon as the year turns.'

'I'd be grateful for that.' The baby wakened and began to whimper restlessly. Juliet seized the moment to make her excuses. 'I'd better be going.' She stood up. It was stuffy in the caravan and the palm reading had shaken her. She felt she couldn't breathe and longed to be out in the fresh air of the heath again. 'Goodbye,' she said. 'I hope little Clover will soon be better. Thanks for the tea – and for the reading, Celina.'

'Just you remember what I said,' the older gypsy woman told her. 'Maybe you'll thank me and mean it one day.'

Outside Juliet took a deep breath of the cold peat-scented air and began to walk back to Heathlands. She noticed that the foundations of the new houses, intended for the gypsies had already been dug. The council must be very serious about moving the gypsies if they'd obtained a building grant from the Ministry of Works to re-house them. At least the council was recognizing their squatters' rights to the common land and weren't intending just to move them on. They must genuinely feel they were doing them a favour, but Juliet knew better. The gypsies had been here at Heathlands for as long as she could remember and she knew for sure that no one would ever persuade the Lees or any of the other families to move into bricks and mortar houses; it would be like expecting fish to live on dry land. Where would they go, she wondered? They would most certainly leave and the heath wouldn't be the same without them.

In bed that night she found that sleep evaded her. In the dark she tossed and turned restlessly, unable to dismiss the thoughts that Celina had put into her head that afternoon. What had she meant when she said that her mother had been wronged? And what could she have been grieving about? It was only the ramblings of a gypsy fortune teller, of course, but why had she always been kept in the dark about her mother's absence from her life? Why did her father never mention her, and why were there no photographs or other mementos? Juliet had only the vaguest of memories of her mother. Marion had said it was time Marcus told her what really happened all those years ago and the true reason for her desertion. Perhaps during the coming holiday, while they were together, just the two of them, she could broach the subject and get him to tell her the truth.

*

When Juliet arrived at the Theatre Royal next afternoon she found Max sitting four rows from the front in a dimly lighted auditorium. When he spotted her coming down the centre aisle he beckoned her to sit beside him. Juliet slipped into the seat and took out her notebook. Harry, the musical director, was at the piano in the orchestra pit, coaching a young actress in a song he had written.

'None of the cast has any musical training,' Max whispered, 'Not many can even read music, so Harry has to teach them note by note. We've had a few surprises.' He nodded towards the stage. 'Maddy for instance. Madeleine Fielding; she's playing Alice and it turns out that she has a really lovely voice.'

Harry began to play again and, as Max had said, the girl sang his song in a sweet but strong soprano voice. As the rehearsal progressed Juliet began to see that this production was going to be something really special. The Pier Theatre was advertising a well known singing star playing the lead part of Cinderella in their production. Obviously she would draw the crowds and sing all the popular songs she was famous for, but Juliet had a suspicion that those who saw this pantomime would remember it far longer. The music was brilliant and evocative and the effects, though unsophisticated, were clearly going to be pure magic. The transformation scene where Dick heard the bells telling him to 'turn again' was done simply with gauze curtains and special lighting but it was breathtakingly effective. And Tommy, the cat, who insisted on rehearsing in the skin was acrobatic and endearingly amusing. At the end of the rehearsal when his head came off Juliet was surprised to see that inside the skin was a very young girl.

'That's Petra,' Max told her. 'She's not a member of the cast. We've borrowed her from the local ballet school. Brilliant, isn't she? We're having a troupe from the school to dance the fairies in the transformation scene. Their teacher is doing the choreography for that, but we won't be rehearsing the whole thing with them until next week.'

Juliet could imagine how magical the effect would be and she looked forward to seeing it. The Pier Theatre was advertising a 'flying ballet' but she felt sure it wouldn't be as magical as this and she said so. Max looked pleased.

'Glad you think so. I certainly hope you're right. This is a bit of a gamble for me. My first civvie job. If it bombs it's going to make me look like a massive flop.'

'I'm sure it won't.' Juliet bit her lip, hoping against hope that she wasn't going to have to let him down over the publicity.

When the rehearsal came to an end, Max invited her to join him for tea in the greenroom and meet the cast. After introducing her to the principals he suggested she join him at a table in the corner.

'When do you propose to start your interviews?' he asked. 'After all, there isn't a lot of time left and we have quite a busy schedule.'

Juliet felt her stomach turn over. 'Well, I'll have to see what my editor has lined up for me,' she hedged. This was the time to come clean and warn him that she might not be able to keep her promise, but she couldn't quite bring herself to do it.

'Right, well if you could let me know as soon as possible,' he conceded. 'Then I can organize something.' He drank his tea, regarding her thoughtfully over the rim of the cup. 'You seem quite knowledgeable about the theatre,' he said. 'Do you have some theatrical connections?'

'My father is an actor – Marcus King,' she added the name tentatively, remembering Gerry Bates's put-down on the only occasion she had mentioned her father's name.

'Marcus King! He's your father?' Max's eyes widened.

'You've heard of him?' Juliet asked.

'More than heard of him. He was my inspiration,' Max told her. 'I saw him play *Hamlet* at the Old Vic when I was still at school before the war. He was brilliant. That was when I knew for sure that I wanted to be an actor. I saved up all my pocket money and saw him play as many times as I could after that; *Henry V, Richard III, Coriolanus.*' He leaned towards her. 'What's he doing now?'

'He joined ENSA and toured with them all through the war,' she told him. 'Since then his career has been in the doldrums I'm afraid.'

'That's a shame. He's a fine actor.'

'Yes I know, but – well, you know how it is,' she said. 'Difficult to get back into the swim when you've been out of the public gaze for so long. Playing farce and romantic comedy is miles removed from everything he made his name doing.' She couldn't tell him what she would hardly admit to herself, that Marcus had lost his confidence – that he was close to giving up and becoming a depressive drunk who could barely bother to get dressed in the morning. 'I worry about him,' she confessed. 'I've managed to persuade him to come and spend Christmas with me. I thought it might cheer him up.'

'Then you must certainly bring him along to the show,' Max said. 'It'd be an honour to meet him.'

Juliet wondered unhappily if he would be so enthusiastic when he saw what a shadow of his former self Marcus was or – worse – when she let him down over the double-page spread she had rashly promised, but she smiled and said, 'He's going to love the show and he'll be so interested to meet you too.'

Next morning she arrived at the *Clarion* offices early. She had spent the previous evening writing the preliminary piece she had promised about the Theatre Royal panto and she was quite pleased with it. While the reporters' room was quiet she typed up the piece at a desk in the corner and hoped that Gerry Bates would soften a little when he read it. She didn't fool herself that he would reconsider his refusal to let her have a double-page spread, but even if he allowed her a single page or even half she would feel a bit better.

She heard the door open behind her and looked up to see Fred coming in. His eyebrows rose when he saw her.

'You're an early bird, beavering away over there in the corner,' he said.

She nodded. 'I wanted to get this piece about the panto written up while there was a machine free and the place was quiet.' She sniffed. 'And smoke free. Sometimes you can hardly see across this room, what with pipes and cigarettes and those awful little cigar things that Bill Martin smokes.'

He laughed. 'I have to agree with you there.' He drew up a chair and sat beside her. 'What's that you're doing?'

'It's a preliminary piece about the Theatre Royal Christmas show,' she told him. 'I haven't even been given a desk of my own yet and I needed to get in before anyone else to type it up.'

'You went along to the rehearsal then?'

'Yes, and I'm more convinced than before that they deserve a good write-up.' She pulled the finished article out of the typewriter and handed it to him. 'Tell me what you think.'

He took his glasses out of his top pocket and slipped them on, then read through the piece she had written. 'It's very good, Juliet,' he told her looking up at her over the tops of his spectacles. 'Certainly enough to whet the appetite.' He gave her back the sheet of paper and removed his glasses thoughtfully. 'As a matter of fact I had a talk with Gerry yesterday. We both belong to the same golf club and I managed to buttonhole him at the "nineteenth".' When she looked puzzled he laughed. 'That's golf speak for the clubhouse bar,' he explained.

'Ah!' She frowned. 'I hope he wasn't over indulging again. I was banking on his being in a good mood this morning.'

'No, just a pre-prandial pint. Anyway, I brought the subject round to the *Clarion*'s youngest trainee reporter. In other words, a certain Miss Juliet King. I told him he wasn't giving you a fair crack of the whip and that he was going the right way to stifle your enthusiasm.'

Juliet's eyes widened. 'You're brave.'

'Not really.' He smiled. 'As I told you, Gerry and I go back a long way. Besides I'm far too good a photographer for him to get stroppy with. I'm getting close to retiring age and I could always make a good living doing freelance work, a fact of which he's well aware.'

'So, what did he say?'

He tapped the side of his nose. 'Let's just say that I'm glad you've written this nice little piece. Show it to him when he comes in and broach the subject again. I think you'll find him a bit more reasonable.'

The reporters arrived one by one and Juliet put the kettle on for coffee. She heard Gerry Bates arrive at about a quarter to ten and, after giving him half an hour to look at his post and settle down, she knocked on his door.

'How would you like your coffee this morning, Mr Bates?' she asked, looking in tentatively.

He looked up at her in the act of lighting his pipe. 'Just as it comes, girl, just as it comes.'

'White or – er – black?'

He took his pipe out of his mouth and one corner of his mouth twitched. 'In other words have I got a Monday-morning liver?'

'No, I just wondered.'

'White then. And one of those biscuits – the dead-fly ones.'

When Juliet returned with his coffee and a Garibaldi biscuit, she put the tray down on his desk and took a deep breath. 'I-I've written a preliminary piece about the Royal's panto,' she said, taking the folded paper out of her pocket. 'I thought you might like to have a quick read – perhaps while you're having your coffee.'

He bit a piece off his biscuit and eyed her. 'You don't give up easily, do you, Juliet?'

He was calling her *Juliet*. That was a good sign. 'Well, no,' she conceded. 'I went to one of their rehearsals yesterday and I think they deserve some publicity. After all,' she added daringly, 'The Pier Theatre doesn't really need it. Everyone goes to their show anyway.'

'And that's your considered opinion, is it?'

'Yes. It's going to be a very good show at The Royal,' she told him. 'Different; innovative. Rather special, I think.' She swallowed hard. 'I think it would make a very interesting feature for the paper.'

'Oh, you do, do you?'

'Yes. I mean, after all, what can you say about the Pier Theatre's panto? It's the same old format every year.'

He pointed suddenly to a chair opposite him. '*Sit down*,' he barked. She sat down gratefully, her knees suddenly wobbly. As she watched he took a deep draught of his coffee and picked up the typewritten paper she had laid before him on the desk. She held her breath as he read it. When he had finished he put it down.

'I said an inch and a half,' he said. 'This is too long.'

Her heart plummeted with disappointment. '*Oh*! I – thought—'

'You said something about a double-page spread; interviews with this new producer bloke.'

'I know but—'

'A double is out of the question, of course, but we might stretch to a full column, we'll see. Right then. Talk to Bill Martin, the features editor, about it and we'll see if any of your crazy ideas stand up.'

'A full column? Could we possibly stretch to two with – er – a photograph? Max Goddard was in the RAF. He-he's a war hero.' She bit her lip hard. Why had she said that?

He glared at her. *'Don't push your luck, girl!'* he roared. He thrust her article back at her across the desk. 'I must be out of my mind! Just get out of here. Oh, and next time you buy dead-fly biscuits, make sure there are more currants in them!'

CHAPTER SEVEN

Bill Martin was enthusiastic about Juliet's ideas for a feature on the Theatre Royal's pantomime, but he had reservations about making a spread of it.

'The Pier Theatre has always been a good patron,' he explained. 'They buy a large amount of advertising space. Apart from the theatre there's their restaurant, for instance, and their coffee lounge. We have a permanent weekly ad for those and at the moment they're all being refurbished so they're bound to splash out on the grand opening. Then there are all their dances in the ballroom – both weekday evening hops and tea dances. And the large functions they cater for.'

'It's all right for them,' Juliet added. 'They are subsidized by the local council.'

'I know, but that's not the point. We have to keep our advertisers sweet. There'd be no *Clarion* without them.' He looked at her downcast face. 'Tell you what, why don't we sneak these interviews of yours in, one each night, under the heading of – say . . .' He chewed his lip and looked at the ceiling. ' "WARNECLIFF'S UP AND COMING TALENT"?'

Juliet brightened. 'And link it to the panto write-up at the end? And maybe Fred could take a couple of photos at the dress rehearsal. I'm sure Mr Bates will agree.'

Bill gave her a cynical smile. 'I've got to hand it to you, girl,' he said. 'Ever the optimist, aren't you? Let me work something out and we'll talk about it later. Meantime we can put your prelim' piece in at the weekend and you can make a start on the interviews any time you like.'

Juliet was elated. In her lunch break she rang Max. 'Hi, it's Juliet. I'd like to start the interviews right away if it's all right with you,' she told him. 'So if you could arrange something—'

'You can start with me if you like,' he told her. 'Next week we'll be closed for rehearsals so everyone else will be more flexible, but I'll be free after curtain-up this evening.' When she didn't reply immediately, he said, 'Sorry, that's in your free time, isn't it? I tend to forget that other people work nine till five.'

'Oh no, that's OK,' she said quickly. 'Anyway, journalists don't keep to strict office hours.' She felt a little frisson of pride in referring to herself as a journalist. This was her first assignment; her chance to show what she could do and she was determined to make her mark with it. 'Shall I see you in the theatre greenroom?'

'No. Better to find a quiet corner somewhere. Tell you what, there's a pub called The Swan opposite the stage door. Suppose I see you there, in the lounge bar at about eight? It should be quiet at that time and if I'm wanted at the theatre I'll be close by. We could have a bite to eat too, if you like. They do really good sandwiches.'

'Fine. I'll see you at eight then.'

The reason for Juliet's slight hesitation when Max had suggested that evening for the interview was that Sylvia had called round to see her the previous evening and suggested a girls' night in to catch up on all their news. They'd agreed that Sylvia would drop round at about half past seven. Juliet felt bad about putting her off, but it was work after all. As soon as she got home she rang the Trents' number. Sylvia answered.

'Hi, Ju. I've just got home from the office. Soon as I've had my tea I'll be round.'

'That's what I was ringing you about,' Juliet said. 'I'm sorry, Sylvie, but I can't make it this evening after all. Got to work.'

'What, this evening? I hope you're getting overtime.'

'I'm doing an interview actually,' Juliet explained. 'It's not at the office.'

'Where are you doing it then?'

'At The Swan, in the lounge bar,' Juliet told her.

'In a pub?' Sylvia snorted. 'Doesn't sound much like work to me. Who are you interviewing?'

'Max Goddard, The Theatre Royal's producer.'

'Oh, I see. Are you sure it's not a date?'

'Of course it's not a date, Sylvia. It's my first assignment. I'm doing a feature on the pantomime. It's really important to me.'

'More important than me, obviously.'

'Oh Sylvie, of course it isn't. It is my job though. We'll get together another night. What about. . . .'

'I'll let you know when I'm free. Got to go now, tea's ready.' There was a click at the other end and the line went dead. Juliet stared with dismay at the buzzing receiver. She couldn't believe that her old friend was taking it so badly. They hadn't arranged anything special, just a cup of coffee and a gossip. They could do that any time. Surely she could understand that working on a newspaper was slightly different from being a typist in a solicitor's office.

She thought long and hard about what to wear. As it was evening she didn't want to appear too formal so that ruled out her one and only suit. After trying and rejecting several things from her limited wardrobe she decided that, as soon as she'd saved up enough clothing coupons she would go shopping for some clothes that were more suitable for a career girl than a teenager who had just left school. After all, it would be her twentieth birthday soon and everything she had looked hopelessly unsophisticated. Luckily Marion had given her one or two items before she went to Canada. One was a garnet-red wool dress which looked good with her dark hair. She decided on that. Over it she wore her navy reefer jacket winding her brightly coloured sixth form scarf around her neck to relieve the sombreness.

She arrived in the lounge bar of The Swan at five past eight and found Max waiting at a table in the corner of the room. He stood up when she came in.

'Hello. Can I get you a drink?'

'Just an orange juice, please.' He wore one of his signature roll neck sweaters underneath a black leather jacket, which he removed before going to the bar for her drink. Juliet took off her own jacket and took out her notebook and pencil, laying them on the table. As he put her drink down on the table Max noticed them and raised an eyebrow.

'You're not in a hurry, are you?'

'No.'

'Only I thought we could have something to eat when you've got all the stuff you want about me. After all, it is after hours and you have to relax sometime.'

She blushed, remembering Sylvia's slightly insulting suggestion that she was putting her off in favour of a date. However, the idea of relaxing with a good-looking man like Max was not exactly repugnant to her. 'That would be nice,' she said.

He leaned back in his chair and took a sip from what looked like a glass of whisky. 'I must say I find all this a bit embarrassing,' he said. 'I'm more used to being the interviewer than the interviewee. Where do we start?'

Juliet smiled. 'Why don't you just tell me about yourself?' she suggested. 'Where you grew up – went to school; how you got your first job in the theatre. You know – just ramble.'

He shrugged. 'OK, you asked for it so here goes. I grew up in a London suburb, which was handy for the West End theatres. My mother was a keen theatre-goer so I was taken to plays from an early age. I went to a boys' grammar school in Hammersmith and moved on to RADA at eighteen. I'd had just over a year in a repertory theatre in the Midlands when the war broke out and I was called up.'

Juliet was scribbling furiously, hoping she'd be able to read her slightly dodgy shorthand later. 'Did you play any important roles when you were in the rep'?' she asked.

He chuckled 'I never got further than ASM,' he told her. 'Assistant stage manager. It's a rather grand name for a general dogsbody, as I'm sure you know. I did get to play a few walk-on parts and on one memorable occasion I was a body that fell out of a cupboard.'

She looked up at him. 'Then you were called up?'

'Yes, for the RAF. I volunteered to train as a pilot,' he told her. 'My mother nearly had a fit. I wanted to fly Spitfires and I was lucky enough to be selected. It was desperately hard but madly exciting. Quite a few didn't even last through the training, but fortune must have been smiling on me.'

'You must have taken part in the Battle of Britain?' she said.

'Yes, but I'd rather draw a veil over that time if you don't mind. There's a limit to how long a pilot can last – if he doesn't get killed, I mean. A lot of the chaps got ill in various other ways and I was one of them. I crashed my kite on the home airfield through my own stupid fault.' His hand went involuntarily to the silver streak in his hair. 'I was lucky to get out with a few burns and scratches and after that there was no more flying for me.' She was guessing that he was playing the incident down deliberately when he suddenly looked up at her. 'You won't put any of that in, will you? You did say ramble. Perhaps it's time I stopped.'

'No! Please go on,' she said. 'I read about the documentaries you were involved with. How did that come about?'

He explained that when he was convalescing from his injuries a representative from a film company came round enquiring whether anyone had experience in acting. He gave her a lopsided smile. 'Yes, you've guessed; I volunteered again. This time it was slightly less dangerous than the flying. I was involved in several short films, two of which I got to direct, and one feature-length one, *Dawn Flight* in which I played a major role. At the end of the war I came out of the service, found myself an agent and the rest, as they say, is history.'

Juliet closed her notebook and smiled at him. 'Thanks. That was fascinating. I'll write it up later. And I promise I won't put in anything you don't want me to.'

He tossed back the last of his drink. 'You won't make me out to be some sort of war hero, will you?' he asked. 'Because I wasn't. And anyway, this is about the future, not the past and in particular the coming panto.'

'Just as you say.'

'Right. Let me get you another drink and what about something to eat?'

'That would be nice.'

'Sandwiches it is then.' He stood up. 'I don't know what's on the menu this evening. Spam's OK but I can recommend the cheese and pickle.'

Juliet smiled. 'Sounds delicious.'

When he came back with the drinks and sandwiches he looked at her. 'What about you? I know about your father, of course, but what's your story? Didn't you ever want to follow in his footsteps?'

She shook her head. 'I'd had enough of being an actor's daughter by the end of the war,' she told him. 'I was sent off to boarding-school –

hardly saw my family except in the holidays, which were mostly spent trailing around with Dad in ENSA – when he was still in this country. I grew really sick of it.' She took a bite of her sandwich and chewed thoughtfully. 'Though I have to admit that coming to the Royal has made me feel quite nostalgic. There's a certain atmosphere – a smell about backstage in theatres. I don't know, a mixture of greasepaint, coffee, cigar smoke and . . . something else. I can't put my finger on it.'

He laughed. 'Fear!' he said. 'Pure unadulterated terror.'

'I don't believe you.'

'It's a bit like flying; you get addicted to the adrenalin.' He looked at her. 'I take it your mother was an actress too.'

'No.'

'Oh.'

He did not pursue the question and Juliet said, 'She wasn't around when I was a child. I guess she must have grown tired of being married to an actor. She left us when I was two. Dad's with someone else now. My grandmother and an aunt were all the family I had and when I wasn't with Dad I was with them.'

'Do you see her – your mother, I mean?'

'I don't remember much about her,' she told him. 'I don't even know whether she's still alive.'

He shook his head. 'Sorry. I didn't mean to pry.'

'It's all right. We've all got things we don't really want to talk about.'

'Right. So who would you like to interview next?'

'Whoever is available.'

'OK, I'll telephone you and let you know who, when and where.'

When Juliet had finished her sandwiches she got up to go. 'Thank you for giving up your time and letting me interview you,' she said, holding out her hand. 'I'd better get home now and write this up while it's still fresh in my mind.'

'How did you get here?' he asked. 'Does the *Clarion* run to a car?'

'There is an old banger at my disposal, but I don't drive as yet,' she told him. 'My predecessor was going to teach me to drive but he's doing his National Service and he's been posted to Yorkshire so that's on hold for the time being. I usually get around on a bike but I came here this evening on the bus.'

'Then you must let me walk you to the bus stop.'

'No, really, I'll be fine.'

'I insist.'

He stood waving to her as the bus pulled away. She waved back, feeling slightly foolish. He was so nice. And so attractive. She wondered just how bad were the injuries he had suffered in the plane crash and if it had really been his fault. Clearly a head injury had caused the streak of silver in his hair. She remembered how warm and strong his hand felt as it held hers – held it for just a *fraction* longer than necessary as they said goodbye. Or was she imagining it? She brushed the thought away, thinking instead about the notebook nestling in her handbag and resolving to write the best, most truthful, yet complimentary write-up she could.

Over the days that followed she interviewed both male and female principals from the pantomime and Harry, the musical director. Her last interview was with Maggie Johnson, the wardrobe mistress. They met in a café next to the bus station where they had a fish and chip lunch.

She took an instant liking to Maggie, a straight talking Yorkshire woman in her late thirties who had spent the war in the ATS. She told Juliet that she had studied costume design at art school and worked before the war for a large West End theatrical costumier.

'I didn't want to go back to that when I came out of the service though,' she told Juliet. 'I'd had enough of London – fancied a quieter life. My husband was killed in North Africa. We married the year the war started. We had such plans for a home and kids for after the war, but it wasn't to be. Now I have to make myself a new life. These young actors are my family now and I want the best for them just like any mum would.'

She explained to Juliet how she got her ideas and showed her some of the sketches she had made of the costumes for the coming show. Juliet could see that she was talented, but more than that she was a wise mother figure to the company, dispensing down-to-earth common sense and advice to any young actor who came to her with worries or problems. When the interview was over they ordered coffee and Maggie lit a cigarette. As she blew out the smoke she looked at Juliet apologetically.

'Hope you don't mind,' she said. 'I can't have a fag when I'm working – too dangerous – all that fabric. So I confine it to when I'm away from the theatre.' She regarded Juliet. 'You're very young to be working on a newspaper,' she observed bluntly.

Juliet nodded. 'My first job.'

'Ah, thought so.' Maggie tapped the ash off her cigarette into the ashtray. 'An all-male environment, I bet. All of them old enough to be your grandad and resentful of a slip of a girl muscling in on their territory? I hope you don't let them bully you.'

'It was a bit difficult to begin with,' Juliet admitted, 'but I'm just discovering that I can be tough too. And actually one or two of them are really nice.' Her eyes narrowed. 'I'm still working on the editor.'

'Good for you!' Maggie laughed. 'You know, ever since I first came here I've been saying that what that paper needs is a woman's page. And now I've met you I reckon you're just the girl to handle it.'

'A woman's page?'

'Yes. There you are – something for you to think about for next year.' She stubbed out her cigarette. 'What do you think of Max?'

To her horror Juliet felt herself blushing. 'Max? Oh, I think he's very talented.'

Maggie nodded. 'You're right.' Her eyes twinkled. 'Quite a hunk of man too, though unlike most hunks he's totally unaware of the fact, which is just as well with so many young women lusting after him. We're all excited now that he's taken over the company with his brilliant new ideas,' she said. 'Fresh blood. New ideas. It's what the theatre – what the *country* needs now that the war is over. Can't cling onto the old ways. Have to move forward.' She smiled at Juliet. 'And if you play your cards right, girl, you can give that stuffy old newspaper a run for its money. If you ask me it's about time someone gave it a kick in the pants!'

When Juliet came away from her meeting with Maggie Johnson she wasn't absolutely sure just who had interviewed whom. She also wondered who the young women were who were 'lusting after' Max.

Juliet was washing up after her evening meal a few days later when there was a knock on the back door. Ever since she had cancelled her evening with Sylvia the other girl had maintained a sulky silence and

Juliet immediately thought her friend had come round to make up. She dried her hands quickly and opened the door. Outside, to her surprise, she found Marcus standing, suitcase in hand, his collar up against the rain.

'Dad! Come in out of the wet.' She drew him into the warm kitchen. 'I wasn't expecting you till next week.' She helped him off with his coat and draped it over a chair in front of the Aga.

'I know. I should have telephoned, but I just got fed up and lonely and I thought it would be nice to be with my best girl.'

'Oh, Dad! Why on earth didn't you let me know?' She hugged him. 'Well, never mind. It's lovely to see you anyway. Sit down and I'll find you something to eat.'

She rustled up beans on toast for Marcus and while he ate she proudly showed him the copies of the *Clarion* that carried the profiles she had written of the Theatre Royal's company.

'There's going to be a spread about the panto with photographs taken at the dress rehearsal.' Suddenly something occurred to her. 'Oh! It's great that you've arrived early. You'll be able to come with me now. Max is dying to meet you.'

He looked up. 'Who's Max?'

'He's the new producer at The Royal. He's just out of the RAF and he tells me that you're his hero. It was seeing you at the Vic before the war that made up his mind to train for the theatre.'

She'd expected Marcus to look pleased, but instead he groaned and rolled his eyes. 'Lord preserve me from over enthusiastic, starry-eyed youngsters,' he said.

'He's not all that young, Dad,' she told him. 'He's twenty-nine.'

'Why wasn't he in ENSA then?'

'Because he was in the RAF; a Spitfire pilot actually. But he plays that down. I can't wait for you to meet him. He's very talented. Just wait till you see the show. It's a really new slant on the tired old pantomime format.'

'He sounds a bit of a pain in the backside to me.' Marcus said grumpily.

Juliet stared at him. '*Dad*! You haven't even met him yet. It's not fair to make judgements like that.'

He pushed his chair away from the table and took out his cigarette case. 'Can you imagine what it's like?' he asked, taking out a cigarette and tapping it on his thumbnail. 'Having some bright-eyed, young smart aleck who thinks he knows it all trying to teach his grandfather to suck eggs.'

'Max has nothing but respect and admiration for you, Dad,' Juliet said. 'And I'd really rather you didn't smoke in here if you don't mind.' She stood up. 'I'll go and make up the spare room bed. Make yourself a cup of tea if you want, the kettle's boiling.'

While she was making up the bed Juliet regretted her angry remark. It must be galling for Marcus, seeing younger actors, full of hope and enthusiasm, building a career for themselves when with all his experience he was unable to get a job himself. Clearly he felt a failure and she had done nothing to boost his confidence by praising Max. Back in the kitchen she found him sipping a cup of tea. She noticed that the unlit cigarette lay on the table in front of him. She smiled apologetically.

'Sorry, Dad. I shouldn't have snapped at you. Light your cigarette if you want.'

He looked up at her with a wry smile. 'You had every right to put me in my place,' he said. 'I'm rapidly turning into a grumpy old curmudgeon. It's all just sour grapes as I'm sure you've guessed.' He put the cigarette back in the case. 'High time I gave up those coffin nails anyway. They're ruining the poor old larynx.' He grinned the familiar wry grin that twisted her heart. 'I remembered to bring my ration book by the way. Oh and I made a pot of tea. Want one?'

There were to be two dress rehearsals of *Dick Whittington*; one just for the company and another to which pensioners and children from a local children's home would be invited free of charge. Juliet took Marcus along to the first, which took place on the following Monday evening. Fred looked in during the evening to take photographs for the final piece, which was to appear in the *Clarion* in two days' time, the day before Christmas Eve. There were very few hitches during the rehearsal, most of them technical and quickly ironed out by the stage manager.

Throughout the whole rehearsal Marcus was quiet, making few comments. Juliet looked at him several times, trying to assess his thoughts, but his face gave nothing away. Afterwards Max had invited them to meet him in the greenroom for a drink and, as the company stood at the end to receive their producer's comments, she touched her father's arm.

'Shall we go, Dad? We can wait for Max in the greenroom.'

He nodded abstractedly. 'What? Oh, yes, all right.'

Seated at a table in the corner she asked him what he thought of the show. He nodded.

'As you say, it's a whole new slant. A bit risky, I'd say, but I hope it pays off for them. They've obviously worked hard.'

'What did you think of the effects?' she pressed him. 'So simple and yet effective.'

He nodded. 'Yes, I'll give you that.'

'And the script? Max wrote it himself.'

Marcus pulled down the corners of his mouth. 'That explains a lot,' he said.

Juliet frowned. 'What do you mean by. . . ?' Before she had time to finish her sentence Max appeared. He smiled and held out his hand to Marcus.

'Marcus King! It's a pleasure to meet you at last. Juliet might have told you that I was lucky enough to see some of your performances at the Vic before the war.'

Marcus winced. 'Back in my heyday, you mean – before the flood.' He rose and shook Max's hand. 'A lot of rather murky water has gone under the bridge since then.'

'Never mind, you're here. That's the main thing.'

Marcus nodded. 'Yes, I'm here, a piece of rather battered flotsam washed up on a muddy shore.'

Max shot Juliet an uncertain look. 'Right – so – what can I get you both to drink?'

When he had gone to the bar Juliet nudged her father. 'Dad! Did you have to be quite so caustic?'

'Was I?' He sighed. 'Sorry.'

'You know you were. Honestly, you've only just met him. What on earth must he think? If I didn't know you better I'd say you'd developed a massive chip on your shoulder.'

He gave her a cynical smile. 'Look on the bright side,' he said.

'Nothing's wasted. I'll be able to play *Richard III* – or *The Hunchback of Notre Dame.*'

'It's not funny, Dad,' Juliet whispered. 'Look, he's coming back. Please try to be pleasant. I have to live here, remember; and work with these people.'

To his credit Marcus behaved himself for the rest of the evening, chatting to Max and generously answering questions about his past career when Juliet knew he hated being reminded of the success he had once been. He complimented Max on the show and wished him success.

When Juliet announced that it was time they left Max asked her when the spread about the show was scheduled for publication.

'Day after tomorrow,' she told him. 'We'll be editing it in the morning. I think Fred's photographs will be good, but I'm not sure how many will be used or which ones.'

He walked up to the street entrance with them and at the door he took Juliet's hand. 'Thanks for all you've done for us, Juliet,' he said. 'I can't wait to see the *Clarion*. It's going to make all the difference to our bookings. They've already picked up just from the profiles you did.' He lifted the hand he held and kissed her fingertips. 'Thanks again.'

She blushed scarlet and was grateful for the one dim light over the door. 'It's n-nothing,' she stammered. 'Just doing my job, that's all.'

'A bit more than that, I know,' he said. 'Anyway, thanks for bringing your father to meet me. Goodnight, Juliet. See you on the first night. I'll put a couple of front row stalls aside for you at the box office and, of course, you're both invited to the first night party after the show.'

The following day Juliet was irritated when she was sent off to interview the widow of a local councillor who had died suddenly. She had been looking forward to helping edit the piece on the pantomime. By the time she got back to the office most of the other reporters had gone for their usual liquid lunch and she took the opportunity to type up her obituary while she could still decipher her shorthand. Fred looked in just as she was finishing. He seemed surprised and a little put out at seeing her.

'Oh – Juliet!'

'Hi, Fred,' she said without looking up. 'How did the editing go? I was disappointed at not being here to see the finished article.'

'Yes.' He shuffled some papers on his desk, avoiding her eye.

She looked up. 'So, was everything all right?'

'It was OK, I suppose.'

She frowned. 'Only OK?' She got up to move across to him. 'Fred, am I missing something? I did get my spread, didn't I?' She touched his shoulder, forcing him to look at her. As soon as she saw his expression it confirmed her worst fears. 'Right, you'd better tell me,' she said.

He sighed. 'A story broke. An unexploded bomb from 1942 was found on the beach during the clearing of the defences late yesterday afternoon. The UXB chaps worked on it most of the night by floodlights – very dramatic. It took up the whole of the front page and half of page two.'

'Her heart sank. 'Are you trying to tell me my piece had been discarded altogether?'

'Oh, no. It's not that bad.'

'Fred. Look, please, just what did I get?'

'Heavy editing and an eighth of page ten – the entertainments page. No photos, I'm afraid.'

Juliet swallowed hard. 'I worked so hard on that,' she said. 'A lot of it in my own time too.'

Fred patted her shoulder. 'I know, love, but I'm afraid this kind of thing goes with the territory. You'll have to get used to it.'

'Can I see the mock-up?'

He shook his head. 'It's already gone to press.'

Her eyes narrowed. 'That's why I was sent off to do that obituary this morning, isn't it, to get me out of the way? Mr Bates might have had the decency to tell me.'

Fred gave her a rueful grin. 'I think he knew he'd have a fight on his hands,' he said. 'In a way you should take it as a compliment.'

Juliet shrugged. It didn't feel much like a compliment to her.

That evening she got little sympathy from Marcus who was preoccupied. He'd spent much of his day trying to telephone Olivia. It seemed that when he eventually got through they'd had some kind of row and he was in no mood to listen to anyone else's problems.

She hardly slept at all that night, imagining Max's dismay when he opened the *Clarion* in the morning and found the show relegated to an eighth of page ten along with the Christmas Fairs and the Bring and Buy sales.

She was first in the office next morning, snatching a copy of the paper from the front office as she went through. There it was, all her work edited to within an inch of its life; every bit of style stripped out of it. No headline and no photographs. It was even worse than she'd imagined, a total fiasco. She could have wept.

At eleven o'clock Bill Martin came to find her. 'Sorry about your panto piece, Juliet,' he said. 'I think Fred's already told you why we had to re-shuffle everything.'

'The unexploded bomb,' she said flatly. 'It was certainly a bombshell for me. My first serious assignment and it blew up in my face.'

'At least it wasn't discarded altogether,' Bill pointed out. 'Gerry was all for ditching it, but I argued on your behalf.'

'You needn't have bothered,' she said. 'Hardly anyone will notice it now anyway, buried at the bottom of page ten. And my name will be mud as far as the Theatre Royal goes.' She looked at him. 'Sorry, Bill. That was rude and ungracious. Thanks for speaking up for me. And I know it's par for the course as far as journalism goes, but that doesn't make me any happier about it.'

Juliet was kept busy all morning, out and about on her bicycle doing wedding reports and covering the opening of a new grocery shop in the High Street but when one o'clock came round and she found that for once she actually had an hour to spare for lunch she made her way round to the Theatre Royal, determined to speak to Max and explain what had happened. In the greenroom she found several of the pantomime cast having sandwiches and coffee. Normally they were friendly but today they looked through her as though they'd never seen her before. She noticed a copy of the *Clarion* on the bar and was relieved when Ben, the barman smiled at her.

' 'Morning, Miss King. What can I get you?'

She glanced around her self consciously. 'I wondered if Max – Mr Goddard – was about,' she said quietly. 'I need to speak to him.'

He put down the glass he was polishing. 'I'll just go and see,' he said. 'Would you mind keeping an eye on the bar while I'm gone?'

'Yes, of course.'

But Ben was back very quickly, a rather embarrassed look on his face. Juliet said, 'I take it he's out.'

Ben shook his head. 'No, miss. He asked me to tell you that he hasn't time to speak to you.'

'But surely . . . it's lunchtime?'

The man looked even more awkward. 'I think it might have something to do with what's in there,' he said, inclining his head towards the newspaper.

'I know, and that's exactly why I'm here,' Juliet said 'to explain. There was an unexploded bomb. It was beyond my control.'

Ben shrugged. Leaning forward so that the others wouldn't hear he whispered, 'You know what these arty farty types are like, miss. All mouth and no trousers, if you ask me. If I were you, love I'd let him get on with it.'

Juliet got down from her bar stool. 'Thanks, Ben,' she said. 'I'll leave it.' She had just reached the door when she noticed a figure in the corner get up and move towards her. It was Maggie Johnson. She panicked. Dangerously close to tears, all she really wanted was to get away, but, as she put her hand on the door, Maggie called out to her.

'Juliet, wait.'

There was no escape. She turned. 'Oh, Maggie, hello.'

Maggie took her arm and steered her firmly through the door into the corridor. 'I can guess why you're here,' she said. 'Naturally everyone is terribly disappointed over the panto write-up, especially Max.'

'So I gather. He won't even speak to me,' Juliet said, her throat tight. 'There was nothing I could do about it. They even got me out of the way yesterday morning while the editing was going on – sent me off to do an obituary. It was the bomb story that ruined everything.'

'Of course. I realized that and so will Max when he's had time to calm down,' Maggie said. 'It's just that he's been so looking forward to this spread the *Clarion* was giving us – we all were. He feels—'

'Betrayed,' Juliet said bitterly. 'Believe me, I know the feeling.'

'If you take my advice you'll let sleeping dogs lie,' Maggie said. 'It'll all blow over, trust me.'

Juliet smiled at her. 'Thanks, Maggie,' she said. 'I don't think I've got much option.'

'Fancy a spot of lunch? My treat.'

Juliet shook her head. 'It's sweet of you, Maggie, but I'm not very hungry and I'm sure I'd be rotten company.'

Maggie smiled. 'Well, you know where I am, love, if you want to talk.'

As Juliet left the theatre it began to snow. She turned up her coat collar and walked to the end of the street. Turning the corner with her head down, she almost collided with someone coming in the opposite direction. Looking up she saw with a start that it was Max. She opened her mouth to speak, but he stepped back and, with a muttered apology, walked past quickly, looking through her as though she were a complete stranger.

'Who the hell do you think you are, coming in here and criticizing the contents of my newspaper?' Gerry Bates's face was purple as he addressed Juliet across his desk. 'Do I really have to remind you that you are the youngest and most inexperienced member of my staff? You are extremely lucky to have been given a job at all, never mind the assignment you bamboozled me into allowing you. Get out of my sight, girl. Remember on which side your bread is buttered, or find yourself a nice soft job that's within your capabilities – behind a shop counter somewhere.'

Juliet swallowed her pride, determined to stand her ground. 'I know I'm inexperienced,' she said as calmly as she could. 'And I'm grateful for the chance you gave me. But I worked very hard on the project and now everything I promised has come to nothing. These people will never trust me again. Any integrity I had will be—'

'*Integrity?*' Gerry gave a snort of mirthless laughter, spitting the word out as though it had a bad taste. 'No one expects *journalists* to have integrity. It's a luxury we can't afford. News breaks and everything else goes out of the window. The sooner you get that fact through your fluffy little head the better.' He looked at Juliet's pink cheeks and seemed to relent a little. Leaning forward he said, 'Juliet – grow up. Remember, never make promises then no one will be disappointed. Newspapers are about today and tomorrow, not yesterday's mistakes and failures. Dwell on those and you'll miss all the opportunities.' He saw her mouth begin to open and nipped any further argument in the bud. 'Right,' he said briskly. 'If there's nothing else . . . He looked up. 'Oh for God's sake, girl, it's not the end of the world. Cheer up, it's Christmas.'

CHAPTER EIGHT

'But the thing is I didn't *make* any mistakes, Dad. My write-up on the panto wasn't a failure either. It was damned good if I do say it myself. Or it would have been if—'

'Juliet!' Marcus looked up from the sprouts he was peeling. 'Give it a rest, darling, will you? You've been going on about it ever since you came home yesterday.'

They were preparing their Christmas dinner together in the kitchen. Juliet had managed to get a chicken from one of the local farmers and it was already in the oven, complete with the stuffing she had made from herbs from the garden. The rest of the Christmas fare she had bought with her collected points coupons. Marcus – typically – hadn't realized that his ration book alone was no use and that he should have gone to the food office before he left London to apply for emergency cards. But Juliet had managed somehow to make her own rations stretch to feed the two of them, mainly by going without lunches herself.

Marcus looked at her hurt expression and relented. 'I'm sorry, darling, but it does start wearing a bit thin when you've heard it for the umpteenth time.'

'A bit like you going on about not being offered any good parts,' she snapped. The moment the words were out of her mouth she was sorry. 'Oh, Dad, I'm sorry. I didn't mean that. It's just. . . .'

He put down his knife and put his arms round her. 'I know you didn't, love. It's this Max Goddard character, isn't it? You've fallen for him in a big way.'

She stared at him. '*What*? No! Of course I haven't.'

He grinned. 'No? Well, you could have fooled me. Why did you go to so much trouble for him then?'

'It's my job. It was my first professional assignment and I wanted to make a success of it. I promised him—'

'Ah! Never make promises unless you're absolutely sure you can keep them.'

'That's more or less what Gerry Bates, my editor said.'

'Well, he's not wrong.' He tipped the prepared sprouts into a saucepan. 'There, anything else I can do?'

'No, I think that's all.' She smiled. 'I managed to get a bottle of sherry. It's in the sideboard, why don't we have one now?'

Marcus fetched the bottle and two glasses, but when Juliet poured them a glass each she found that there was barely enough. She shook her head at him. 'I see you already found it.'

He looked shamefaced. 'I only had a couple of snifters, just to lift the old spirits. I got lonely on my own all day.'

'No, Dad, it was a full bottle. I was saving it.'

'Well then, I don't know how it happened.' He assumed his naughty little boy expression. 'Mice?'

In spite of herself she laughed. 'Dad! You really are incorrigible. Well, it's a good job I'm not all that keen on booze because there's nothing else.'

'That's where you're wrong!' Marcus left the kitchen to reappear a few minutes later with a bottle of brandy which he waved aloft. 'For the pudding,' he announced. 'Never touch the stuff myself as you know, but you can't have plum pudding without brandy, can you?' He looked at her. 'Am I forgiven, dear heart daughter mine?'

She took the bottle from him, noting as she did so that it was only half full. 'OK, you're forgiven, even if you don't deserve it.'

He sipped his sherry smacking his lips appreciatively. 'Maybe when we go to the panto tomorrow evening Max will speak to you again,' he said.

'We're not going.'

He stared at her. 'But he said he'd put two stalls aside for us at the box office.'

'Well, he won't do that now, will he?' she said. 'It was by way of a thank you. He's got nothing to thank me for now.'

Marcus frowned. 'But we'll still go,' he insisted. 'If I remember rightly he said something about a party. Never let it be said that Marcus King turned down the offer of a good first night party. Anyway, if you don't show up you're going to look guilty and as you've said, you've nothing to be guilty about.'

'I'm not going to risk being ignored again,' she said.

He gave her shoulder a push. 'Come on, don't be so stuffy. A couple of drinks and you won't give a damn who's speaking to you and who isn't.'

'If we go it'll be because I want to see the show,' she said. 'I shall pay for our tickets ... and I won't be going to any party afterwards. You can if you like, but I shall be coming straight home.'

He smiled and began to rub his hands together, but one look at her face told him he'd better take her at her word. 'All right, you win; stand on your dignity if you must. But I still think—'

'Dad!'

He held up his hands in a gesture of surrender. 'OK, OK, the panto incognito it is,' he conceded. 'With carriages before midnight for Cinderella.'

After they'd eaten they exchanged presents. Marcus was delighted with his book and in return he handed Juliet an envelope.

'I didn't know what to get you,' he said. 'And, as you know, the old coffers are a bit empty at the moment, so I thought you might appreciate some clothing coupons. I don't need them so you might as well have them. I know you girls are always needing to keep up with the fashions.'

Juliet opened the envelope to find an untouched book of coupons. 'Oh, Dad, thank you. They're just what I need, but what about you? If you get an important audition. . . .'

He held up his hand. 'Not very likely. Anyway, I've got plenty of things to wear.'

Juliet tucked the book of coupons away in her bag, feelings of sadness for her father mingling with the excitement of going shopping for the new clothes she had promised herself.

The following evening at the Theatre Royal Juliet did not enquire for the complimentary tickets Max had promised but bought two stalls tickets several rows back for herself and Marcus. They were almost the last available seats and, as they settled in their row, she was pleased to note that the auditorium was almost full. At least her sadly mutilated write-up on the production hadn't done too much damage to the bookings.

They both enjoyed the show enormously. In the interval they went to the bar where Juliet had a coffee and Marcus a whisky and soda. At the end of the finale the company took six curtain calls and the audience clapped and whistled appreciatively. Marcus glanced at her as they rose from their seats.

'Are we really going straight home?'

'Of course we are.'

'Right. Will you wait for me in the foyer.'

'Why? Where are you going?'

He raised an eyebrow at her. 'Really, Juliet, do you *have* to know my every move? If you must know your dear old papa's plumbing isn't what it was and I'll never make it back to Wycombe Heath on a jolting omnibus without a visit to the little boys' room first.'

She smiled. 'OK then, but don't be long.'

In the greenroom Marcus scanned the crowded bar. It was full of friends and family of various members of the company and it was several minutes before he spotted Max, laughing and chatting to a group of people on the other side of the room. Going up to him he tapped him on the arm.

'Can I have a quick word, old boy? Shan't keep you from your friends for long.'

Max looked surprised. 'Of course. Shall we sit over there? I can see a free table. Can I get you a drink?'

'Nothing, thanks. I've only got a minute. I just wanted you to know that Juliet was devastated about the write-up she prepared being cut like that. It wasn't her fault – something about an unexploded bomb that suddenly took precedence. When you refused to let her explain—'

'That was wrong of me,' Max put in. 'Stupid and childish. It was just that she promised such great things and when I opened the paper – well, it took me all my time to find it at first.'

Marcus nodded. 'Can you imagine how *she* felt after all the work she'd put in? She's very young you know and this was her first professional job. It meant a lot to her. She put her neck on the line for you and your show – worked long hours of her own time. She even had a go at her editor and risked losing her job when she discovered the hatchet job they'd done on it. And all for you to ignore her when she came to apologize.'

'I know.' Max ran a hand through his hair. 'I behaved badly.'

'I'm afraid you did.'

'I'm really sorry. Will you tell her for me?'

'I can't tell her anything.' Marcus stood up. 'She'd be furious if she knew I was here. The remedy is in your own hands.'

Max looked up. 'Was she here this evening? Did she see the show?'

'She certainly did. Wouldn't have missed it for the world after all the interest she'd put in. And by the way, she insisted on paying for our seats; wouldn't accept the complimentary tickets.'

Max sighed. 'I did notice the two empty seats in the front row.'

'Well, I've said what I came to say, so I'll leave you to it.' Marcus began to move away then turned. 'But I can't go without congratulating you on a first-class show. You deserve better than the *Clarion* gave you and you would definitely have got it. But who can compete with unexploded bombs?' He held out his hand. 'Sorry to interrupt your celebrations, but I couldn't go back to London without putting you straight about Juliet. It was good to meet you, Max. Who knows, maybe our paths will cross again one of these days.'

Max shook the hand he offered. 'I hope they do, Marcus. I really do. And thanks for coming. It was good to meet you, too. And you can rest assured that I'll make it up to Juliet one way or another.'

Juliet was waiting in the empty foyer when Marcus joined her. 'Dad! There you are. I was getting worried about you.'

Marcus was shrugging into his coat. 'There was a hell of a queue,' he said. 'Seems there are a lot of old codgers like me around.'

Juliet had to return to work the next day. It was quiet after the holiday and she found herself being sent on trivial errands most of the day. Bill Martin's wife had a birthday coming and she was delegated to find a suitable card and present. Fred had developed a bad cold over the Christmas break and Juliet was dispatched to the chemist to buy aspirin and cough linctus for him.

She had time to think during the day. Marion had said she should ask her father to tell her the truth about her mother's reason for leaving them. Soon Marcus would be itching to get back to London. Whatever he might say about how much he was enjoying the peace and quiet he was showing all the signs. She decided that if she was going to broach the subject it would have to be this evening.

At home she made a fricassee with the remains of the chicken. Marcus was sprawled, unshaven on the settee in the living room, looking morose. When she called him to the table and put his plate in front of him he stared at it, then at her.

'What is it?'

'Fricassee of chicken. It's one of your favourites.'

'Who said?'

Juliet put down her fork. 'What's the matter, Dad?'

'Who said there was anything the matter?'

'Your face – everything about you. I've hardly had one word out of you since I got home.'

He laid his own fork down. 'Sorry, love. It's Libby,' he confessed. 'I rang her this morning. I thought I'd go up there and see the show – stay a few days. I was foolish enough to think she might be missing me as much as I'm missing her.'

Juliet looked at him. 'And. . . ?'

'And she obviously isn't.'

'Did you have a row?'

He nodded miserably. 'I was really looking forward to going up there – to seeing her in the show – being together again.'

'Well, why don't you just go anyway?' Juliet suggested. 'I daresay you both said things you didn't mean. The telephone's no good. You need to sort it out face to face.'

He looked uncertain. 'Do you really think so?'

'Yes. Go tomorrow. But eat your dinner now before it gets cold.' She glanced at him as he began to eat. Was this really the right time to ask him about her mother? But it was the only chance she'd get. Goodness only knew when she'd see him again. Besides, she'd prepared herself for it now. It would be such an anticlimax to lose her nerve and let the opportunity go. Maybe after a good meal he'd have forgotten his row with Olivia and he'd be looking forward to seeing her and sorting things out – or apologizing, if she knew Marcus, whether the row had been his fault or not.

She found a tin of peaches at the back of the cupboard and opened it for dessert. Afterwards she insisted that Marcus relax in the living room and listen to the wireless while she washed up. When everything had been put away she took the coffee tray through to the living room and poured Marcus a cup. He smiled at her.

'Thanks for having me, darling,' he said. 'Sorry I've been like a bear with a sore head this evening. I've really enjoyed spending Christmas with you. I thought the panto at the Royal was very good indeed and I like your Max Goddard. I think he's really going places.'

'He's not *my* Max Goddard,' she told him, sitting down with her own coffee. 'But I'm glad you've enjoyed your stay. It was great having you, Dad. We haven't spent nearly as much time together as I'd have liked.'

'I know, darling, but, as you know, that hasn't been entirely my fault.'

Juliet put down her cup. It was just the cue she needed. Her heart was beating faster as she said, 'Dad, don't you think it's time you filled me in on what really happened all those years ago – between you and my mother, I mean?'

Immediately his mood changed. 'It's better you don't know,' he told her. As he put down his coffee the cup rattled in the saucer. 'There's a well worn phrase – let sleeping dogs lie.'

'I'm not a child any more,' Juliet insisted. 'I have a right to know. She was my mother and she left – apparently abandoned me. That's all I know, but there has to be more to it than that. Is she still alive? Do you know where she is? I need to know, Dad. Even Marion thinks it's time you told me.'

Marcus stood up suddenly, startling her. '*The devil she does*! It's all right for her, isn't it, thousands of miles away in Canada? If she wanted you to know why didn't *she* tell you?'

Juliet stared at him. 'You mean – you mean she knew – *knows*?'

Marcus shrugged. 'Your grandmother knew and I'd be surprised if she didn't confide in her only daughter once she was a responsible adult. But Mother and I decided all those years ago that it was better for you never to be told. Believe me, you wouldn't like it. It's not a pretty story.'

'I can take it. I'm an adult now.' Juliet shook her head. 'Dad, Marion has never lied to me. I'd trust her with my life, and she told me that my mother loved me – was a devoted mother. So why?'

'*Huh*!' Marcus gave an explosive grunt. 'She had a funny way of showing her so-called devotion!' He looked at Juliet. 'I'm saying no more so please don't push it. I'm going to pack.' At the door he turned. 'I'm adamant about this, Juliet. I don't want to hear another word about your mother and if you can't promise not to ask me again I'm afraid it's going to be impossible for us to go on seeing each other.'

'*Dad*!' She jumped up from her chair. 'Please don't say that. I'm sorry if I've upset you. Don't let's part on bad terms. If it hurts you so much I won't mention it again.'

He paused for a moment in the doorway then his expression softened and he crossed the room to hug her close. 'I'm sorry, angel, but it does hurt, yes. It still hurts intensely and if you and I had to part company it would break my heart. If it hadn't been for – for what happened I'd have been able to play a bigger part in your upbringing. We'd have had a proper father-daughter relationship. We've both missed out on so much and I can't help being bitter. But it's all in the past and that's where I want it to stay. I don't want to talk about it any more.'

Juliet kissed his cheek, tears trembling on her eyelashes. 'If it's what you want then we'll forget it,' she said. 'But don't let it spoil our time together. I can't remember the last Christmas we shared and it's been such fun. Go and do your packing. Go and make it up with Olivia, but please keep in touch – promise?' She drew back her head to look at him pleadingly.

He smiled. 'I promise. Of course we'll stay in touch. I couldn't bear to lose you, too. You'll always be my dearest girl.'

'I know. I love you, Dad.'

He kissed her forehead. 'Love you too, darling.'

Juliet really missed Marcus. He had only been with her for a few days and yet it seemed strange to come home to an empty house each evening. He telephoned to say that he'd arrived safely in Hull and that Olivia was very good in her pantomime. She asked if they had resolved their differences, but he hedged a little over that, saying obliquely that he was sure it would all be fine – given time. Olivia always knew how to make Marcus grovel. She'd milk the situation for all she was worth and come out on top just as she always did. Juliet shivered, wishing her father would drop the wretched woman once and for all.

After Christmas the weather took a turn for the worse. Sleet and rain, icy pavements and dark mornings and evenings did nothing to lift Juliet's depression. Clearly Marcus was determined to keep whatever had happened between him and her mother all those years ago to himself. What Marion had told her about her mother was at odds with what Marcus indicated – that her mother had been a bad, uncaring parent. And all the time niggling away at the back of Juliet's mind were Celina's words that afternoon at the caravan. *She loved her babby – still does. I see her grievin' sore.* Juliet kept reminding herself that Celina was just a gypsy fortune-teller and couldn't really know anything for sure, but she couldn't help wondering if her grandmother had confided in Marion, and whether Marion in turn had told the secret to Celina. She had become close to the gypsy woman when her young son was ill. Then there was the fact that Celina had spoken in the present tense, so could her mother still be alive somewhere and maybe even wondering where *she* was and how she'd grown up? The thought refused to be shaken off and invaded her thoughts and dreams constantly.

She went round to see Sylvia on New Year's Day, taking with her the small present she had bought her; a little powder compact with a pink rose on the lid. In the Trents' kitchen she heard about their busy Christmas, which as usual had been full of family parties and visits. When Sylvia walked down to the gate with her she confided that she had met someone special.

'His name is Derek,' she said. 'He's just come to work for the same firm as me and he's hoping to be made a partner some day. Trouble is he'll be called up any day now to do his National Service. He got a deferment because he was still at university.' She giggled shyly. 'Fancy me going out with a boy who's been to university.'

'That's wonderful, Sylvie,' Juliet said. 'I'm really pleased for you.'

'What about you and that chap from the paper – Nigel, isn't it?' Sylvia asked. 'Didn't you say he was going to teach you to drive?'

'He's been posted to Yorkshire,' Juliet told her. 'So I haven't seen him for a while.'

'Oh, that's a shame. I expect you miss him.'

'He's not a boyfriend or anything like that,' Juliet said quickly. 'I'm grateful to him for helping me get my job. I took his place at the *Clarion* as I expect I told you. But we're just good friends.'

Sylvia looked at her. 'And what about the chap at the Theatre Royal, the one you stood me up for?'

'Sylvie! I didn't stand you up,' Juliet insisted. 'It was work. I had to interview him for the paper and the only time he could spare was that evening.'

'So you're saying you don't fancy him then?' Sylvia said, with a maddening smirk.

'I've just said, haven't I?'

'OK. No need to get touchy about it.'

'Well, we're not all boy mad, you know.'

Sylvia bridled. 'Like me, you mean?'

'No, of course not. I'm really pleased you've met someone special, Sylvie. It's just that at the moment I'm concentrating on trying to make a career.'

Sylvia was only half appeased. 'Right. So, there's no one special?'

Juliet thought for one fleeting moment of her father's words about Max. *You've fallen for him in a big way.* Why did everyone get the impression that she was keen on Max? It was ridiculous. It seemed that a girl couldn't even *speak* to a member of the opposite sex without everyone thinking she was keen on him. 'No,' she said firmly. 'I'm much too busy with work.'

'That's a shame,' Sylvia said. 'I'd suggest we got together some evening soon, but Derek seems to have all my evenings tied up at the moment.'

'That's OK,' Juliet said. 'As you know a lot of my work is out of hours anyway. Free evenings are almost a thing of the past.'

As she walked the few yards home she thought about her friend's words. This Derek seemed to have a tight hold on her already, but then that was all she really wanted from life, wasn't it? To be the average housewife like her mother, with a husband and two point four children. It was quite sad really.

As January thawed into February and the days began to lengthen a little, Juliet's job at the *Clarion* remained frustratingly a cross between errand girl and tea lady. She was pedalling her bicycle down the High Street one morning when Maggie Johnson hailed her from the other side of the road.

'Hi there – Juliet!'

Juliet dismounted and crossed over. 'Hello, Maggie. How nice to see you.'

'Got time for a coffee?'

Juliet looked at her watch. She was returning to the office to type up an account of a forthcoming wedding, but there was no hurry. 'Why not?' she said, nodding towards a nearby tea shop. 'Shall we go in there?'

Seated at a table in the window they ordered coffee and buns. Maggie looked at her. 'It was a shame about your panto feature after all the work you put in on it, but I expect you're busy on some new project by now.'

Juliet sighed. 'Not really. And not everyone saw it as you did, Maggie. I'm afraid Max felt badly let down.'

'Well he needn't have,' Maggie said, pouring them a cup of coffee each and passing Juliet the plate of buns. 'We've done fantastic business throughout the run and the show that opens next week is almost sold out too. The profiles you wrote about us all seem to have been a big help.'

Juliet sipped her coffee. 'Well, that's something, I suppose.'

Maggie smiled. 'So how's the career going?'

'It's good of you to call it that,' Juliet said. 'I'm back to being the errand girl.'

'Why are you riding a bike? Don't they let you have the use of a car?'

'There is an old pre-war bone shaker at the disposal of the junior reporter but I can't drive,' Juliet told her. 'Nigel, whose job I took when he went into the army, was going to teach me, but now he's been posted to darkest Yorkshire and doesn't get home often.'

'That's not a problem,' Maggie said. 'I'll teach you. I was a driver instructor in the ATS and if I do say it myself I'm pretty damned good.

Sundays any good for you?'

Juliet's eyes lit up. 'Oh, Maggie! That would be marvellous. Yes, Sundays would be wonderful. Thank you so much.'

'If we're quick we might get you your licence before they bring back testing,' Maggie said. 'It was suspended for the duration of the war, but I've heard it could be back in place later this year.'

'Mmm, that would be ideal,' Juliet said, her mouth full of bun.

Maggie looked thoughtful. 'What about that women's page we talked about for the paper?' she asked. 'Have you done anything about that yet?'

Juliet gasped. 'Do you know, I'd forgotten all about that. It's a great idea. I'm not exactly my editor's favourite person at the moment but it might be worth a go. Thanks for reminding me, Maggie.'

'What d'you mean, *women's page*?' Gerry Bates was staring at her, his eyes bulging in the way she was becoming accustomed to. 'We cover all the weddings and christenings already, don't we? What else is there for women to be interested in?'

'Lots,' Juliet told him. 'Make-up and fashion, cookery and slimming diets, hairstyles. But not only that, women are interested in the arts too – theatre and cinema. Then there's handicrafts, embroidery, knitting, dressmaking – not to mention horoscopes and competitions.'

'You're suggesting I fill up the paper with the kind of stuff they can get from any women's magazine, are you?'

'Ah, but ours would have a local slant,' Juliet told him. 'We could feature local art and craft courses, exercise classes, what's on at our own cinemas and theatres; what the local fashion shops have for the new season.'

'You're talking about establishments who already advertise and *pay* us,' he pointed out. 'Why should they do that if you're planning to do it for them for free?'

'You're missing the point,' Juliet said daringly. 'They'd be even keener to advertise in the *Clarion* if we *reviewed* their films, plays and fashion collections,' she said. 'And we could always point out tactfully that we'd only supply that service for our *regular* advertisers.'

In spite of himself the corners of his mouth twitched. He laid his pipe down on the overflowing ashtray to allow himself a pause.

'You've put a bit of thought into this, haven't you?'

'Yes, I have,' she admitted. 'Someone pointed out to me recently that the *Clarion* needed a women's page and it made me think. The readership is out there for it. Now that the war is over women want to accentuate their femininity again.'

'Do they, b'God?' He considered for a moment then looked up at her. 'All right then. Put your money where your mouth is and do me a mock-up.'

'Really?' Her heart leapt. 'I'll do it this weekend.'

He held up his hand. 'Don't go counting any chickens.' he warned. 'I'm making no promises and don't you go making any either. I think you know where that can lead. I'm the editor, remember. I have the final word.'

'Yes, Mr Bates. I'll remember.'

'Another thing to remember is that there's still a paper shortage and it'd have to fit into the present format. It might have to be more like half a page than a whole one.'

'I understand,' she said. 'I'll have it on your desk first thing on Monday morning.'

'No need to rush. There's . . .' but she'd already gone. He stared at the swinging office door. 'No hurry,' he finished lamely. Bloody girl'd be after *his* job next!

Juliet was busy working on ideas for the women's page at home on Saturday evening when the telephone rang. She was tempted to let it ring, unwilling to disturb her train of thought. But then she thought it might be Marcus so she laid down her pen reluctantly and went to answer it.

'Hello.'

'Juliet? Juliet King?'

'Speaking.' She'd already recognized the voice and her heart quickened.

'Hello, Juliet. It's Max Goddard here. I've been meaning to ring you ever since Christmas, but we've been so busy rehearsing the new play and playing the panto at the same time.'

'I can imagine,' Juliet said guardedly. 'What can I do for you?'

'Well, I'm ringing to ask if you're free tomorrow evening.'

She paused. 'Well, yes.'

'Then would you like to have dinner with me? Sunday evening is my one free evening.'

'Dinner? Oh, I don't know.'

'Of course if you'd rather not I'd quite understand,' he said. 'Our last meeting was a bit of a disaster – on my part, I hasten to add. I was unforgivably rude, but I would like to make it up to you.'

'Well. . . .'

'Please say yes, Juliet.'

The 'please' did it. She wanted to have dinner with him, of course she did, but she wasn't going to allow him to patronize her. But his 'please' sounded so genuine.

'All right, I'd love to,' she said. 'Thank you for asking me. Where shall we meet?'

'I'll book a table at The Feathers. Shall we meet in the bar at seven-thirty?'

'All right. I'll see you there at seven-thirty then.'

The Feathers was the town's best hotel and Juliet was impressed. When she replaced the receiver her thoughts were no longer on the mock-up for the women's page but on what she would wear tomorrow evening.

In the end she decided on the garnet red dress that Marion had given her. She hadn't yet had time to go shopping for new clothes and it was the only really smart item in her wardrobe. She pressed it carefully and hung it up on the wardrobe door.

Her first driving lesson with Maggie on Sunday morning went well. The older woman had a pre-war Austin Seven which she had christened Monty after her favourite field marshal. She pronounced Juliet 'a natural' and prophesied that eight to ten lessons should be enough to make her proficient enough to get a licence. It had occurred to Juliet that Maggie might have had something to do with the sudden dinner invitation from Max and, during the course of the lesson, she tactfully quizzed the older woman. However it seemed that she'd had the last few days off after the busy Christmas rush and hadn't seen or spoken to Max since the previous week.

Juliet dressed for her dinner date in the best of moods. She had a good chance of pulling off the women's page with Gerry Bates; she was learning to drive at last and she was being taken out to dinner by Max, who had actually apologized for his bad behaviour.

She made sure she was five minutes late arriving at The Feathers. She didn't want to be first and have to hang around in the bar on her own. She needn't have worried, he was already there, sitting at the bar and chatting to the barman in a totally relaxed way as though he dined at The Feathers every day of the week. He wore a dark grey suit and tie and looked somehow different – more formal. When he turned and saw her hovering in the doorway he smiled and stood up.

'Juliet! Come and have a drink while you look at the menu. It's looking particularly tempting tonight.' He raised an eyebrow at her. 'What will you have?'

Suddenly orange juice seemed childish and unsophisticated and she smiled at him and said, 'A sherry would be nice – thank you.'

She hoisted herself onto a bar stool next to him and took the outsized blue leather menu, scanning its contents. The prices astounded her, but she tried not to show it.

'The roast chicken sounds nice,' she said at last.

'And to start?'

She looked at the menu again. Everything seemed to cost the earth. Soup was the cheapest and she decided that rather than have him think she was exploiting him she'd have that. 'The vegetable soup sounds' – she blushed, realizing that she'd already said nice twice. – 'delicious,' she substituted quickly.

Max ordered for them and she sipped her sherry. Nervous about her driving lesson, she hadn't eaten anything since breakfast and it made her feel slightly light-headed. When Max suggested another she began to shake her head and, to her relief, a waiter appeared to say that their table was ready and Max took her arm and escorted her through to the restaurant.

The carpet was deep and dark blue and the walls satiny white. Subdued lighting came from pink-shaded wall lights. The tables with their pristine white cloths, sparkling glass and gleaming cutlery made Juliet feel slightly intimidated. Her thoughts went to the bus station café where she and Maggie had eaten fish and chips and the Spartan dining hall at school, all scrubbed tables and chunky white crockery.

The waiter pulled out her chair for her and shook out her napkin, spreading it over her skirt. Max smiled at her from the other side of the table.

'All right'

'Fine, thanks.'

A wine waiter appeared and handed Max the wine list. He looked across at her. 'As you're having chicken I expect you'd like white,' he said. 'A nice Chardonnay perhaps?'

Juliet had no idea what that was, but she nodded, hoping she wouldn't have to drink something horrible. Max ordered and sat back, smiling at her.

'I've been meaning to get in touch with you ever since Christmas,' he said. 'I was very rude to you and I can't tell you how bad I feel about it.'

Embarrassed, she shook her head. 'No need,' she told him. 'I saw Maggie the other day and she told me that you played to full houses all through the panto run. I was relieved that I – we – the *Clarion* hadn't let you down too badly.'

'You didn't let us down at all,' he said. 'Business really picked up after the profiles you wrote. Bookings are good for the next show too. I know there was no excuse for my behaviour. Put it down to the stress of my first important production for the Royal.'

The wine waiter brought the uncorked wine and poured a little into Max's glass. He took a sip then nodded. Juliet was dismayed to see the large goblet in front of her filled to the brim. Max raised his glass.

'Here's to the *Clarion* and the Royal,' he said.

Juliet lifted her glass and repeated the toast, touching her glass to his with a clink. She took a sip and tried not to grimace. The level of the wine hardly seemed to move. Perhaps the food would help it down.

The vegetable soup and the roast chicken were delicious and Juliet, by now very hungry, did them justice. She chose sherry trifle for dessert and enjoyed that too. In fact she couldn't remember when she had enjoyed a meal so much. She was so engrossed with the food that she hardly noticed that she'd finished her wine or that Max had refilled her glass a couple of times. She didn't notice his amused glances either as he watched her clear her plates with obvious relish.

They took their coffee in the lounge and Juliet sank back against the cushions of a comfortable armchair feeling relaxed and replete. Somehow she seemed to be having trouble concentrating on what Max was saying and preventing her eyelids from closing.

'Enjoy your meal?' Max asked.

She nodded, making a supreme effort to sit up straight and look alert. 'Very much. Thank you, Max.'

'You're looking very attractive this evening,' he said softly. 'That shade of red really suits you.'

'Does it? Thanks.'

He poured her a black coffee and passed the cup across to her. 'Drink that up, Juliet.'

She frowned. 'I don't like coffee without milk.'

'Yes you do,' he insisted. 'Tonight you do, I promise.'

She blinked, suddenly realizing what he was getting at. Picking up the cup she drank it down quickly. 'I don't drink alcohol normally,' she told him. 'I think the wine has made me a bit . . . tired.'

'You should have told me.' He refilled her cup. 'There's no rule that says you have to drink if you don't like it. Here, have some more coffee. It'll help.'

It did help and, as the mist inside her head cleared a little, Juliet looked at her watch. 'Heavens! It's a quarter to eleven,' she said. 'I really should be going. In fact I think I might have missed the last bus.' She began to get up but he reached out to touch her arm.

'It's all right. Relax. I'll take you home in a taxi. There's no hurry, is there?'

'Not really.' Relieved, she sank back in her seat.

'You haven't mentioned your father. How is he?' he asked. 'Is he still with you?'

'No. He went back right after the holiday. Olivia, his girlfriend, was in pantomime up in Hull and he went up there to join her.'

'Is he working?'

She shook her head. 'He's finding it hard to get parts since ENSA,' she told him. 'He wouldn't want anyone to know it but he's losing his confidence and his self esteem. To tell you the truth, he's beginning to neglect himself and I worry about him a lot.'

He frowned. 'I had no idea. He hides it well.'

Suddenly Juliet's head cleared. Why on *earth* had she said that about

Marcus – and to Max of all people? These things got about in theatrical circles and Marcus would never get work if it became known that he was losing his self-belief. She forced a laugh which turned into a hiccup. 'Listen to me,' she said. 'Take no notice. It's just a bit of typical daughterly fussing. Dad would be furious if he could hear me.'

He stood up and held out his hand. 'Come on, Juliet. Time I took you home.'

While Juliet went slightly unsteadily to the cloakroom for her coat the receptionist telephoned for a taxi which arrived within minutes. Max helped her into the back and then followed.

'Are you sure you're all right?' he asked as he closed the door.

She nodded. 'I'm fine, thank you. In fact there's no need for you to come with me. I'll be perfectly all right on my own.' She was by now beginning to feel foolish and humiliated. And when she saw him smiling in the dimness of the cab her irritation mounted.

'I'm sure you live in town.' she said. 'The taxi can easily drop you off first.'

'Relax!' He took her hand and squeezed it. 'Juliet, you may have a low opinion of me, but never let it be said that I'd let my date travel home by herself.'

She was silent, biting her lip and wishing the taxi ride could be over quickly.

'I really did appreciate all that you tried to do for us at Christmas,' he went on. 'I was unforgivably boorish and I wanted to make it up to you.'

'And you have,' she said. 'Very generously. It was a beautiful meal and I enjoyed it very much.' She looked at him. 'So now we're quits.'

He frowned. 'You make it sounds as though I thought of it as repaying a debt.'

'Weren't you? Not that it wasn't kind of you,' she added quickly.

'There was nothing *kind* about my invitation this evening, Juliet,' he said. 'I wanted to see you again.'

'Oh!'

'Is that so hard to understand?'

'Well. . . .'

'It's true. I wanted to see you again – very much.' To her surprise he cupped her chin with his hand and bent forward to kiss her gently.

'*Oh!*' she said again.

'I was disappointed about the panto write-up at the time and I knew that I must have upset you. But when your father said you were *devastated. . . .*'

'*What?*' She pushed him away violently. '*Dad* said that? He spoke to you about me? But when was this? And where?'

Realizing his gaffe he tried hard to back pedal. 'He only meant to make me understand how badly—'

'I said where?'

'After the show in the— It was on the first night of the panto.'

'When he said he was going to the gents!' She stared at him. 'And you thought you had to butter me up in return!'

'No! It wasn't like that.'

'Why else would you ask someone like me out to dinner in a place like The Feathers and – and *kiss* me?' She was close to angry tears now. 'You must have thought I'd be flattered to be wined and dined *by you*. How arrogant can you get? You must think you're God's gift to women. Well, you're not. You're just a – a *wolf!*' The moment she'd uttered the word she cringed with embarrassment. And when she heard his smothered laugh she wanted to jump out of the moving cab.

The moment it pulled up outside Heathlands Cottage she opened the door and jumped out, slamming it behind her and running up the path. Standing in the shadow of the porch she heard the cab pull away and drive off. Fumbling in her bag for her key she swallowed hard at the lump in her throat. She'd never been so shamed and mortified in her life. '*Damn bloody Max Goddard*,' she said between clenched teeth. '*And damn Marcus too for sticking his nose in. In fact, to hell with all men!*'

CHAPTER NINE

It was a couple of weeks later that Juliet looked up from her desk one Monday morning to see a familiar face smiling down at her.

103

'*Nigel!*' He was wearing his uniform, which now sported a single stripe on the sleeve. 'Why didn't you let me know you were coming home on leave?'

'Thought I'd surprise you,' he said with a grin. 'I've seen all the chaps. I was purposely leaving you till last.' He looked at his watch. 'It's almost one o'clock. Do they let you off the chain to graze midday?'

She laughed. 'I usually bring some sandwiches, but I am entitled to an hour.'

'Good, then why don't we go and find ourselves a café where you can fill me in on all the news?'

Since Gerry Bates had agreed to give the women's page a month's trial Juliet had been allotted an office. It was really the cubby hole that Gerry's secretary used when she came in for two hours each morning to deal with the post and type any letters he needed to send.

Miss Yates was a tiny, birdlike woman of indeterminate age. No one had ever known her Christian name and no one really knew anything about her. She scuttled in at nine o'clock each morning and was gone by eleven, her tasks neatly and efficiently completed, letters left on Gerry's desk for signing and copies carefully filed. Juliet was allowed to use her room, desk and typewriter once she had left. It wasn't ideal, but it was better than nothing as she told Nigel over coffee and sandwiches at the Jersey Cow milk bar in the High Street.

'I understand that the panto spread you planned didn't quite come off,' Nigel said.

Juliet sighed. 'An unexploded bomb turned up on the beach when they were clearing the defences and that took over the whole of the front page, which meant—'

'No need to go on,' he said holding up his hand. 'That's journalism for you. You can't rely on anything.' He looked at her. 'Was the Theatre Royal producer upset at the cut in your review?'

Juliet winced at the memory. 'You could say that. He completely cut me dead afterwards, though he took me out to dinner a couple of weeks ago to make amends.'

Nigel raised an eyebrow. 'Really? So you and he are now on a slightly different footing?'

Juliet shook her head vigorously. 'No! It was just his way of apologizing for his rudeness.' She carefully omitted that the evening had been a total disaster, or that the real reason for Max's invitation was that her father had intervened.

Still smarting over the humiliation she had telephoned Marcus and told him in no uncertain terms not to interfere in her life again. She hadn't heard from him since.

Keen to change the subject she looked up at Nigel with a smile. 'Guess what, I asked Gerry if I could start a women's page, and he agreed.'

'Wow! Good for you,' he said. 'You know you really can't grumble. You've done better than I ever did, persuading old Gerry the Terrible to let you do the panto review *and* have a whole page to yourself.'

'Half a page actually,' she said. 'And I'm not counting my chickens over that any more after the panto débâcle so I shan't be surprised if that gets cut in half too. You know I feel a bit of a fraud really.'

'How come?'

'Well, reviewing the panto was your idea and the women's page was suggested to me by the wardrobe mistress at the theatre. Neither idea was mine.'

'Doesn't matter, it was you who spotted the potential and followed them through. It's a pity about the driving lessons. Four wheels would be a big help to you now.'

'I've even got that organized,' she told him excitedly. 'Maggie Johnson, the wardrobe mistress at the theatre, whose idea the women's page was, is teaching me. She was a driver instructor in the ATS.'

'A driver/instructor eh?' He pulled a face and made a mock salute. 'Better sit up straight and do as you're told then.'

Juliet laughed. 'No, she's a lovely person. Not a bit bossy.' She looked at him critically. 'You're looking really well, Nigel. The army life obviously suits you.'

He shrugged. 'It's OK; not as bad as I expected. I've made some good friends. I was fed up not getting home for Christmas though. I got a forty-eight hour pass but it takes all day getting down here from Yorkshire.'

'Your family must have been disappointed.'

He smiled. 'Well, I've got seven days this time, so how about letting me take you out for a slap-up meal one evening?'

'That sounds lovely.'

'And you can tell me how the first issue of the women's page kicks off.'

'Yes. I can't wait to see what kind of feedback we get,' she pulled a face. 'If any.'

'Don't be such a pessimist. Did you say it's to go in once a week?'

'Yes. On Wednesday – the day after tomorrow.'

'Why Wednesdays?'

'It'll give me a chance to see the latest film or play and write a review. I'll only be able to take one theatre or cinema a week. Then there'll be recipes to dream up. That was a problem to begin with. I looked out one of my gran's recipe books but they all seem to be pre-war and demand loads of butter and eggs. I thought it might be a good idea to ask cooks and chefs from local restaurants to contribute those.'

Nigel looked doubtful. 'Aren't they usually a bit cagey about their precious culinary secrets?'

'That'll be where my charm comes in,' she told him with a grin.

He laughed. 'Well, you've certainly worked it on Gerry successfully.'

'We're inviting readers to write in and say what they think, so I'll have to make it good.'

'And I'm sure you will.'

By the time they parted company back at the *Clarion* office Juliet had arranged to meet Nigel for a meal on Friday, which would be his last day. He told her he would book a table and would come and pick her up in his father's car which he was hoping he'd be allowed to borrow.

Juliet spent the afternoon getting her first women's page ready to go to press. Her page was to be entitled *Juliet's Jottings*. It had been Gerry's choice and she hadn't been too sure about it. It sounded a bit like *Peg's Paper* but, as the fate of her brain child already hung in the balance, she kept quiet about it and let him have the last word.

For the first week she had chosen to include a fashion item and some beauty tips, supplied respectively by the fashion buyer and the beauty consultant at Brightwell's, the department store. There was to be a review of the film currently showing at the town's largest cinema: *The Wicked Lady*, with Margaret Lockwood and James Mason, which she had seen the previous evening. The recipe was for bread and butter pudding, taking into account the new rationing restrictions which had been brought in at the beginning of February. She had persuaded the cook at the bus station café to supply that, promising to mention her by name. There was also a simple competition, the prize for which was a ticket for the show at the Pier Theatre, which Juliet had persuaded the front-of-the-house manager to part with, reminding him that it was by way of being a free advertisement.

As the paper was put to bed she watched the sub editors anxiously in case any of her precious copy was cut and she was in the office bright and early on Wednesday morning to grab a copy of the paper and see her handiwork.

'Looks pretty good, eh?' She turned to see Bill Martin looking over her shoulder.

'Not bad,' she said. 'I only wish I had more space. I could have included so much more.'

He shook his head at her. 'If I were you I'd hold your horses on that one,' he advised. 'At least for the time being. I don't know how you managed to persuade Gerry to let you have even half a page. Do you realize he's actually cut his precious fat stock prices for you? Greater love hath no man!'

They laughed together and Bill patted her shoulder. 'Well done, girl, but seriously, I'd rest on your laurels for a bit and see how things go.'

She nodded. 'Thanks for the tip, Bill. I will.'

Nigel was allowed to borrow the family car and arrived on Friday evening at eight o'clock to take her out to dinner. As she settled into the passenger seat of his father's much cherished 1937 Hillman, which had spent the war years on blocks in his garage she asked where they were going. Nigel shook his head.

'Wait and see,' he told her mysteriously. 'But I'm sure you'll like it.' He smiled at her. 'I like your outfit, by the way.'

Juliet had spent some time in the fashion department at Brightwell's and, while she was there, she had decided to treat herself to one or two items with the help of Marcus's clothing coupons. She'd bought a very smart dark suit to replace her old one. She felt it would be useful for interviewing important people for the paper. On the more frivolous side she had been unable to resist a dress in a pretty shade of pale green; filmy georgette over a silky under slip with two little diamante clips at its square neckline. There was a little jacket to go with it and she found perfect shoes in a darker shade of green suede. It was the first really sophisticated outfit she had ever possessed and it made her feel confident and special. She smiled at Nigel's compliment.

'Thank you,' she said. 'I'm really looking forward to this evening.'

'Me too.' He looked at her. 'Well, how did the women's page go down?'

'Well enough, so far.' Juliet held up crossed fingers. 'If we get some favourable feedback I'll get to keep it. If not, it'll be the panto all over again.'

Nigel grinned. 'Don't be such a pessimist. You'll get your feedback all right. I read the page myself and tried it out on Mum. She thought it was just what the stuffy old *Clarion* needed.'

'Really?' She searched his face. 'You are telling me the truth, aren't you? Not just saying that.'

He turned to her with a look of horror. 'Would I lie to you? No, you did a good job, Juliet. I'm sure it's going to be a success.'

When he parked the car at the rear of the hotel she still didn't know where they were going, but as soon as they walked round the corner her heart sank.

'We're not going in there, are we?' she asked him as she looked up at the Georgian façade of The Feathers.

He looked dismayed. 'Well, yes. I've booked a table. Don't you like it? It's the best hotel in Warnecliff.'

'Yes, I know.' She swallowed hard, remembering her last visit. 'And of course I like it,' she said quickly. 'But it – it's terribly expensive.'

'You can let me worry about that,' he said with a smile. 'There's nothing much to spend my army pay on up in Yorkshire anyway. I promised to give you driving lessons and I had to let you down. This is to make up for it.'

'There's no need, honestly. I'd be quite happy with fish and chips.'

He looked aghast. 'What, in that outfit? Come on now.' He took her arm and steered her firmly towards the entrance. 'No arguments.'

They ordered and sat in the lounge bar, waiting for their table to be ready, Nigel with a lager and Juliet with her usual orange juice. This time she was determined not to touch any alcohol and make a fool of herself. Nigel looked at her.

'Are you all right? You look a bit on edge.'

She nodded. 'Of course. It's really nice of you to bring me here, Nigel, but something simple would have been just as good.'

He narrowed his eyes at her. 'I sense that there's a reason for you being this uncomfortable,' he said. 'Have you been here before?'

She chewed her bottom lip, torn between denying it and telling him the whole story. In the end she said, 'Yes – once.'

He nodded. 'Ah, I get it. *He* brought you here, didn't he, this producer bloke? Was there a bit more to the evening than you've told me?'

Reluctantly she nodded. 'Oh, Nigel, it was *awful*,' she confessed. 'He asked me what I wanted to drink and I said – God knows why – *sherry*. And then he ordered all this wine with the meal and I—'

'Got a bit high?' he finished for her.

She nodded miserably. 'The worst part was that he noticed and made me drink two cups of black coffee. Then he took me home in a taxi because I was in no fit state to go on the bus. Then, in the taxi – he kissed me.'

'He *did*? The rotten scoundrel!'

Juliet glanced across at him. Was he laughing at her? But his face was completely straight. She went on hurriedly, 'No. It was only a peck, nothing heavy. What really annoyed me was that he let slip that Dad had told him how upset I was that he'd ignored me after the thing with the panto review. I got *really* angry then and I called him – I called – I—'

'Go on,' Nigel urged. 'I can't wait to hear what you called him.'

'I called him a *wolf*,' Juliet said, her cheeks reddening at the memory.

Unable to contain himself any longer Nigel burst out laughing. 'Oh, Juliet! I'd have given anything to have been a fly on the wall. You're priceless, you really are!'

'Don't *laugh*. It was dreadful. I curl up every time I remember it.'

'Well, if I were you I'd forget it,' he advised. 'Chalk it up to experience. We all make mistakes and do embarrassing things that make us want to crawl under the carpet. It's part of life.'

She nodded. 'I suppose you're right.'

'Anyway, I daresay he's already forgotten it,' Nigel said lightly. 'Oh look, the waiter's beckoning us. Our table's ready.'

Juliet got up and followed him into the restaurant. She wasn't sure about his last remark – wasn't sure that she wanted Max Goddard to have forgotten her, written her off as a naïve little fool. On the other hand perhaps it would be best if he had.

The meal was delicious. Juliet enjoyed it even more with Nigel as her companion. She could relax with him, knowing she didn't have to impress him, or pretend to be more sophisticated than she was. When they'd eaten they took their coffee in the lounge and this time Juliet was able to enjoy her coffee laced with cream just as she liked it. Once she glanced up at the clock over the bar and was astonished to see that it was already half past ten.

'Heavens! I don't know where the time has gone to this evening,' she remarked.

Nigel smiled. 'Good food and even better company. No need to worry about buses tonight, anyway. Dad's trusty Hillman awaits you in the car-park, so we can sit here as long as we like.' He sighed. 'This time tomorrow I'll be back in barracks so I'm savouring every minute of this evening.'

She nodded. 'Two years is an awful long time out of your life when you could be getting valuable experience in your career. It hardly seems fair.'

'Well, at least they let me finish my training,' he said.

Juliet poured the last of their coffee and sat back to enjoy it when suddenly she caught a movement out of the corner of her eye. A couple had just come in and walked up to the bar. Nigel gave a low whistle and she turned to see Madeleine Fielding, who had played a major part in the Theatre Royal panto standing at the bar. She wore a slinky black cocktail dress and patent court shoes with high heels. Her gleaming blonde hair, piled on top of her head, displayed her elegant neck and the sparkling jewels in her ears.

'She's from the theatre,' Juliet whispered.

'She certainly stands out in a crowd,' Nigel said softly. 'What a figure!'

Madeleine moved slightly and Juliet drew in her breath sharply as she saw for the first time who her companion was. She turned away quickly, trying to hide her face in her coffee cup, but she was too late. Max had seen her and was heading straight for them, Madeleine following reluctantly.

'Juliet! How nice to see you,' he said.

He glanced across the table at Nigel and Juliet said, 'This is Nigel Foreman, I took his job at the *Clarion* when he was called up for his National Service. He's home on leave.'

Max reached out a hand to Nigel. 'Nice to meet you, Nigel. I'm Max, by the way; Max Goddard and this is Madeleine Fielding.' He turned to Juliet. 'You remember Maddy, don't you, Juliet? She played Alice in the panto.'

'Yes, I remember.' She smiled at the other girl who smiled back frostily. She looked up at Max. 'Well, we mustn't keep you. We were just leaving anyway, weren't we, Nigel?'

Max bent forward and laid an arm across her shoulders. 'Juliet, I've been meaning to ring you – is your father working?'

'Not as far as I know – at the moment,' she said.

'I'll get his address from you some time,' he said. 'I'd quite like to keep in touch.' He looked at Madeleine who was tapping her foot impatiently and then at Nigel.

'We're too late for dinner, but we thought we might get sandwiches and a nice bottle of wine,' he said. 'I'd better let you go. Nice to see you, Juliet. I'll ring you soon.'

'Don't bother,' she muttered under her breath, as she watched him cross the lounge, his arm round Madeleine's waist. Nigel looked at her.

'So that's the famous Max Goddard,' he said. 'I have to say that he didn't look as though he's written you off – far from it. In fact I'd go as far as to say that he seems rather taken with you.'

'Not a chance!' Juliet blew out her lips. 'He hero-worshipped Dad when he was a boy. Now he seems to think some of his talent might rub off, that's all it is. It's not me he's taken with.' She picked up her jacket and bag. 'Shall we go?'

In the car on the way back to Wycombe Heath Juliet was quiet. When he drew up outside Heathlands Cottage Nigel switched off the engine and turned to her.

'He really gets to you, doesn't he?'

'Who?'

'*Who*!' He laughed. 'Come off it, Juliet, Max Goddard of course.'

'He does *not* get to me!'

'No? You could have fooled me.'

She smiled at him. 'Sorry, Nigel. All he does is makes me cross. I refuse to let him spoil the lovely evening we've just had. Do you want to come in for a last cup of coffee?'

He shook his head. 'I'm really tempted, but I've got a five o'clock start in the morning.'

'Oh, that's a shame. When do you think you'll get home again?'

He shrugged. 'Before too long, I hope.' He paused. 'Juliet, will you write to me? Oh I know you have dropped me the odd line, but it would be nice if you could make it more – well – regular.'

'Of course I'll write, Nigel.'

He touched her hand. 'What I'm really saying is that I'd like to think of you as my girlfriend. Is that a horrifying thought?'

She laughed. 'I already think of myself as your friend and, as I'm also a girl I suppose that makes me a girlfriend.'

He laughed and squeezed her hand. 'You know damned well that's not what I had in mind.' He leaned across and cupped her chin, looking into her eyes. 'If I were to kiss you – just a peck, nothing heavy,' he added, quoting her, 'would you scream, or faint and have an attack of the vapours, or would you just call me a wolf?'

'Why don't you try it and see?'

He kissed her, very gently at first, then, moving closer he pulled her into his arms and kissed her again more deeply. Drawing his head back to look at her he said, 'At least you didn't faint. Is that a good sign?'

'I'm not really the fainting type,' she told him.

'You didn't call me a wolf either.'

She sighed. 'I'm never going to live that down, am I?'

'Afraid not. Have you got a photograph of yourself, Juliet?' he asked. 'It'd be nice to show off to the other blokes.'

'Nigel! I'm no pin-up girl,' she said. 'You should have asked Madeleine Fielding. She's much more the type. You said yourself that she had a lovely figure.'

'Not a patch on yours,' he said. 'I much prefer your looks to hers anyway. She looks as though she could be a really heartless one.'

'How do you know I'm not?' she challenged. He sat back and looked at her.

'Are you trying to tell me something, Juliet?'

'Just that I made up my mind a long time ago that I'd never marry, or get into a serious relationship,' she said. 'So anyone who gets close to me will have to understand that.'

'You're a bit young to make a decision like that,' he said. 'Don't you want to have kids some day?'

She shook her head. 'I've seen what a mess a broken marriage can leave, for everyone, children especially. My parents split up when I was little. Even Dad's relationship with Olivia doesn't make him happy. He's just so entrenched in it now that he can't live without her however miserable she makes him. I just think it's wrong – and sad – to have to rely completely on one other human being for your happiness. It makes you so . . . so vulnerable.'

'How cynical for one so young,' he said.

She shook her head. 'I'm just trying to save myself and others a lot of unhappiness.'

He gave her a quick hug. 'Well, let's take things as they come, shall we?'

She nodded. 'Just as long as you know how I feel.' She touched his cheek. 'I am very fond of you, Nigel.'

He grinned ruefully. 'Well, that's a start, I suppose.'

In the kitchen Juliet was thoughtful as she put the kettle on for a bedtime drink. Nigel had surprised her with his sudden request for her to be his girlfriend. She had misgivings, hoping it wouldn't spoil the easy relaxed friendship they already had. She was fond of him, but so far she couldn't imagine falling in love with him – or anyone else for that matter. Men were far too complicated for her to puzzle out. She wasn't even sure she wanted to be bothered trying.

Marcus sprang into her mind. What had Max really meant when he said he wanted to keep in touch with him? Maybe she should offer him this opportunity. Max was a contact after all – young and with a finger on the current pulse. Maybe she should ring her father and ask him whether he wanted her to give Max his address. Switching off the kettle she went into the hall and dialled the number. When Marcus answered it was immediately clear that he'd been drinking.

'Juliet! My own angelic baby daughter!'

'Dad, listen, I saw Max Goddard this evening and he asked me for your address. Do you want me to give it to him?'

'Does 'is mean that you've f'given your stupid old dad? I've missed you so much, my darling Ju-ju.'

Juliet winced. Marcus always got maudlin when he'd had too much to drink. *'Dad!'* she said severely. 'Did you hear what I said? Max Goddard has asked me for your address. Do you want me to give it to him?'

'Wass'e want my address for?' Marcus slurred. 'A place to doss down when he's in Town?'

'Of course not. He just said he'd like to keep in touch with you.' There was no response at the other end of the line and she said, 'Dad, are you still there?'

'Wha'? Yeah, still here.'

'Are you working?'

He gave a half snort, half laugh. *'Working*? Could call it that, I s'pose. Just finished another deadbeat session in a film.'

'Oh, well that's something.'

'Not even a proper film this time, one of those advertisement things they show in the interval at the cinema,' he said. 'I played a patient in a dentist's chair. All you get to see of me is my molars and a tasteful shot of my nasal hair. Needless to say I didn't get any lines to say – not even *aaargh!*' He made a gargling sound that would have made Juliet laugh if she hadn't known her father in this mood so well.

'Don't worry, Dad. I just know you'll get that break soon.'

'Really? Well, you know a bloody sight more than I do.'

'At least I've got some good news, Dad,' she said. 'I've been given a weekly women's page at the *Clarion*. The first one went in this week.'

There was a pause, then she heard a strange snuffling sound at the other end of the line. 'Are you all right?'

'Libby's left me,' he said, his voice husky with misery. 'She met some fellow up in Hull and he's offered her a part in a touring play.'

Juliet's heart sank. She couldn't pretend to like Olivia or to think she was good for her father, but she knew how deeply this would affect him. 'Never mind,' she said breezily. 'She'll be back, you know she will. She's left you before.'

'Not like this,' he said. 'She's totally besotted with this chap. He's directing the play and she thinks he's heading for the big time. I daresay she's hoping to ride on his coat tails like she once did with me.

That's all she ever wanted me for – have to face up to the fact now.'

'No, Dad. She loved – *loves* you,' Juliet said, against all her convictions. 'She'll soon realize that and come back begging for forgiveness.'

'And if she did I'd be fool enough to let her,' he moaned. 'Whass *wrong* with me, Ju? Am I just a washed-up old has-been who nobody wants any more?'

'No!' Juliet was really worried now. 'Stop it, Dad!' she said. 'You're just feeling sorry for yourself and I won't have it. You're one of the finest actors this country has ever had so pull yourself together and get out there looking for work again. Stop taking anything that idiot of an agent chucks at you. Get yourself a new agent. Demand the kind of work you're worthy of.'

'I can't – not any more. Not even sure if I want to.'

'Then get on the next train and come down here to me,' she said. 'Let me look after you and feed you up. You've got to stop drinking, Dad, and I bet you're not eating properly.'

'Don't boss me about. You're worse than your Aunt Marion.'

'You need taking in hand,' she told him. 'Now, are you coming or do I have to come and get you?'

'You don't want a boring old fart like me cluttering your life up.'

'Are you listening? If you're not here by lunchtime tomorrow I'm coming up there to fetch you.'

'OK, OK, you win.'

'You'll come?'

'Yeah, I'll be there.'

It was only after she'd put the receiver down that she realized he hadn't even acknowledged the fact that she'd had a small success of her own.

True to his word Marcus arrived early on Saturday afternoon, looking hung over and depressed, his jowls dark with five o'clock shadow and his eyes bleary. Juliet had a hot meal waiting and made him sit down and eat it. He saw her looking at the two large suitcases he'd brought with him.

'I've given up the flat,' he said by way of explanation. 'Couldn't afford to keep it on when I wasn't there. Hated the bloody place anyway – full of memories; mostly bad ones.'

Juliet was a little dismayed. 'You know you're welcome to stay here as long as you want, but is it a good idea to be away from London for too long?' she asked. 'It's important to keep your face in front of the people who matter.'

He gave a cynical little laugh. 'The *people who matter* as you call them seem to be sick and tired of this worn out old *visage*.'

'Suppose Olivia comes back?' she asked. 'Won't she wonder where you are?'

Marcus smiled. 'It's a lovely idea darling, but A, she won't *be* back. She made that more than clear. And B, if she did decide to return it wouldn't be to find yours truly. I've got to acknowledge the fact that she's gone this time and I'm going to have to face a future life without her.'

'You seem very sure.'

'Couldn't be surer, my love.'

'Well, you won't want to hear this, Dad, but I'm glad it's over,' Juliet said. 'She was no good for you. She was dragging you down, undermining your confidence. Look on tomorrow as the first day of the rest of your life.' A sudden idea hit her. 'You can even help me. On Monday evening I have to see the latest play at the Theatre Royal and write a review. Who better to help and advise me but the famous Marcus King?'

He brightened. 'Well now, you know I'm always happy to do anything to help.'

'Dad. . . .' She knew what she was about to say would not be popular. 'Look, you'll have to go to the Labour Exchange first thing on Monday morning and sign on. If you don't you're soon going to run out of money.'

His eyes widened. '*What*? Stand there in a queue with hoi-polloi holding my hand out like a beggar?'

'Of course if you've got enough money to keep you going indefinitely.'

He sighed. 'To be brutally honest, angel, the train fare just about cleared me out.'

She gasped. 'Did Olivia clear the bank account before she left?'

'No.' He paused, looking down at his hands. 'But her brother came round, demanding money for her.'

'And you gave it to him?' Juliet could hardly believe her ears.

Marcus got up from the table. 'Look, never mind all that.'

'You're talking about Adam Kent, aren't you? Did he come round looking for Olivia?'

He turned to stare at her. 'You know him?'

'I met him once,' she told him. 'It was when I was staying with you last autumn. He was looking for Olivia that time too. Actually he was at the flat the day before. I came in and heard them having a row about something. I didn't like him.'

'What did he say to you?'

'Nothing much, I was just about to leave to catch my train so I gave him rather short shrift. Why on earth did you give him money, Dad?'

Marcus shrugged. 'Mainly to get rid of him. I'm putting Olivia and everything to do with her behind me now. For the time being no one knows where I am and it's better that way. Just let me stay and recharge the batteries for a couple of weeks then I'll high-tail it back to London, find a cheap room somewhere and start pounding the Charing Cross Road again.'

By Monday morning there was quite a postbag of letters at the *Clarion* commenting on *Juliet's Jottings*. One or two had misgivings; one thought that the new page was 'condescending'; another that 'modern women were more interested in politics and current affairs'. But on the whole the letters were complimentary and enthusiastic. Gerry called Juliet into his office on Monday morning.

'Looks as though you've pulled it off,' he said gruffly. 'I have to say it went down pretty well. Even my wife liked it – said it was about time that the paper gave some space to the distaff side.' He looked up at her. 'So you'd better get on and prepare this week's page,' he said. 'Normally you'll have more time, but as the first week was a trial you've only got today and this evening to come up with your copy. It's a challenge for you. And it had better be as good or even better than last week's.' He glowered at her. 'So, what are you waiting for?'

Juliet worked like a beaver all day, collecting fashion and beauty tips from her contacts at Brightwell's. She interviewed the housekeeper at The Feathers, getting some useful spring cleaning advice from her;

whilst there she also persuaded the restaurant manager to provide a meal for two as that week's competition prize.

Marcus came into town and met her for a snack lunch at the Jersey Cow. She was pleased to see that he looked much better; his eyes were clearer and there was more colour in his cheeks.

'Did you go to the Labour Exchange?' she asked him tentatively.

He nodded. 'I decided it was my right to get some money from the government,' he said. 'After all that serving my country during the war – it was that that wrecked my career, wasn't it?'

'No, it was not,' she told him firmly. 'You've got to start being more positive, Dad. It'll pay off. You see if it doesn't.'

As they ate he came up with the suggestion that she might review a novel once a month for her page. Seizing on the idea, Juliet went off to the largest bookshop in town and bought the latest novel published by Willis and Rooney the popular romantic publisher, determined to read it in bed, ready for next week's page. She spent the afternoon at the office, preparing the material she had already accumulated and she was busy typing up her copy when the telephone rang. She lifted the receiver.

'*Daily Clarion*. Juliet King speaking.'

'Hello, Juliet. It's Max – Max Goddard.'

She almost dropped the receiver. His was the last voice she had expected to hear. 'Oh, Max – hello,' she said, quickly recovering.

'If you remember I said I'd ring,' he said. 'To get your father's address.'

'Yes, I remember.'

There was a pause and then he prompted, 'So, may I have it? Or is there a problem?'

'Oh – no. The fact is Dad is staying with me at the moment. He's – er – between flats and – er – jobs at the moment.'

'I see.'

'As a matter of fact we're coming to the theatre this evening. I'm going to review the play for my page in the paper.'

'Your page?'

'Yes. I'm editing the weekly women's page. It's called *Juliet's Jottings*.'

'Juliet's Jottings eh?' to her annoyance he sounded amused. 'That sounds very professional. Congratulations!'

'Thank you,' she said stiffly.

'You said *we*. Does that mean you'll be bringing your father with you?'

'That was the plan, yes.'

'I'm honoured. And that's ideal. Why don't you both join me for a drink after the show?'

She couldn't refuse knowing that Marcus would want to see him. She told herself that she could always make herself scarce and leave them to chat. 'Thank you,' she said. 'That would be very pleasant.'

When she replaced the receiver she found to her intense annoyance that her hand was shaking. Why did she allow him to have this effect on her? *That sounds very professional* indeed. Who did he think he was?

CHAPTER TEN

Kiss Me Quick, the play at the Theatre Royal was a farce. The plot was flimsy and rather silly and Juliet wondered how she was going to write a complimentary review of it. But she made notes, remarking on the scenery and costumes and the antics of the company's elderly character actor who made the most of his mediocre script to get as many laughs out of his part as he could. She hoped that Max would appreciate the fact that she was sacrificing her own good taste for him. During the performance Marcus shot her a few looks that told her plainly that he shared her view. When the curtain came down at the end of the first act he gave a sigh of relief.

'Don't know about you but I could use a drink after that.'

Juliet nodded. 'A coffee would be nice. We're meeting Max later, remember. When we do you won't be too disparaging about the play, Dad, will you?'

He raised an eyebrow at her. 'What do you take me for? I can see he's done the best he can with it, but it is a stinker, isn't it?'

She laughed. 'I'll certainly have my work cut out writing the kind of review he'll like.'

'I have to say that the cast is good,' Marcus observed. 'They're not a bad lot actually, 'specially the old boy playing the vicar. You have to be good to wring laughs out of rubbish like that.'

When the final curtain came down they took themselves off to the greenroom.

'Thank God for that,' Marcus muttered under his breath. 'I don't think I could have sat through another five minutes.'

Max was waiting for them, sitting up at the bar. He stood up and held out his hand to Marcus.

'Good to see you again. What can I get you?'

Marcus smiled. 'Very good of you, old boy. I'll have a whisky and soda.'

Max glanced at Juliet with a smile and said, 'Orange juice?'

Determined not to be patronised she said quickly, 'No. I think I'll have a lager, please.'

His eyebrows rose fractionally but he made no comment.

They took their drinks to a table in the corner and Max said, 'I shan't ask you what you thought of the show. Ghastly, isn't it?' He looked at Juliet. 'I shan't blame you if you condemn it as a load of you-know-what.'

'Dad and I both thought that the cast handled it very well,' Juliet said.

'Mmm.' Max took a long draught of his drink. 'Trouble is I don't always get the choice of what plays we put on,' he told them. 'The theatre is run by a committee and occasionally they insist on having their own way.' He grinned ruefully. 'On this occasion they were of the opinion that I'd had my own way a bit too often lately and that we were getting too highbrow.' He smiled at Juliet. 'So that being the case, you giving the play a less than rave review would do me a favour.'

She smiled back. 'I'll try to be tactful.'

'One thing I did get my own way about was our summer special,' Max went on. 'We're to get a six week run during the summer season: a really recent play with a special guest star in the lead. They gave me carte blanche – of both play and star.'

'Oh, really?' Marcus looked interested. 'Have you decided what to put on?'

Max nodded. 'I've chosen *House Guest*. It's a new play by Peter Longhurst. It's about a family who enter a competition, the prize for which is to have a celebrity to stay for a weekend. The celebrity turns out to be Frank Langley, a best-selling author who turns out to be an absolute monster who makes all kinds of outrageous demands on his hostess and generally turns the whole household upside down. It's very funny.'

'Sounds like a sure-fire hit,' Juliet said.

Marcus leant forward. 'I've heard of the play,' he said. 'Actually I know Peter Longhurst slightly. We met once when I was touring with ENSA.'

'Then you'll probably know that the denouement is that when the weekend is over and the family are heaving a sigh of relief at the thought of getting rid of him, the celebrity slips on his way to his taxi and breaks his ankle, meaning the family are doomed to be stuck with him for weeks.'

Marcus laughed. 'Longhurst is a superb playwright,' he said. 'I should imagine it's a first-class script.'

'Oh, it is.' Max looked thoughtful. 'The thing is, Marcus, it struck me that you would handle the part of Frank Langley superbly. I know it's only six weeks' work, plus a couple of weeks' rehearsal on half pay, but if you're not doing anything else. . . .' He looked up hopefully. 'Does it appeal at all?'

Juliet looked at her father. She knew he must be highly delighted at the prospect but he was frowning uncertainly.

'Well,' he said, stroking his chin, 'I am waiting to hear about a possible film deal at the moment. If it comes off I wouldn't be available.'

Juliet could hardly believe her ears. 'That was only a faint possibility, Dad, wasn't it?' she put in quickly. 'You said yourself that you weren't all that keen on the part anyway.'

Marcus nodded, playing along, every inch the consummate actor. 'That's very true,' he said. He looked at Max. 'When would you require me to begin rehearsals?'

'We open mid-May, so we're starting rehearsals at the beginning of the month,' Max told him.

'And are you making me a firm offer?'

121

Max nodded. 'Oh yes indeed. If you are agreeable we could work out some details right away. But if you'd like to sleep on it, why don't you come and see me in the morning?' He glanced from one to the other then added, 'Of course the pay would reflect your standing as a celebrity – ex-Old Vic and so on, though it will be negotiable. I have to warn you that the committee always has to have the last word.' He smiled at Juliet. 'And I'm sure you'd get a favourable write-up from your daughter.'

'Naturally.' Juliet took a sip of her lager and tried not to shudder. 'I noticed that Madeleine Fielding wasn't in the play tonight,' she remarked.

'No. She's left the company,' Max told her. 'She's got a very small part in a new West End musical, *Bless the Bride*. Finding out that she could sing when she was in the panto encouraged her to audition and she got the part. That's what we were celebrating at The Feathers when I saw you the other night.'

'Oh, I see.' Juliet bit her lip. 'You must miss her.'

He looked surprised. 'Yes. As a matter of fact it's been very inconvenient. She was required for rehearsal very quickly and I had to get another female juvenile lead in a hurry.' He nodded towards her barely touched drink. 'Don't drink that if you don't like it. Let me get you something else.'

Juliet coloured. 'What? Oh no.' She picked up the glass and took a large mouthful, swallowing it down bravely. 'It's delicious.'

Max walked out to the street with them and bade them goodbye on the pavement. 'See you in the morning then, Marcus – about eleven.' He held out his hand. 'And I do hope that your answer will be yes.'

Marcus shook his hand. 'Till the morning.'

When they were out of earshot Juliet nudged her father in the ribs. 'What was all that about a film offer?' she asked. 'Is there one?'

'Of course there isn't, but it doesn't do to appear too keen,' Marcus told her. 'Don't want the fellow to think I'm on my uppers do I?'

'Oh no, heaven forbid,' Juliet said, adding, 'Even if you are.'

On the bus on the way back to Wycombe she thought about Madeleine Fielding. So she'd left the Theatre Royal. Why should that fact please her, she asked herself? It was a matter of supreme indifference to her whether the girl was here in Warnecliff or on the moon. And the fact that Max missed her simply as a 'female juvenile lead' was of no consequence at all, was it?

Juliet sat up till the small hours composing her review of *Kiss Me Quick* for the women's page and almost overslept the following morning as a result. Snatching a quick breakfast she reminded Marcus that he had a date with Max at eleven.

'You will go looking decent, Dad, won't you?' she said, her mouth full of toast.

'*Decent?*' Marcus looked outraged. 'Don't I always look decent? Did you think I was going to turn up in my underwear?'

'You know what I mean,' she said. 'To begin with, you could do with a haircut. Wear your good suit and try not to cut yourself shaving.'

'For heaven's sake, girl, you make me sound like a dissipated old slouch!'

Looking at him across the table in his tattered dressing-gown, his hair awry and his cheeks dark with stubble she had to restrain herself from saying that right now he looked like one. Popping the last of the toast into her mouth she got up. Dropping a kiss on his forehead she said, 'You can look very handsome and distinguished when you put yourself out, Dad. I've got to fly. See you for lunch?'

He nodded, only half reassured. 'One o'clock, if you can bear to be seen with an old has-been like me.'

She laughed, pulling on her coat. 'Oh, pass me my violin! Bye.'

The second edition of *Juliet's Jottings* went to press and Bill Martin congratulated Juliet on her quick presentation of it.

'You've done well, considering you had so little time,' he said. 'I think this is going to be a winner. Well done, Juliet.'

When one o'clock came round she was feeling very up-beat and went off to meet Marcus with a spring in her step. He was already at the Jersey Cow when she arrived. Before he caught sight of her she stood in the doorway, looking at him. He wore his dark-grey suit and she was surprised to see that he had actually had his hair cut. He must have hurried round to the barber's soon after she left for work. He looked smart and well groomed and she felt her heart swell with love at the sight of him. He looked every inch the man-about-town, handsome and debonair; more like the father she used to know. Now that he was wearing his suit she noticed for the first time that he had

123

even lost some of the excess weight he had put on. She guessed it was not intentional – more likely the result of fretting over Olivia, but nevertheless it was an improvement. He looked up and saw her and his face broke into a beaming smile.

'*Juliet*! Over here, darling.'

Several heads turned at the sound of his melodious actor's voice and Juliet joined her father slightly self-consciously. 'Hi, Dad. I take it your meeting with Max went well.'

He nodded. 'Everything is settled. I'm to begin rehearsals on May the third. I have to say that it won't pay the best money I've ever earned, but it's better than standing in a queue at the Labour Exchange. It'll be nice to be solvent again.'

'That's great news.' She looked at him as a suspicion occurred to her. 'Dad, do you owe any money to anyone?'

He stared at her aghast. '*Owe* anyone? Certainly not!'

'You paid the rent on the flat up to date when you left, did you?'

He paused. 'Yes, well sort of.'

'What does "sort of" mean?'

He shrugged. 'They were stuffy about me not giving notice – wanted a month's rent in lieu. A whole *month*! I ask you!'

She sighed. 'And you left without paying it?'

He shook his head. 'I simply didn't have it, poppet. I told you, the train fare just about cleaned me out.'

'So why on earth did you give Olivia's brother money?' She looked at him closely. 'He didn't threaten you, did he?'

'Threaten?' Marcus bridled. 'He wouldn't dare. I'd have had the police onto him instantly, and he knew it.' He took out a cigarette and lit it. 'The fellow knows other ways to get what he wants.'

'Which are?'

Marcus shook his head impatiently. 'Oh for heaven's sake, Ju. Why are we talking about that miserable little toad when we're supposed to be celebrating?'

'You'll have to give up those.' Juliet indicated the cigarette in his hand.

He sighed. 'Don't be such a bore, Juliet. Today's special.'

'All right, you win – just this once. But I'm watching you from now on. This could be just the break you're looking for and I don't intend to let you do anything to spoil it. You've got four weeks to get yourself fit. No more drinking or smoking and I'm going to make sure you get exercise, good food and plenty of sleep.'

He groaned and clutched his forehead. 'Dear God, girl. It sounds more like a penance!'

That weekend Juliet noticed for the first time that the fruit trees in the garden had been pruned. The grass had been cut too. Danny must have been coming to tend the garden while she was at work and he hadn't knocked once for payment. She must put it right.

Sunday morning dawned fine and sunny. The sky was a clear blue and the birds were singing. It was a perfect spring morning and Juliet put on her coat and walked down the garden and across to the gypsy encampment. The upper half of the Lees' caravan door was open and a delicious smell of frying bacon floated out. Juliet tapped gently and called out, 'Imelda, it's only me, Juliet King.'

The gypsy girl appeared at the door, the sleeping baby wrapped snugly in a plaid shawl tied firmly around her body. ''Mornin', Miss King,' she said with a smile. 'Come in and have some breakfast with us.'

Juliet shook her head. 'Oh no. I can't eat your rations.'

'You won't,' the girl assured her. 'The farmer Danny works for gave us a big piece of bacon and some new-laid eggs. We don't have breakfast like this very often. Come and share it with us.'

Inside the caravan it was warm and snug. Imelda laid the baby in her little crib and dished up the bacon and eggs frying on a little oil stove. Danny sat waiting, his knife and fork at the ready. Juliet took the money she had brought with her from her pocket and put it on the table.

'I was so pleased when I saw what you'd done in the garden,' she said. 'You should have asked for your money. I hope this is enough.'

Danny looked at the money, then at her, his dark eyes twinkling. 'More'n enough thanks, Miss King. I done the trees back afore Christmas – thought I'd better see to them, or you wouldn't get no fruit this year.'

'I'm so glad you did. I'm ignorant about such things. In future when you come to do the garden will you knock on the door and tell me?' she asked. 'It isn't right, going away without being paid.'

Danny stuffed the money into the pocket of his check shirt and began to tuck into his breakfast. 'Right you are, miss. 'S'long as you say so.'

Juliet ate her own breakfast, relishing the delicious taste of the home-cured bacon and the rich new-laid egg. For a few minutes no one spoke as the three of them ate, then Juliet said, 'Actually, Danny, you can do me a favour.'

He looked up. 'Oh yeah, what'd that be then, miss?'

'My father is staying with me,' she told him. 'He's going to be working in a month's time and he really needs to get fit. Will you let him help you in the garden?'

Danny looked puzzled. 'Will I *let* him? If he wants to work alongside me I can't do nuthin' to stop him, can I, miss?'

Juliet laughed at the logic of the remark. 'No, I suppose not. What I really meant was that I need you to *encourage* him to help. I'll do my part too, of course. He really does need to get in shape.'

Danny grinned at his wife. 'Reckon I could do that, miss. S'long as it's what you both want.'

'Oh, it is,' Juliet said, with grim determination. 'I'll make sure it is.'

Marcus wasn't too pleased when he heard Juliet's plan for him to spend some time working in the garden.

'For God's sake, girl, I don't know one end of a spade from another,' he said.

'That's all right, Danny knows and he's going to teach you,' Juliet told him. 'By the time the next few weeks are over you'll be as fit as the proverbial flea.'

'It's a bloody conspiracy!' Marcus complained. He looked at his watch. 'I think I'll go for a walk.'

'Don't be long. I've got a driving lesson at two.'

'You usually go in the morning before I'm up.' Marcus went into the hall and returned with his coat.

'Yes, but Maggie couldn't manage the morning this week,' Juliet told him. 'You'll get the chance to meet her at last.'

'Right.' He glanced at Juliet as she peeled potatoes for lunch. 'Well, aren't you going to congratulate me? I said I'm going for a walk. That's exercise, isn't it?'

'Yes.' As he opened the back door, Juliet said, 'Only one drink at the Wagoner's Rest, Dad. Back here for lunch at one sharp or I'll come looking for you.'

Marcus made no reply but closed the door with a flourish that was almost a slam. Juliet smiled to herself. Did he really think she didn't know what he had in mind? Walk indeed!

She had just finished preparing the vegetables when the telephone rang. Picking up the receiver she was surprised to hear Marion's voice at the other end of the line.

'Marion! What a lovely surprise.' Something suddenly occurred to her. 'Oh, you are all right, aren't you? It must be really late over there. Nothing's wrong, is it?'

'Everything is fine,' Marion assured her niece. 'I just thought it would be nice to hear your voice before I went to bed. How are you? I want to hear all your news.'

'I was going to write to you this afternoon,' Juliet said. 'Life is quite hectic here at the moment.' She poured out all her news, from her success with the women's page at the *Clarion* to Marcus's forthcoming part in the summer season at the Theatre Royal. Marion sounded delighted.

'I do hope it will lead to more permanent work for him,' she said. 'Is Olivia getting a part too?'

'No. She's left him,' Juliet said. 'Gone off with someone who offered her a part in a touring play. Dad was pretty cut up about it but this new offer is helping to take his mind off it. Marion . . .' she said. 'I asked Dad when he was here at Christmas about my mother. He got quite angry and refused to discuss it. But he said he'd be surprised if you didn't know – if Granny hadn't told you.'

'She didn't, darling,' Marion said sadly. 'As you know I was very young at the time it all happened. It was decided never to tell you and Mother never disclosed anything to me.'

'Promise?'

'I promise you, Juliet. All I can tell you is that I was very fond of your mother and I know that she loved you.'

'I was over at Imelda's a few weeks ago. Celina was there and she told me one day that my mother had suffered a lot – "grieved sore" were the words she used. It made me wonder if you had said anything to her.'

'No. Celina sees things that others don't see. I don't know what you'd call it. Maybe it's a kind of psychology – vibrations she picks up from people. I'm sorry if she upset you.'

'She didn't. She aroused my curiosity though. I need to know, Marion. And I will find out somehow.'

'Sometimes it's better – less hurtful – not to probe too deeply,' Marion said.

'Nevertheless I have the right to know,' Juliet insisted. 'And someday I will.'

'Is Marcus there?' Marion asked. 'Could I have a word with him?'

'I'm afraid you've missed him,' Juliet told her. 'He's gone for a walk. At least that's what he called it. I think you could translate it as "gone for a drink at The Wagoner's Rest".'

Marion laughed. 'Sounds like you've got the measure of him.'

'I have, and I'm determined to get him fit before he starts rehearsals at the beginning of May,' Juliet said. 'Or perish in the attempt.'

They had just finished lunch when Maggie arrived to take Juliet for her driving lesson. Marcus was drying the dishes as Juliet washed them. Juliet introduced them.

'Maggie this is my father, Marcus King. Dad, this is Maggie who's teaching me to drive.'

They shook hands and Maggie said, 'As a matter of fact I've seen you before.'

'Really, when?' Marcus asked.

'When I was in the ATS and you and your company came to entertain us. We were stationed in the north of Scotland at the time,' Maggie told him. 'Miles from anywhere and it was such a treat to be able to go to a show.'

Marcus pulled a face. 'What were we performing?'

Maggie smiled. '*Charlie's Aunt*,' she said. 'I laughed till the tears ran down my cheeks. You were wonderful.'

Marcus winced, but he looked pleased with the compliment all the same. 'My one and only attempt at dressing in drag,' he said. 'So, you're teaching this girl of mine how to drive. How is she getting on?'

'Fine,' Maggie said. 'She's well on the way to being a competent driver.'

'Maggie is wardrobe mistress at the theatre, Dad,' Juliet put in. 'So you'll soon be seeing quite a bit of her.' She turned to Maggie. 'Dad is to play the lead in the summer season production,' she explained.

The older woman smiled. 'I had heard and it's marvellous news. I'm sure it'll be a big success.'

During the weeks that followed Marcus worked quite hard with Danny Lee in the garden. Juliet made sure she got him out of bed at half past seven each morning and put him on his honour to work for as long as Danny worked. To her surprise he obeyed her and to *his* surprise he found himself enjoying the work, even though for the first few days he insisted that his back was broken and all his joints were on fire. Gradually his skin took on a healthy colour and Juliet could see his body firming up as he lost weight and grew stronger. Retiring to bed each night before eleven was no hardship for him. He was usually yawning by the time ten o'clock came round.

One morning towards the end of April, Max Goddard telephoned Juliet at work and asked her to meet him for lunch.

'I've got a script for your father,' he explained. 'And I thought he might like to study it and maybe make some notes about his character. I tried to ring your home number but there was no reply.'

'No, he'd be busy in the garden,' Juliet told him. 'He's been working hard getting himself fit.'

'Right. Good for him. So, where shall we meet, Juliet?'

'There's no need for you to take me to lunch,' she told him. 'I only have an hour anyway. You could just give me the script.'

'That's rather ungracious of you,' Max admonished. 'As a matter of fact I'd rather like to have your company for lunch, but, of course, if you've got something more interesting to do. . . .'

She winced. Why did she have to put it so bluntly? He was right. She did sound ungracious. Now he had that against her too! 'Sorry, that came out all wrong,' she said quickly. 'Of course lunch would be nice. Thank you.'

'Good. Shall we say the Red Lion in the High Street? Nothing fancy, just a sandwich and – a *lager* perhaps.'

She could picture his smug smile. 'Sandwich and a lager would be lovely,' she said firmly. 'I'll see you at one then, Max. Goodbye.'

The Red Lion was crowded with lunchtime drinkers but they

managed to find a couple of seats in a corner well away from the bar. Max opened his briefcase and took out a covered ring binder.

'I'd better give you this before I forget,' he said.

Juliet opened it and flipped through the pages. 'I hadn't realized it was quite such a long part,' she said.

Max nodded. 'Langley is hardly off the stage. That's why I thought Marcus would appreciate getting to grips with it before we begin rehearsals.' He glanced at the menu chalked on a blackboard above the bar. 'I see they've got ham, cheese or tomato sandwiches,' he said. 'What do you fancy?'

'Tomato please.'

'And to drink?'

Inwardly she dared him to mention lager again. It must have been obvious from her expression because his eyes danced with mischief. 'Don't tell me – orange juice, right?'

'Right.' She smiled in spite of herself.

'So, what have you been doing since we last met?' Max asked, when he returned with their sandwiches and drinks.

Juliet shrugged. 'Working, looking after Dad and learning to drive.'

'Sounds like a full-time occupation.'

'It is, though Maggie tells me I'll soon be competent enough to apply for my licence. As for Dad, he's been as good as gold; working hard in the garden and getting very fit.'

'Glad to hear it. He'll need plenty of stamina for this part. Only another couple of weeks before we start rehearsing.'

Juliet shot him a sideways glance. 'Have you heard from Madeleine?' she asked.

He looked surprised. 'Maddy? No, only a brief phone call to say that things were going well. I expect she's been too busy.'

'She must have been very excited. Her first West End show.'

He looked at her thoughtfully for a moment. 'Why the sudden interest in Maddy. I didn't know you and she were friends.'

Juliet blushed. 'We're not. I only know her by sight. It was just that we met that evening at The Feathers when you and she were ... celebrating.'

He smiled. 'So we did; when you were having dinner with your boyfriend.'

'He's not my boyfriend.'

Max's eyebrows rose. 'That was a hasty denial. You looked quite – close.'

'Close? I wouldn't put it quite like that. Nigel was called up to do his National Service and I took his job at the *Clarion*. We met at my aunt's wedding when he came to do the write-up. We're good friends, that's all. He's a very nice person.'

'OK.' He looked amused. 'There's no need to sound so defensive.' He took a bite of his sandwich and regarded her silently. 'You know,' he said at last, 'I'm quite surprised that you've never been tempted to follow in your father's footsteps.'

She shook her head firmly. 'It's too precarious a life for me. I've seen too many careers crash, too many hopes dashed; too many inflated egos. I've always wanted to do something creative, but not in the theatre.'

'You think it makes people egotistic then?' He raised an eyebrow.

'I know that's a bit of a generalization, but on the whole I believe it does. It's necessary I suppose, a case of survival of the fittest.'

He laughed. 'You make it sound like the law of the jungle.'

'In a way it is.'

He let that go. He finished his sandwich, then he asked, 'So your mother wasn't an actress?'

'No.' She looked up at him. 'I don't remember much about her. I think I told you, she left Dad and me when I was very young.'

'Yes, you did. I'm sorry. I suppose that's another reason why you're so averse to the theatre.'

'It doesn't seem to make for successful marriages, or long-term relationships either.' She looked at him. 'The temperament it takes to be an actor depends largely on self interest.'

He winced. 'That's a very cynical attitude for one so young.'

'I don't feel all that young,' she told him. 'When I look at other people of my age they seem very . . . I don't know, naïve, immature.'

He drew the corners of his mouth down. 'Oh dear, we are getting serious.' He nodded towards her empty glass. 'Want another one of those?'

She shook her head. 'There's only so much orange juice a girl can drink.'

He laughed. 'I can see it might get boring. Why don't you try a shandy? That's half lemonade and half beer.'

'Yes, I know what it is. All right, go on then.'

He stood up. 'Good for you. We'll make a boozer out of you yet!'

CHAPTER ELEVEN

A week after her lunch with Max Juliet came home to hear voices coming from the living room at Heathlands Cottage. She went through to find Maggie with Marcus in the living room with a tray of empty coffee cups on the table between them. Maggie was hearing Marcus's lines for the play.

Juliet had noticed an instant rapport between them on the Sunday afternoon when she first introduced them. She knew that they had met for coffee or a drink several times and she was pleased. Maggie was closer to Marcus's generation and she was by temperament his complete opposite; down-to-earth and level-headed – just what he needed to keep his feet firmly on the ground.

'Hi, Maggie,' she said.

Maggie looked at her watch in surprise. 'Juliet! Heavens is that the time? I should be going. I have to be at the theatre at six.'

'Stay and have a bite with us,' Juliet invited. 'Then you can go straight there.'

'I might come with you,' Marcus said. 'We start rehearsals next week. Time I familiarized myself with the back-stage geography.'

While he went off to get changed, Maggie joined Juliet in the kitchen. 'I hope you don't mind me keeping your father company,' she said.

Juliet smiled. 'Not at all. I think it's great that you get along so well. He's on his own all day while I'm at work. He's enjoyed working in the garden, but there's nothing much to do now for the time being and he needs someone to keep him in line.'

Maggie laughed. 'I'm not so sure that I'm doing that. Working hard in the garden has done him good though,' she added. 'He's beginning to look really well.'

'Yes. He surprised me with the way he got down to it,' Juliet admitted. 'But he's certainly a lot fitter than he was when he first arrived.'

'Breaking up with his girlfriend must have got him down.'

'He told you about Olivia?'

Maggie nodded. 'A long-term relationship like that takes some getting over.'

'Not for Olivia apparently. Between you and me, Maggie, Dad splitting with her was the best thing that could have happened to him. They hadn't been getting on for some time anyway.'

Maggie sighed. 'I haven't been close to a man since Don, my husband was killed.'

Juliet didn't know quite what to make of that remark. Was Maggie trying to tell her that she felt close to Marcus? And was that a good idea? Juliet knew her father so well. He could be mercurial, thoughtless at times. She would hate to see Maggie get hurt.

'Dad's not the easiest man to understand,' she said. 'Or to put up with. There are times when he drives me barmy.'

Maggie laughed. 'Working as wardrobe mistress teaches you all about temperamental actors,' she said. 'I tend to take it all with a pinch of salt.'

After Maggie and Marcus had left for the theatre, Juliet got down to finishing her copy for *Juliet's Jottings*. She had almost finished when the telephone rang.

'Hi, guess who.'

Juliet didn't have to guess. 'Nigel! I'd know your voice anywhere. Where are you?'

'At home. I've had a new posting. Much nearer to home this time – Southampton. It means I'll be able to get home most weekends now.'

'That's a bit of luck.'

'Isn't it? So what about meeting me for a drink?'

'Right. When?'

'Now, of course. Dad says I can have the car so I'll come and pick you up.'

Juliet glanced at the clock. 'It's a bit late – almost nine o'clock.'

'Oh, listen to you,' Nigel said. 'Do you turn into a pumpkin after nine or something? I'll be there in fifteen minutes,' he added, without waiting for a reply.

'So what's new?' Nigel asked as Juliet settled into the passenger seat of the Hillman.

'Nothing much,' she told him. 'You know Warnecliff. I daresay once the summer season gets going the place will liven up a bit.'

'I love your letters,' he told her. 'From what you say Gerry doesn't change much, or any of the others.'

The bar at The Wheelhouse was crowded, but they managed to find a couple of seats. 'What'll you have?' Nigel asked.

Juliet considered. 'I'll have a shandy, please.'

He looked at her in surprise. 'Shandy eh? Have you been getting into bad company?'

She laughed. 'Someone persuaded me to try it and I quite liked it.'

'Right, a shandy it is then.'

Nigel watched with amusement as Juliet lifted the glass to her lips and sipped. 'Hey, you really do like it, don't you?'

'Yes, I told you.'

Nigel shook his head at her. 'We'll have to watch you. You could be on the way to turning into a secret drinker.'

'Why everyone finds it so funny, I can't understand,' Juliet said, slightly peeved. 'Is it so unusual for a girl to drink something as harmless as a shandy?'

'Ah, but it's the thin end of the wedge,' Nigel said. 'Before we know it you'll be drinking the beer without the lemonade.' He shook his head. 'After that it's all downhill I'm afraid.'

She gave him a playful punch on the arm. 'Oh, shut up! I tried lager and it tasted like nasty medicine to me so no worries there.'

She looked up to see someone waving to her from the other side of the room. It was Sylvia with a young man. He was tall with red hair and, like Nigel, he was in uniform. She assumed this must be the 'Derek' she'd heard about. Nigel had noticed them too. He looked at her.

'Someone you know?'

'It's Sylvia, an old friend of mine,' she explained. 'We used to play together as kids. She and her family are neighbours. She told me she'd met someone.' As she spoke Sylvia and her escort began to cross the room towards them. 'Looks like we're about to be introduced.'

'This is Derek,' Sylvia said proudly. 'Or I should say Private Derek Summers. Derek, this is my oldest friend, Juliet and. . . .' She looked at Nigel.

'Nigel,' Juliet quickly intervened. 'Or perhaps I should say, Lance Corporal Nigel Foreman.'

The two young men laughed and shook hands. 'I'm sure we'd both rather forget the formalities,' Nigel said. 'I don't know about you but I can't wait for my two years to be over.'

'Can we join you?' Sylvia said, sitting in the chair next to Juliet without waiting for her assent. 'Derek is on leave. We're off down to Cornwall for a few days' holiday the day after tomorrow, aren't we, Del?' She looked across the table, but Derek was already deep in conversation with Nigel and hadn't heard. She shook her head. 'Look at them. They're well away.' She smiled at Juliet. 'So, how are you? I love your weekly column, Ju. Never miss it. You're doing really well, aren't you?'

'I'm trying,' Juliet said. She lowered her voice. 'Derek looks nice. You're going on holiday then?'

Sylvia nodded. 'It was my idea. I thought it would be nice for us to get to know one another better. Now that Del is away I hardly see him. He's stationed right up in Scotland.' She glanced across the table at Nigel. 'How about you two?'

'We're just friends,' Juliet said. 'We write and I see Nigel when he manages to get home. Nothing serious.'

In the car on the way home Nigel told Juliet that Derek had confided in him that he was about to be sent to France for three months.

'Oh, poor Sylvie,' she said. 'She didn't tell me that. She was only saying that she hardly sees him.'

'Did she tell you that he's a musician?' Juliet shook her head and Nigel went on, 'He's with the regimental band, which is part of the reason he's going to France. It sounds like a great opportunity.'

Juliet was puzzled. 'She didn't tell me any of this. All she could talk about was the holiday they're about to have and how they mean to get to know one another better.'

Nigel said nothing, but the look on his face was sceptical.

Outside Heathlands Cottage he kissed her goodnight. It was a gentle kiss that she knew could have turned into something more passionate if she hadn't pulled away. 'Thanks for a lovely evening, Nigel,' she said, her hand on the door handle. 'Will I see you again before you have to go back?'

'No, more's the pity. I have to report back first thing tomorrow.' He gave her a wistful smile. 'I was hoping I might get invited in for coffee.'

'Of course you're welcome to come in,' Juliet said. 'I thought you'd want to get off if you have an early start in the morning.'

'Not as much as I want a few minutes more of your company.' He leaned in and kissed her again.

'You know that Dad will be there, don't you?'

'I'm sure he's the soul of discretion.' He looked into her eyes. 'Or are you eager to get rid of me?'

'Of course not.' A sudden tapping on the car window made her jump. She wound it down to see Sylvia's distraught face peering in at her.

'Oh, Ju, I'm sorry to interrupt, but I need to talk to you.'

'Well . . .' Juliet glanced at Nigel and hesitated. 'I'd ask you in only Dad's inside, and—'

'Get in the car,' Nigel said. 'That's if you don't mind talking in front of me. I'm a very good listener. I don't make judgements and I'm hardly going to gossip about you, am I?'

Sylvia opened the door and tumbled into the back seat where she burst into noisy tears. 'It's Del,' she hiccupped. 'He doesn't want to go on holiday. He doesn't even want to see me any more. He's going . . . going to . . . to *France!*'

Juliet glanced at Nigel. 'Oh, Sylvie, I'm so sorry.'

Without a word Nigel passed Sylvia a large handkerchief. She snuffled into it and blew her nose hard.

'Sorry. I'll take it home and wash it,' she mumbled, then burst into fresh tears. 'Oh Ju, what am I going to do?'

'Are you sure he said he doesn't want to see you again?' Juliet ventured. 'Maybe he just meant he wouldn't be able to see you for a while.'

'You weren't *there*,' Sylvia wailed. 'He dumped me. He thinks I'm trying to tie him down – that I'm too . . . too clingy. Honestly, Ju, I never meant to be.'

Nigel turned round. 'Look, Sylvia, some chaps are cautious; they get the wind up when a girl starts making too many plans. It makes them feel sort of trapped.'

'Oh *no*! You're saying I scared him off. If only he'd told me more about himself. I never even knew he was a musician. Why did he have to be so secretive? I told him everything about me.' The tears continued to flow and Juliet and Nigel looked at each other helplessly.

'What can I *do*?' Sylvia implored. 'What can I do to get him back? Nigel, you're a man; you must know.'

'Sorry. Without actually talking to him, I can't say,' Nigel said awkwardly.

'Look, come inside both of you,' Juliet suggested. 'I'll make some coffee. You can't go home in this state, Sylvie. Your mother would have a fit if she saw you like this. You can wash your face and calm down. You'll feel better after some coffee, I promise.' She looked at Nigel. 'Don't you think so?'

'Excellent idea,' he said firmly. 'Afterwards I'll walk you home.'

'What about your dad?' Sylvia asked, only partly appeased.

'Leave him to me. I'll see he doesn't disturb us,' Juliet promised.

Indoors Juliet left the other two in the kitchen while she went to find Marcus and warn him to keep out of the way. She didn't have to look far. He was clearly in the bath. As she stood on the landing his melodious baritone voice floated out through the keyhole accompanied by the vigorous splashing that Marcus always made.

'*Where the bee sucks there suck I. . . .*'

Juliet had a mental picture of sopping towels on the wet bathroom floor and a ring round the bath. But at least he would be occupied for at least the next half hour or so. Marcus always made a production out of having a bath. She went back to the kitchen where Nigel was sitting side by side with Sylvia at the kitchen table, his arm around her shoulders. Juliet filled the kettle and put a pan of milk on to warm.

'Dad's in the bath,' she said. 'But you can use my bedroom to freshen up.'

The three of them drank their coffee to the accompaniment of

Marcus's muted rendition which penetrated the ceiling. It was almost impossible to think constructively to the strains of: *Merrily, merrily shall I live now. Under the blossom that hangs on the bough.* Then, with renewed gusto, *UNDER the blossom that hangs on the BOU . . . OUGH.*

After a strong cup of coffee and a brief repair session in Juliet's bedroom Sylvia felt composed enough to venture home. Nigel offered to walk with her. They said goodnight and Juliet saw them out of the back door with some relief. As she closed it behind them Marcus appeared clad in his dressing-gown.

'Hello! Visitors? Why didn't you call me?'

Juliet shook her head. 'Not exactly visitors, Dad. Sylvia had a bit of a crisis and Nigel and I were trying to sort her out.'

Marcus sat down at the table, taking the lid off the coffee pot and peering inside. 'Crisis – what kind of crisis?'

'With her love life,' Juliet told him.

'Ah, no one knows more about those than me,' he said, with a resigned sigh. 'Why didn't you call me? I could have offered her the benefit of my experience and wisdom.'

Juliet couldn't think of anyone less qualified to give advice to the lovelorn, but she didn't say so. 'You sounded as though you were enjoying your bath,' she said. 'I didn't want to disturb you.' She lifted the coffee pot. 'This is cold now. Shall I make some more?'

'That'd be lovely, darling.'

'Did you have a good evening at the theatre?'

He smiled and rubbed his hands. 'I can't tell you how wonderful it is to feel a living part of it all again,' he said. 'Max is a damned good fellow. I'm to get the best dressing room, right next to the stage because I'm hardly off, you know. It's a hell of a part, but this afternoon when Maggie was hearing me I was almost word perfect.' He reached out and grasped her hand. 'And it's all thanks to you, my darling. Don't think I don't appreciate that because I do. You're the best daughter a fellow could have; bless you.'

The following Monday morning on her way to work Juliet noticed the first of many posters that had been distributed around the town advertising the Theatre Royal's summer production.

HOUSE GUEST
A comedy by acclaimed playwright Peter Longhurst.
Starring Marcus King

It was a colourful, eye-catching poster with a photograph of Marcus as its central feature and Juliet felt a small stab of pride. She wondered if Marcus had seen it. It would be a tremendous boost for him.

At the office, Jim, the office boy, told her that Gerry wanted to see her as soon as she got in. The news brought her up sharp. What had she done now? She took off her coat, smoothed her hair in the cracked cloakroom mirror and walked down the corridor to tap on his door.

'Ah, Juliet.' Gerry looked up as she came in, removing the pipe from his mouth. Juliet was relieved to see that he looked fairly calm. 'Everything going to plan, eh?' he asked with what passed for a smile.

'Yes, thank you.'

'Copy in for this week's JJ?' The name of her women's page had been condensed to initials now, which she took to be a sign of success.

She nodded. 'Almost. I'm hoping to finish this morning. Just one more interview to do and then when the office is free I shall finish typing it up.'

'Excellent, excellent!'

She was beginning to wonder where the conversation was leading when he suddenly said, 'There's something I think might be up your street, so if you're not tied up this afternoon I'd like you to handle it for me.'

'Y-yes?' It sounded suspiciously like the kind of thing that nobody else wanted to do. 'What is it?' she asked, holding her breath.

'A Dr Galbraith who lives on the outskirts of Warnecliff has been awarded the George Cross,' he explained. 'Sterling work with the victims of the London blitz, apparently. I thought you might like to write a piece for the paper.'

Juliet frowned. 'Do you think I'm the best member of staff suited for this?' she ventured.

'Eh?' Gerry looked up in the act of refilling his pipe. 'Oh, I forgot to mention that Dr Galbraith is a woman. Doctor Felicity Galbraith to give her her full title. I thought that as well as writing a biographical piece you might like to feature her in JJ as well.'

'Oh, I see.' Juliet smiled, her spirits rising. 'I'd like that very much.'

Gerry pushed a piece of paper across the desk at her. 'Here's her telephone number and address,' he said. 'Give her a ring and arrange something. If she can fit it in this afternoon it'll go in the paper this week so try and twist her arm.' He looked up at her as she studied the address on the paper. 'All right, girl. That'll be all. Run along with you,' he said irritably.

Juliet looked at him. 'She lives out at Hemsbury,' she said.

'I'm aware of that.'

'But it's at least ten miles. How – how do I get there?'

'Oh, for heaven's sake girl, can you *still* not drive?'

'I'm hoping to g—' He stopped her with a wave of his hand.

'Ever heard of the *bus*, girl?' He shook his head. 'Don't look at me like that. You'll have to take Fred with you anyway. We'll want a mugshot. He'll drive so you've no worries. Off you go now.'

Doctor Galbraith agreed to be interviewed that afternoon. Juliet and Fred drove out to the village of Hemsbury in Fred's old MG and found Dr Galbraith's house quite easily following the instructions she had given Juliet on the telephone. Standing on the edge of the village it was a Georgian vicarage, the new one having been built adjacent to the church just before the war. Juliet stood at the white painted five-bar gate inhaling the fragrance of the laburnum that grew by the gate. Wisteria climbed the stone walls of the house in abundance, clothing it in purple.

'What a beautiful spot,' she remarked to Fred, as he hauled his camera and tripod out of the boot. He looked up.

'A bit off the beaten track for my taste,' he said. 'But I suppose after spending the war in London it's exactly what she wanted.'

Dr Felicity Galbraith opened the door to them herself. She was a heavily built middle-aged lady with a fresh complexion and close-cropped iron-grey hair. She wore crumpled trousers and a brown cable-knit sweater. At her side were two golden Labradors.

'Warnecliff *Clarion*?' she barked. Juliet nodded and she opened the door wider. 'In you come then. Don't stand on ceremony.' She glanced at the dogs. 'And take no notice of Samson and Delilah. Soft as grease, the pair of them. Lick you to death if you're not careful.'

She ushered them into a pleasant drawing room furnished with shabby chintz chairs and a comfortable-looking sofa that the dogs were clearly not barred from. Two long windows looked out over a garden tumbling with spring flowers. Clematis climbed the trunk of an ancient cedar tree and lilac trees dripped their blossom, purple, white and mauve over an emerald lawn. Juliet was enchanted.

'How beautiful,' she said.

For the first time Dr Galbraith smiled. 'My pride and joy,' she said. 'Can't spend enough time out there. Just me and the birds and these two daft devils.' She bent to pat the dogs who seemed to follow her everywhere like shadows. 'And having said that why don't we get down to this interview nonsense so that I can get back to what's important?'

Juliet glanced at Fred. 'My colleague is here to photograph you, Doctor.'

'Call me Fliss. Everybody does,' she ordered.

Juliet bit her lip, not knowing quite how to phase her next question. 'So – er – do you want to cha— er get ready?'

'Think I look a mess, eh? Well, I suppose I do. But this is me. I can't be any different.' Dr Galbraith looked at Fred with a twinkle in her grey eyes. 'So do your best, my friend – or worst as the case may be – and the best of British luck!'

Juliet smiled. She was beginning to like this odd woman. Fred clearly liked her too.

'Right,' he said. 'I think we'll have you sitting over there. And we must have the dogs in too. I'll just set up the equipment and off we go. It shouldn't take long.'

Fred took three carefully angled shots of the doctor. 'There. I think that ought to do it,' he said at last. 'I've got to wait for Juliet here, so do you mind if I take a walk round your garden and have a smoke, Doctor?'

'Not a bit and I said to call me Fliss.'

When Fred had taken his leave the doctor patted the sofa cushions and invited Juliet to sit down. 'Might as well be comfortable,' she said. 'Fire away. Just ask me what you want to know and I'll do my best to make the answers sound interesting.'

Juliet learned that the doctor had spent her war working as a general surgeon at St Bartholomew's Hospital in London and had been involved in the worst of the London blitz, going out with the ambulances, helping victims – clearly saving many lives, though she deliberately and frustratingly played down her part in it all.

'I can't think what all the fuss is about. I only did my job,' she said. 'I did what I was trained to do; what I hope somebody would have done for me.'

She was so self-effacing that Juliet had to resort to quite rigorous questioning.

'But you're being awarded the George Cross, Doctor. You must have had some quite hair-raising experiences. You must have risked your life again and again. Our readers will want to read about all that.'

With great difficulty Juliet wheedled the details of a couple of instances where her life had been in danger and she made notes, reflecting that she had never conducted a trickier interview. Most people were only too eager to talk about themselves.

'Like I said, it's a lot of bloody fuss about nothing,' Dr Galbraith said at last. 'There are other people who deserve it at least as much as me – far *more* in many cases.'

Juliet looked up with interest. 'Would you like to tell me about them, Doctor?'

'Oh for God's sake! Call me *Fliss*. How many times?' Dr Galbraith looked down at her strong hands, now roughened by gardening. 'There are far too many to name them all.'

'Is there anyone in particular?' Juliet's pencil hovered. Maybe at last the doctor would reveal something more stirring that she could write about.'

'Yes, there was one.' The voice suddenly lost its rough edge. 'A woman ambulance driver – little slip of a thing. I've never known such bravery. I lost count of the times she climbed under dangerous wreckage to rescue someone. Once she saved a woman and her two-week-old baby, buried under the rubble of their house. Minutes after she got them out the place collapsed. Another time she pulled out an old man and went back in for his wife seconds before there was a gas explosion.' She shook her head. 'She should certainly have received an award. In fact I recommended her for one.'

'So why didn't she get it?' Juliet asked.

'Because of some damned stupid rule.'

'Rule? There's a rule that says certain people can't be rewarded for bravery?'

'Sodding outrageous, isn't it?' Fliss looked at Juliet, her mouth set in an angry line. 'Truth is, the poor wretched woman had been to prison,' she said softly. 'As it happens she'd been convicted of something she didn't even do. I talked to her later and she told me the whole story.'

'What did she do?'

'She was arrested in a nightclub and charged with possessing stolen goods, but she insisted they were planted on her. I'm utterly convinced she was innocent,' the doctor said. 'It was a gross miscarriage of justice. You only had to talk to the girl for five minutes to see that. But try telling the powers-that-be and see where it bloody gets you!'

'What was her name?' Juliet asked. 'I'd really like to look into it further.'

'Her name was Tina Moore.' The doctor shook her head. 'But don't waste your time; won't get you anywhere. I tried everything at the time. Lobbied MPs, wrote letters – got nowhere with it. It's a closed book as far as the authorities are concerned. She was convicted; she served her time and that's that. A black mark against her for the rest of her life – in spite of her gallantry.'

'She still has the satisfaction of knowing the good she did,' Juliet offered.

'True. And it seems she'll have to be content with that.'

As they drove back to Warnecliff Fred glanced at Juliet. 'Get a good story then? You're unusually quiet. Everything all right?'

Juliet nodded. 'Yes, I'm fine. I did get a story. I almost had to beat it out of her though. It wasn't just a case of modesty, she was downright angry about being awarded the George Cross.'

'Angry?' Fred looked at her with raised eyebrows.

'She insisted that there were others who deserved it more,' she explained.

'Always the way,' Fred said. 'For every case of acclaim there are a dozen whose gallantry goes unsung.'

'So it seems. She told me about one in particular,' Juliet told him. 'I even got a name out of her. I might even try and follow it up.'

143

Fred sighed. 'I'd leave it if I were you. For one thing you haven't the time and for another Gerry's only interested in local stuff.'

Juliet was silent. The story Dr Galbraith had told her haunted her. She was determined to follow it up somehow and find out more if she could.

CHAPTER TWELVE

Marcus had completed one week of rehearsals. To Juliet's relief everything seemed to be going to plan and her father was like a new man. At last he had something to get out of bed for in the mornings. He was off to the theatre by half past nine, shaved, hair brushed and neatly dressed. He knew his lines and had memorized his moves. Everything was going well. But towards the end of the week to Juliet's dismay he had begun to come up with ideas which he would bounce off her during their evening meal, looking for her reactions.

'Dad, don't you think you should leave all that to Max?' she said one evening after he had outlined an idea that threatened to completely alter the mood of act two. 'After all, he is directing the play.'

'I know, but he's very young and comparatively new to the business,' Marcus said. 'I'm only trying to give him the benefit of my experience.'

'Yes, but he may not appreciate it, Dad,' Juliet pointed out. 'He's from a more modern school than you. He has his own way of interpreting a playwright's work.'

'New isn't always best,' Marcus argued, his lower lip protruding stubbornly. 'When I was at the Vic—'

'Dad, take my advice and leave it to Max,' Juliet said. 'You don't want to put his back up at this stage, do you, not just when you're getting on so well?'

Marcus lifted his shoulders in an exaggerated shrug. 'I just can't help offering ideas when I see something that could be done better,' he said petulantly. 'It's in my nature.'

'Well, why not just wait and see how it goes?'

'All right, if you say so.'

Juliet hoped he would stick to his promise not to interfere with Max's direction. He seemed to have quite forgotten how lucky he was to have been given this chance. Why could he never leave well enough alone? Why must he always overstep the mark and spoil things?

She decided to try to smooth the way by having a word with Max and dropped in at the theatre during her lunch break the following day at the time when she knew that Marcus would be in The Red Lion having his usual pub lunch. Backstage at the theatre she asked Harry, the stage-door keeper if Max was in his office.

'Yes, miss. Just down the corridor, second on the left,' he told her.

She tapped on Max's office door and was rewarded by his call of 'Come in.' As she put her head round the door he looked up from his desk, his eyes widening in surprise when he saw her.

'Juliet! What a nice surprise. I thought it was Kenny, the ASM bringing me the sandwich I'd ordered.' He stood up and swept a pile of papers off the only other chair in the room. 'Come in and sit down. What can I do for you?'

Juliet sat down. 'It's nothing really,' she said. 'At least, I hope you'll think it's nothing. It's just that Dad has been telling me all about his ideas for the direction of the play. It's just his enthusiasm, but I was afraid he might have offended you.'

Max laughed. 'I know what you mean. I'm not offended. In fact I'm very well aware of the fact that he's been in the business far longer than me. He probably sees being directed by someone my age a bit like trying to teach your granny to suck eggs.'

'Oh no, I'm sure he doesn't!'

'Actually I always encourage ideas from actors,' Max went on. 'It shows they're getting inside the character they're playing and very often they work very well and I'm happy to incorporate them. The success of the play is the important thing after all. But I have worked quite hard on the direction and I do insist on having the last word, so as long as everyone understands that we're fine.'

'And he ... so he hasn't ... pushed you too hard?'

Max smiled and she noticed for the first time that when he smiled a tiny dimple appeared at the corner of his mouth. 'He hasn't pushed too hard, no. I'm not an easy push-over. And if he did, I think I have enough tact to make it clear that in the end I'm the boss.'

'Right, that's OK then. Well. . . .' She stood up and backed towards the door, suddenly embarrassed and tongue-tied. 'I'll go then.'

'Come and have a bite to eat with me,' he said, getting up. 'You must be on your lunch break.'

'Oh, that would be nice but what about your sandwich?'

'Looks as though Kenny's forgotten about it anyway. Head like a sieve, that boy.'

She hesitated. 'Dad always goes to the Red Lion.'

'I know he does. And you'd rather he didn't know we've been talking about him,' he said, reading her mind. 'Right, we'll go to the Jersey Cow if that's all right.'

'Yes, lovely.'

There was only half an hour of Juliet's lunch break left by the time they had ordered sandwiches and coffee. They didn't talk about Marcus any more. Max asked about her job and how she was enjoying it and she told him a little about Dr Galbraith and her beautiful home and garden. As they went in opposite directions they said their goodbyes in the street outside the milk bar.

'You won't mention to Dad that I came to see you, will you?' Juliet asked.

To her surprise Max took her hand and bent forward to kiss her fingertips. 'I think it was very sweet of you to worry about us getting at cross purposes,' he said. 'You really are a very nice person, Juliet, aren't you?'

To her horror she felt herself blushing furiously. 'Not at all. I can be quite horrible at times,' she said. 'It's just that I love Dad and I know how much this job means to him. I couldn't bear the thought of anything happening to spoil it.'

He looked at her with mock reproach. 'Ah, and here was I thinking you were worrying about me being offended.'

'Oh yes, I was. I mean I didn't want – I. . . .'

He threw back his head and laughed. 'I'm teasing. I think you're very sweet and very loyal, Juliet.' He leaned closer. 'And, by the way, *very* attractive.' He leaned in to kiss the corner of her mouth. 'Bye for now, lovely Juliet. See you again soon, I hope.'

She walked back to the *Clarion* office in a kind of daze. Max Goddard had a cheek, kissing her in the street like that for anyone to see. Who did he think he was? More to the point, said a quiet inner voice, who did *she* think he was? She pushed the question aside, preferring not to probe her mind too deeply for the answer, particularly when the skin at the corner of her mouth where his lips had brushed was still tingling.

That weekend Nigel came home again. He rang her on Saturday evening.

'Shall we go out for a drink?'

'That'd be nice.'

'I thought perhaps a run out somewhere now that the evenings are longer. Stop at a quaint country pub.'

'Sounds lovely.'

There was a pause and then he said casually, 'Oh, by the way I've asked Sylvia to come too.'

'Sylvia?'

'Yes. I felt a bit sorry for her after the way that fellow had let her down. You don't mind, do you?'

'No, of course not.' But she did mind; not so much that Nigel had invited Sylvia but that Sylvia had accepted.

When Nigel picked her up Sylvia was already sitting in the front passenger seat. She smiled up at Juliet through the window.

'It's so sweet of you two to invite me,' she said, making no attempt to relinquish her seat. Then, as Juliet got into the back of the car, 'Are you all right back there, Ju? Not taking your seat, am I?'

'Not at all.' Juliet seethed as they drove. It was kind of Nigel to ask Sylvia to join them, but trust her to take advantage. She'd already noticed that she was dressed to the nines and was wearing lots of make-up.

They stopped at a picturesque thatched pub called The Cat and Cricket. Inside Juliet ordered her usual orange juice while to her surprise Sylvia decided to have a gin and tonic. When Nigel had gone to the bar Juliet looked at her friend.

'I didn't know you drank spirits.'

'I do now,' Sylvia said with a hint of defiance. 'I think your Nigel is

147

an absolute smasher.'

Juliet's eyebrows rose. 'I'm sure he'd be flattered to hear your opinion of him. And he's not *my* Nigel by the way.'

Sylvia eyed her friend speculatively. 'If I didn't know you better, Ju, I'd say you were just a tiny bit miffed.'

'Miffed! What about?'

'About Nigel inviting me along this evening.'

'Not at all. He said he felt sorry for you after the way Derek or whatever his name was, treated you.'

Nigel returned with the drinks before Sylvia could respond and the three of them sat sipping from their respective glasses. Nigel was the first to break the silence.

'Derek must be in France by now.'

'He can be in hell for all I care,' Sylvia said. She drained her glass and held it out. 'Can I have another of these, please Nige?'

He took the glass from her and stood up. 'Of course.'

'A word of advice,' Juliet said when he had gone. 'He hates being called Nige.'

'Really?'

'And isn't it a bit rude, asking for another drink when we've hardly started on ours?'

Again Nigel reappeared before Sylvia could do more than shrug. She drank the second gin and tonic as quickly as the first and suddenly she said, 'So Del is a musician. I wonder why he never told me that. Do you know what instrument he plays, Nige?' She shot a defiant sideways look at Juliet as she used the abbreviation.

'He told me he plays the bassoon,' Nigel told her.

'The *what*?'

'Bassoon.'

Sylvia gave a shrill laugh. 'What's that? Never heard of it. I thought that was some kind of monkey. No wonder he didn't tell me.'

'The bassoon is a woodwind instrument,' Juliet said stiffly. 'It has a beautiful sound.'

'Is that so? What it is to have had an expensive private education, eh, Nige?' Sylvia said waspishly. 'Juliet's favourite pastime is making the rest of us look like Philistines.' She held out her empty glass. 'Maybe if I had another of these I might start to feel more intelligent.'

Nigel took the glass from her, but Juliet put her hand on his sleeve. 'I think Sylvia has had enough,' she said.

'Who are you to tell me when I've had enough?' Sylvia said belligerently.

Nigel winked at Juliet and went to the bar. She guessed he would get her a plain tonic water. She looked at Sylvia. 'You're making a fool of yourself, Sylvia,' she said. 'Don't spoil the evening. And don't accuse me of making you look like a Philistine. You asked what a bassoon was and I told you.'

Sylvia sighed. 'You've changed so much,' she said, shaking her head. 'You used to be such a nice girl, but since you got that job on the *Clarion* it's tuppence to speak to you.'

'Nonsense!'

'Oh! I'm talking nonsense now, am I?' Sylvia's voice rose and people at a nearby table turned to look at her.'

'Why are you being like this, Sylvia?' Juliet asked quietly. 'We've always been such good friends.'

'That was when we were kids,' Sylvia said. 'But there comes a time when *some* of us have to grow up.'

'What's that supposed to mean?'

Sylvia was saved from giving an answer to Juliet's question when Nigel reappeared with her drink.

Juliet looked at him. 'Perhaps we'd better move on,' she said, picking up her bag and coat.

Sylvia tossed back the contents of her glass. 'Yes, come on, let's go,' she said loudly. 'I'm sick of being a sitting target for my so-called friend's bitchy remarks.'

In the car-park she climbed quickly into the front passenger seat, took out her handkerchief and burst into tears. Nigel slipped in beside her and put an arm round her shoulders.

'Don't get upset, Sylvia,' he said. 'Just try to forget about Derek. Put it down to experience. There are plenty more fish in the sea.'

Juliet said nothing, sitting silently in the back seat.

'I know,' Sylvia snuffled. 'I thought I was getting over it. It was so nice of you to ask me out this evening, but I didn't know I was going to be made to feel like an interloper.'

'Of course you're not an interloper,' Nigel said.

'No? Ask your girlfriend then.' Sylvia burst into fresh tears. 'It's at times like this that you find out who your real friends are.'

Juliet had had enough. 'Just take me home, Nigel,' she said quietly. 'Then you can take Sylvia somewhere on her own. I'm sure that's what she had in mind all along anyway.'

To her surprise Nigel turned round to face her with a frown. 'She can't help being upset,' he said. 'Show her a bit of sympathy, can't you? Not everyone has a heart of stone.'

Heart of stone! His words were like a slap in the face and Juliet knew exactly to what he was referring. She'd been unresponsive towards him. It was true. But she couldn't make herself feel something that simply wasn't there. She was fond of Nigel; he was a thoroughly nice person and a good friend. Maybe she'd been unfair to him. The thought wounded her. The last thing she had wanted was to hurt him. She would have liked to talk to him about it. Not just part on bad terms, but with Sylvia there, snuffling self-pityingly into her hanky in the front seat there was nothing she could do or say.

'I'd like to go home now please, Nigel,' she said. 'Maybe we could talk later.'

'Look, wait a minute,' Nigel said.

'Oh, take her home and be done with it,' Sylvia interrupted. 'She's been in a mood all evening. It's just what I can do without.'

Nigel started the car and they drove back to Wycombe in silence. When she got out of the car outside Heathlands Cottage neither Sylvia nor Nigel said goodnight.

Marcus had asked Max for permission to announce his appearance at the Theatre Royal in the theatrical trade paper, *The Stage*. Max had agreed and Marcus's agent agreed to write the article and make sure it was inserted. It appeared the following week and Marcus opened his copy of the paper at the breakfast table, as excited as a small boy at Christmas, his cheeks flushing with pleasure as he read.

'Look, Juliet,' he said. 'What do you think of this?' He passed her the paper, folded at the announcement.

Marcus King is appearing for a short season at the Theatre Royal, Warnecliff playing the lead in the play House Guest *by Peter Longhurst.*

Before the war Marcus King was renowned for his Shakespearean appearances at the Old Vic and on tour, making his name in such roles as Hamlet, Romeo and Henry V. During the war he toured extensively entertaining the troops with ENSA.

Max Goddard, producer and director of the Theatre Royal, is recently out of the RAF and has directed and appeared in several documentary films. He is already stunning Warnecliff audiences with his innovative work. He is delighted to have persuaded a major star like Marcus King to appear for the Royal's summer season and is expecting the show to be a sell-out.

Juliet passed the paper back with a smile. 'It's lovely, Dad. I'm sure there'll be some important agents and producers down from London to see you in the show. Not long to go now eh?'

The smile left Marcus's face fleetingly and just for a moment he looked nervous. 'I wouldn't admit it to anyone but you, darling, but the very thought gives me the collywobbles.'

Juliet gave him a hug. 'You'll be fine, Dad. You know you will.'

On Monday morning Marcus was up early. When Juliet went into the kitchen she found him already dressed and making tea.

' 'Morning, Dad,' she said, yawning. 'Not like you to be up this early. Couldn't you sleep?'

He poured boiling water into the teapot and replaced the lid. 'Never had a wink,' he said. 'Lines just keep going round and round. God! I'll be glad when tonight is over.'

Juliet took cups from the dresser and poured the tea. 'Nonsense,' she said. 'You'll enjoy yourself enormously. It's just that first entrance, isn't it?'

He put a hand to his head dramatically. 'Don't! Don't remind me.'

Juliet sat down at the table with her tea. 'Once you've got that first line out of the way you'll be fine,' she reminded him. 'And I'll be there, remember, somewhere in the centre of the stalls.'

'Yes. Thank God you won't be staring up at me from the front row.'

She laughed. 'You know I wouldn't do that to you. Anyway, you always say the audience is just a blur to you anyway.' She looked at her watch. 'I've just got time to make you some breakfast and then I'll have to go. Can't be late for work, even on the day of my famous father's second debut.'

'Don't call it that,' Marcus said. 'And as for breakfast, don't bother. I couldn't eat a thing.'

Juliet couldn't wait to get in to work that morning. The previous week she'd spoken to Bill Martin about the story Dr Galbraith had told her.

'How would I go about tracing this woman, Bill?' she asked him. 'It would be wonderful to write an article about these unsung heroes and heroines. If I could find her she could tell me so much – might put me in touch with some of the others.'

Bill nodded. 'You might even sell an article like that to a magazine such as *John Bull*.'

She stared at him. 'Could I really? Would that be ethical, when I work for the *Clarion*?'

'Nothing to stop you doing a bit of freelance work,' he told her. 'But you could always clear it with Gerry first as a matter of courtesy.' He looked thoughtful. 'Look, I used to work for the *Daily Post* and I'm going up to London this weekend. I'll be dropping in on all the old colleagues. You say this woman was in prison. If you'd like to give me what details you have I could look up the trial in the paper's archives.'

'Oh, Bill, could you?'

'Yes, it'd be fascinating.'

'All I know is that her name was Tina Moore and she was arrested in a nightclub and convicted of possession of stolen goods.'

'Right. I can't promise anything, mind. Unless it was a dramatic story the paper probably wouldn't report it, but it's worth a try.'

To Juliet's disappointment Bill was on his way out when she arrived at the office that morning. As he got into his car outside she asked him if he'd had any luck with the archives and he nodded.

'I found a report of the case,' he told her. 'Can't stop to tell you much about it now. I'm off all day on an assignment. I can tell you, however, that she was an unmarried mother and as well as being convicted of possession she was found guilty of child cruelty.'

Juliet was shocked. How could the doctor defend a woman like that? Maybe she should go and visit her again, this time when she was off duty. But for now she pushed the story to the back of her mind; Marcus's impending first night was her first priority.

Arriving home that evening she found that he had already left for the theatre. He had left a scribbled note on the kitchen table. She snatched a quick bite to eat and then caught the bus into town.

The stage door-keeper, who knew her by now nodded to her as she went in.

'Evenin', Miss King.'

'Good evening, Harry. Is my father in his dressing-room?'

The man gave her a rather knowing smile. 'Oh yes, miss. He's in there all right. I'd say it's a good job you've come early.'

Puzzled, Juliet went through the corridor and tapped on the door which already had Marcus's name emblazoned on it.

'Wadderyawant?'

'Oh, please God, no!' Juliet's heart sank. Before she'd even opened the door she knew that Marcus had been drinking. She opened the door and looked in apprehensively.

'Dad?'

Marcus sat at the dressing table in his dressing-gown. He had clearly made no attempt to apply make-up or dress for his part. On the dressing table in front of him stood a half-empty bottle of whisky and a glass.

'*Dad*! What do you think you're doing?' Juliet closed the door and stood in front of her father who slumped in his chair. 'You've got a show to do. You're on in just under forty minutes and you – you're *drunk*!' Tears filled her eyes and she swallowed hard at the lump in her throat. 'I can't *believe* this! How could you be so *stupid*?'

He looked up at her blearily. 'S'no good, Juliet, I can't do it. I can't go on.'

'*Yes, you can!*'

He waved a hand at her. 'I *can't*. I can't remember a single word of the bloody script. I'm finished, darling.' He whined. 'Your old daddy is washed up and finished.'

'*No, you're not*! Pull yourself together. Suppose Max saw you like this. You can't let everybody down, Dad. You've no understudy. You *have* to go on.' She picked up the whisky bottle and waved it accusingly under his nose. 'Where did you get this?'

153

He heaved a huge sigh. 'Harry got it for me. Slipped across to the pub. Good chap, Harry.'

'Good chap! I'd like to kill him,' Juliet said under her breath. Aloud she asked, 'How many have you had? Have you drunk all this?' She held up the bottle.

He shook his head. 'Harry joined me for a couple of snifters. Di'nt want to drink alone. Good cha—'

'*Chap* – yes, you said. Just wait till I get my hands on him.' Juliet grabbed Marcus by the back of his dressing-gown collar and hauled him to his feet. Pulling him across to the wash basin she turned on the cold tap and pushed his head under it. He complained loudly.

'Oooh-aarh. Stop it. You're drowning me.'

'Nothing to what I'd like to do,' she said between clenched teeth. Grabbing a towel she wrapped it round his head and pushed him back into the chair. 'I'm going to put the kettle on for coffee and you're going to drink it, black and strong until you're sober.' She looked at him as he sat, head in hands, groaning loudly. Inwardly she felt completely helpless; helpless and terribly afraid. What on earth was she going to do with him? If Marcus disgraced himself this time he would indeed be finished. Max would be devastated. No one would ever employ him again and without his work Marcus would die. She knew it as well as she knew her own name. Suddenly she had a thought. 'Wait there,' she told him. 'Just don't move. I'll be back in a minute.'

Closing the door she went along the corridor and knocked on the door marked Wardrobe. As it was a modern dress play there was little reason to expect Maggie to be there but she prayed with all her heart that she would be in luck. When Maggie opened the door she felt almost faint with relief.

'Juliet! Hello, love.' Seeing Juliet's harassed expression she stopped. 'Oh dear, is something wrong?'

'Are you busy, Maggie?'

'No, not really. I usually just hang around in case someone splits a gusset or ladders a stocking. Why, is there a problem?'

'You could say that.' Juliet lowered her voice. 'It's Dad. He got himself into a panic and I'm afraid he's tried a bit too hard to relax with a bottle of whisky.'

'Oh my God!' Maggie was immediately galvanized into action.

Closing the door she took Juliet by the arm. 'Right,' she said. 'Lead on. I'm a bit of an expert in this field.'

When Marcus saw Maggie bearing down on him he shrank back.

'What's she doing here? Hey! What do you think you're doing?'

His dressing-room was the only one in the theatre with its own en-suite shower room. Maggie hauled Marcus to his feet and turned to Juliet. 'Cold shower,' she said. 'It's the only way.'

To loud protests she ripped off Marcus's dressing-gown and pushed him manually into the shower, turning the cold tap full on while he clung to his under pants with comic desperation. Maggie grinned at Juliet over her shoulder.

'Shows he's not too far gone,' she said. 'That's something at least. See if you can find him some dry undies and make that coffee good and strong.'

Ten minutes later a calm and chastened Marcus sat at the dressing table again, dressed in his costume for act one and sipping black coffee while Juliet combed his hair. Maggie sat beside him, his make-up box open on the dressing table and the script in her hand.

'Now, while you're drinking your second cup I'll hear your first lines,' she said. 'And don't tell me you don't know them because I know better. Then we'll get that handsome physog of yours made-up.' She looked at her watch. 'You've got just fifteen minutes. The call boy will be round any second now.' She peered at him. 'How do you feel?'

'Bloody awful,' Marcus moaned. 'You've half killed me, woman.'

'*Good*!' Maggie said. 'This part requires you to be a bad-tempered, miserable old bugger and you're already more than halfway there!'

The curtain came down at the end of act one to an enthusiastic burst of applause and Juliet let out her breath in relief. She felt as though she'd been holding it ever since the curtain went up. She'd seen Marcus act many times before in every kind of role but this time he really had excelled. As the irascible, idiosyncratic best selling author, Frank Langley he was superb. No one would ever have guessed at the scene in his dressing room a few minutes before curtain-up. Juliet was almost light headed with relief. She went to the bar for a coffee and found Maggie waiting for her there, her face wreathed in smiles.

'How about that then?' she said. 'What a triumph! No one could have played the part better. Aren't you proud of him?'

Juliet sank into a chair. 'I suppose I will be when it's sunk in. Right at this moment I'm just weak with relief and grateful that he made it at all. I was at my wits' end when I arrived and saw the state he was in.' She squeezed Maggie's arm. 'It's all thanks to you. I don't know what I would have done without you. This is really your triumph as much as his.'

But Maggie was shaking her head. 'Rubbish! Glad I was there when I was needed.' She looked at Juliet with a wistful smile. 'It's a long while since I had to do that. My dad was an alcoholic – turned to the bottle after we lost my mum when I was fourteen. He was a night watchman and the times I had to haul him out of the pub and get him sober enough to go to work, God rest him.' She looked up as the warning buzzer sounded for act two. 'Better get back to your seat now. See you at the party afterwards?'

'Yes. See you at the party. And, Maggie.'

'Yes?'

'Dad isn't an alcoholic, you know. He only drinks when he's depressed or scared.'

'I know that love.'

'And you won't mention what happened earlier to anyone, will you?'

'What do you take me for?' Maggie gave her a quick hug. 'My lips are sealed, as they say. I'm too fond of the pair of you to want to rock the boat.'

The stage had been cleared for the party, a makeshift bar set up against the back wall. Juliet found Marcus chatting animatedly to his leading lady. She touched his arm.

'Congratulations, Dad. You were magnificent.'

He turned to smile at her, his face wreathed in smiles and she knew at once that he had completely blanked out his pre-show panic and the shameful scene in his dressing room earlier. 'Thank you, darling,' he said. 'You've met Emma Hardy, haven't you?'

Juliet smiled at the actress. 'Of course. You were very good too. The play went down extremely well.'

'I think we can safely say we had a moderate success. Will you be reviewing for the local paper?' Emma asked.

Juliet shook her head. 'A colleague is doing it this time. I think I'd be a bit prejudiced, don't you?'

Emma smiled. 'I daresay you just might be, but rightly so. You have a very talented father, Juliet.'

Marcus was in great demand and loving every minute of it. Juliet stood back and watched as he enjoyed his special moment. She shared a drink with Maggie who announced that she was tired and heading for home.

'Never did go a bundle on these first-night bashes,' she said. 'Egos anonymous, I call them – or not so anonymous as the case may be.' She tossed back the last of her drink. 'I expect you'll be staying till Marcus leaves.' She raised a cynical eyebrow. 'By the look of it you could be in for a late night. Goodnight love. Take care.'

' 'Night, Maggie, and thanks again.'

'I know what she means about first-night parties.'

Juliet turned to see Max standing behind her. It was the first time she'd seen him all evening. 'Hello. Congratulations. You must be so pleased that it went so well.'

'I am. It's good to see you, Juliet.'

She flushed. 'Good to see you, too.' Her eyes searched the room for Marcus. 'I hope Dad doesn't want to stay too late. I've got to be up for work in the morning.'

'Don't worry about him,' Max said. 'I'll make sure he gets a cab.'

'I know, but I feel I should wait – be here for him when he's ready.'

'You know sometimes I wonder which of you is the parent,' Max remarked. 'He's fine. Just look at him. If you want to go home just go. In fact, get your coat, I'll take you.'

'I couldn't take you away from your own party.'

'It'd be great to get away from the theatre for a while. I've been here since early this morning. Anyway, it's their celebration really; a chance to let off steam, loosen the tension.' He took her arm. 'Come on. Find Marcus and tell him you're off. I'll get the car and wait for you outside.'

She found Marcus in the centre of a group of admirers and he hardly seemed to register the fact that she was leaving.

'You'll get a taxi home, won't you, Dad?'

'What? Yes, yes, don't worry about me. And don't wait up,' he called after her to the accompaniment of gales of laughter. Juliet was briefly reminded of Max's remark about which of them was the parent.

Max's sports car was waiting outside the stage door with the engine running. She got in gratefully. 'It's very good of you to take me home,' she said. 'It's been a hectic day and I'm quite glad it's over.'

'Me too,' he said.

They drove in silence for a few minutes then Juliet said, 'It looks as though you have a hit on your hands. I've a feeling it's going to be a successful summer season. The play is excellent.'

He glanced at her. 'And I'm going to be at a bit of a loose end for a few weeks. Apart from keeping an eye on things and planning for the months ahead, that is.'

'So, you'll have some well-deserved time off.'

'Yes. Which means being able to do some of the things I've been planning.'

'Like taking a holiday?'

He shrugged. 'I might take a trip down to Devon one weekend and see the family.'

'Nothing more adventurous than that?'

'That's what I wanted to talk to you about.' They had arrived at Wycombe and Max drew up outside Heathlands Cottage and switched off the engine. 'One of the things I've been promising myself is to ask you out to dinner again.'

She laughed. 'Is that adventurous?'

'Well, you have to admit that the last time was a bit of a disaster. It must have put you off me in a big way.' He turned to look at her. 'Every time we meet we seem to get off on the wrong foot. So would it be a waste of time asking you to let me try again?'

'That evening – it wasn't your fault,' Juliet said, genuinely surprised. 'I was the one who drank too much.'

'And I was the one who encouraged you to, albeit unintentionally. But let's forget about that.' He leaned forward. 'Please say you'll have dinner with me again, Juliet.'

'I'd like that very much,' she said quietly.

'That's wonderful.' He took her hand. 'I'd like it to be the first of many. Juliet, I know you think that theatrical people are superficial and insincere.'

'That was just a generalization.'

'I know. And I can imagine why you feel that way. Maybe it's why you seem so – so wary, but we can't all be like that, can we?'

'I suppose not.'

'And I'd like you to believe that I'm different – sincere.'

'Of course I believe you – if you say so.'

He winced. 'See what I mean? I can see I'm going to have to work very hard to prove to you that I'm not some kind of Lothario.'

'There's no reason why you should prove anything to me.'

'Oh, but there is.' He cupped her chin with both hands. 'You've already made it clear to me that any kind of relationship with a member of the theatrical profession is doomed to failure. So what chance do you give our prospects, Juliet? I really need to know.'

She took a deep breath. The way he was looking at her was making her heart beat faster. 'Sometimes,' she said slowly, 'sometimes we don't have a choice. Sometimes emotions – *feelings* – wash away everything that seemed to make sense.'

'And I need to convince you that what I feel couldn't be more sincere – because you see, my lovely Juliet, I'm afraid I'm falling ever so slightly in love with you.'

When he kissed her she felt as though her heart had stopped beating. The breath caught in her throat and the world spun madly. She found his closeness as intoxicating as the wine she was so unused to, leaving her with a surreal feeling, like floating through space.

He drew back his head to look at her. 'Juliet.'

She forced herself to open her eyes and look at him. 'Yes?'

'Would you say something please?'

'I-I can't think straight.'

'Are you happy?' When she looked bemused he frowned uncertainly. 'Do you feel anything for me at all?'

'Oh, Max.'

'So, having me falling in love with you doesn't exactly fill you with horror?'

'N-no.' She reached out to touch his face. 'I love you too.'

He stroked her cheek. 'And so, what about all your fears – about fickle theatrical types?' His dark eyes held hers hypnotically.

'Sometimes you have to throw away your fears and take a risk.'

159

'And will you take a risk on me?' he whispered.

Suddenly lightheaded with happiness, she wound her arms around his neck. 'Kiss me again and I'll tell you,' she said, her eyes sparkling with mischief.

CHAPTER THIRTEEN

House Guest had been playing for two weeks to packed houses and Max was even talking of extending the season. Marcus was in his element. There had been no repeat of his attack of first night nerves and neither Juliet nor Maggie had reminded him of it. All that Juliet was dreading now was the end of the season when Marcus would once again be unemployed.

So far there had only been good reviews. Because of her relationship to her father Bill Martin had written one for the *Clarion* and given Marcus a glowing tribute. There had also been one in *The Stage* and in one of the London *Evening News*'s arts column under 'What's on in the Provinces'. Marcus devoured them all avidly and Juliet watched his confidence grow from day to day.

When her driving licence arrived in the post one mid-week morning there was great excitement over the breakfast table.

'Thank goodness you won't have to keep using Marion's old bike,' Marcus said. 'You worried the life out of me on that rusty old thing.'

Juliet agreed, but she was already making plans for her new found freedom of the road that did not include her work for the *Clarion*.

As soon as she arrived at the office that morning Juliet went through to give Gerry Bates her news.

'I'm now officially a legal driver,' she told him, waving the document triumphantly at him.

He removed the pipe from his mouth and grunted, 'Good, but not before time.'

'I wanted to ask you a favour,' Juliet went on.

'Mmm, I knew there'd be a catch.'

'It's just – may I have the car over the weekend?' she said, adding quickly, 'So that I can get some practice in before I use it for work.'

His eyebrows shot up. 'You're asking for out of hours usage already? Bit of a bloody cheek, isn't it?'

'I'll pay for the petrol I use,' she said.

'And who will you pay?' he asked; then at her downcast expression his face suddenly creased into the grimace that passed for a smile. 'Stop looking like someone's just pinched your lollipop, girl,' he said. 'Of course you can take the car for the weekend. I'm only pulling your leg. Just don't smash it up, that's all. Get a chitty and the coupons from the front desk, get the tank filled up and make sure it's still in one piece on Monday morning.'

'Thanks, Mr Bates.'

'Oh, and Juliet . . .'

She paused in the doorway. 'Yes?'

'Tell your father congratulations. The wife and I saw the show at the Royal last night. We enjoyed it very much.'

'Thanks. I'll tell him.' Juliet almost skipped along the corridor. Everything seemed to be going her way for once.

Max was waiting for her at lunchtime as usual in the Rose and Crown. Ever since the first night of *House Guest* they had seen each other almost daily. His face lit up with a smile when she walked into the bar.

'Your dad tells me you have some good news.'

She sighed. 'Trust him to steal my thunder.' She waved her licence at him. 'Look. I've got it at last!'

'Congrats!'

'*And* I've got the company car for the weekend,' she told him. 'I've got something special to do and I'm taking you with me.'

'You're taking me.' He pulled down the corners of his mouth. 'Does that mean *you're* going to drive?'

'Of course. I'll have you know I'm a very good driver. Maggie says I'm a natural.'

He grinned at her. 'Oh, well, if Maggie says you are, then I know I'll be in safe hands.' He passed her the menu. 'What'll you have? And we're celebrating, remember.'

When they'd made their choices he looked at her. 'Right, so where is this somewhere special I'm being taken to?'

'I want to take you out to Hemsbury to meet Dr Galbraith,' she told him.

'Is this to do with the article you wrote for the paper on her being awarded the GC?'

'Partly, but it's not for the paper this time, it's off the record.'

'So what's it about?'

'Something that came out of that interview,' she told him. 'Do you remember me telling you about the unsung heroes she mentioned? There's one in particular that she felt strongly about. Bill looked the court case up in the London *Daily Post*'s archives for me a few weeks ago. There was a bit more to it than I realized and I want to see if she knows any more.'

'Do you think she'd tell you if she did?'

'That remains to be seen. I telephoned her this morning and she said to come over on Sunday afternoon.' She looked at him, her head on one side. 'So, will you come?'

He grinned. 'Are you kidding? I can't wait.'

As they ate Juliet couldn't help watching him. She realized now that she had been in love with him almost since their first meeting, but she was still finding it hard to believe that he was actually in love with her, Juliet King, an inexperienced, unsophisticated girl eight years his junior, when he could surely have his pick of elegant, stylish women. But the more they were together the more she felt they were destined for each other. Being in love with Max seemed to be uncovering so many facets of her personality. So many things were clear to her now, not the least of these being her inability to respond to Nigel. She felt guilty about it and at the very first opportunity she had confessed everything to him. He took it surprisingly well.

'I'd already guessed,' he said. 'That night when he walked into the Feathers with that girl from the company, your face was a study. I could see he was keen on you too.' He smiled a little wryly. 'As a matter of fact I've started seeing someone else myself.'

His admission made Juliet feel much better, but she couldn't help wondering if the 'someone else' he was referring to was Sylvia.

Doctor Galbraith had clearly taken a little more care over her appearance when she opened the door to them on Sunday afternoon. She wore a tweed skirt and a blue sweater which brought out the colour of her eyes.

'Juliet King!' she said with a smile. 'How nice to see you again. Come in, my dear.'

'This is Max Goddard,' Juliet said, turning to Max. 'He is the producer at the Theatre Royal.'

The doctor held out her hand and shook Max's warmly. 'I'm very pleased to meet you, Mr Goddard,' she said. 'The theatre is one of my delights and I go when ever I get the chance.' She looked at Juliet. 'I'm going next week to see your father perform,' she announced. 'Saw him at the Old Vic several times before the war when I lived in London. A very fine actor. Now . . .' She held out her hand towards the drawing-room. 'Come and have a cup of tea and please call me Fliss.' In the drawing-room she pushed the dogs off the sofa. 'Do come and make yourselves at home,' she invited. 'I shall call you by your first names and I'll be most put out if you keep on calling me doctor. Those days are over for me.'

Over tea they chatted about the theatre and Fliss's garden, which was looking even more colourful and beautiful than the last time Juliet had seen it. The tea finished and pleasantries exchanged, Fliss looked enquiringly at Juliet.

'Now, you didn't come here just to exchange small talk with an old has-been like me,' she said. 'You said on the telephone that you wanted to know more about Tina Moore.'

Juliet nodded. 'A colleague of mine once worked for the London *Daily Post* and he looked up the court case in the paper's archives for me a few weeks ago. It said that Tina was an unmarried mother and that she was found guilty of child cruelty. Did you know that?'

Fliss sighed. 'Sadly, it's true that she was charged and later convicted of that. Her young child was found alone in the flat.' There was a pause as she looked at Juliet. 'You're wondering how I could condone that kind of thing. Obviously I don't, but I believe implicitly in Tina's innocence. She insisted throughout the trial that there was a young girl sitting with the child that evening and I believe she was telling the truth, but unfortunately the girl was not there when the

163

police broke in.'

'So what happened exactly?'

'It's all a little hazy.' Fliss shook her head. 'When I met Tina she was determined to make a new life and she was reluctant to talk much about what had happened to her in the past,' she said. 'But I pride myself in being a pretty good judge of character and I'd stake my life on it that the girl was innocent. From what she did tell me I gathered that she'd met a man who appeared to be fond of her and her child. Clearly she'd had quite a hard time of it, bringing up a child alone, and no doubt she thought her luck had changed when she met a man who seemed to want to protect her. So when he arrived one evening and said he had planned a special evening out she was delighted. He'd even brought a young girl – said she was his sister – to sit with the child. To cut a long story short the special surprise turned out to be a visit to a sleazy nightclub, which was later raided by the police. To Tina's horror she could not find her boyfriend anywhere when she was arrested along with many others. At the police station stolen jewellery was found in her handbag, clearly planted, and, as I've already told you, her child was found alone and distressed in the flat. No one believed in the existence of either the man friend or the baby sitter. No one came forward to be a character witness for her. No one believed in Tina's innocence.'

'Was either of them ever found?' Juliet asked.

Fliss shook her head.

'So Tina went to prison.'

'Yes. She was found guilty and sentenced to seven years.'

'What happened to her child?'

Fliss shrugged. 'Taken into care – probably adopted. Tina wouldn't talk about it and I could see how painful it was for her so I didn't press her. She was released from prison two years before the war. She got a job as housekeeper for an elderly man who treated her well. He even paid for her to have driving lessons so that she could take him out. But, when the war began he went to live with his daughter down in Cornwall and Tina joined the ambulance service. That was how we met.'

'Did you keep in touch?' Juliet asked, holding her breath. 'Do you still hear from her – know where she lives?'

Fliss shook her head. 'We exchanged Christmas cards a couple of times, but I don't hear from her any more.'

Juliet took a deep breath. 'I know it's asking a lot – and please say no if you'd rather not – but could you give me her address?'

'It's two years since I last heard from her,' Fliss said. 'Then she was living in a bed-sit in the East End – Hackney. She might have moved of course – married, gone abroad even.' She hesitated. 'And I'm not sure she'd want me to encourage anyone to rake up her past.'

'I thought she might give me some more names to investigate,' Juliet said. 'I'd love to write about the valuable and brave work done during the blitz by ordinary people.'

Fliss looked thoughtful. 'I would like to see her and all the others get the recognition they deserve. If you promise not to mention any of what I've told you I'll find the last address I have for her. But that's not to say she's still there of course.'

'It's a start,' Juliet said. 'Thank you, Fliss. Would you mind if I mentioned your name? I could say it was to do with your citation.'

Fliss hesitated. 'Well, I suppose it would be all right.'

As they drove back to Warnecliff Max looked at her. 'What are you going to do?'

'Get a couple of days off and go up to London,' she told him. 'Try to find Tina Moore and get her to talk. Maybe she'll point me in the direction of some of the people who worked with her during the blitz.'

'And if you can't find her?'

She turned to look at him. 'I'll meet that when I come to it.'

He laughed. 'Well, you're nothing if not determined, Juliet King,' he said. 'I'll give you that.' He paused. 'Can I come too?'

She looked at him in surprise. 'Why would you want to?'

'Because I want to be wherever you are,' he said simply. 'It's ages since I saw my agent, so I could do that while you were busy. Just think, Juliet, it would give us some free time to ourselves. With Marcus so ever-present we never seem to get a chance to be alone. I know a nice little hotel in Earls Court – very respectable, single rooms – if you like.' Mischief danced in his eyes as he looked at her. 'We could see a show – anything you fancy.'

Juliet's heart missed a beat. 'Oh, Max, it sounds wonderful.' She drew the car up smoothly outside the block where Max had his flat. He looked at her enquiringly.

'Are you coming in?'

'I'd love to, but I'd better get back to Dad.'

He sighed. 'See what I mean? So, how do you feel – about a weekend in London together?'

She switched off the ignition and looked at him with shining eyes. 'Do you think we could?'

He reached across to kiss her. 'Just get the time off and say the word, darling. I'll sort the rest out. I can't wait.'

'Neither can I,' she said happily.

To Juliet's surprise Maggie was in the kitchen making a pot of tea when she arrived home.

'Maggie, this is a surprise. I didn't know you were coming today.'

'I wasn't.' Maggie closed the kitchen door. 'I was on the way to have tea with a friend and I thought I'd pop in,' she said. 'I don't know what made me feel there was something wrong, but I was right.'

Juliet's heart sank. 'Dad? Is he all right?'

'He's a bit upset,' Maggie said. 'He won't really talk about it, but I gather he's had a visitor, someone he clearly didn't want to see.'

'Who?' Juliet asked.

Maggie shook her head. 'He wouldn't tell me; said it wouldn't mean anything to me anyway. All I know is that whatever happened between them seems to have upset him.'

Juliet took off her coat. 'You get off now, Maggie,' she said. 'Your friend will be wondering where you are.'

'I will now that you're home, love, but let me know if there's anything I can do, won't you?'

Juliet found Marcus in the living-room. He sat staring at the wall, his face chalky white. She went to him.

'Dad! Are you all right? What's happened?'

'He's been here; he's found me,' he said numbly.

'Who, Dad – *who*?'

For the first time he looked at her. 'Kent,' he said. 'That slimy little toad Adam Kent.'

She gasped. 'Olivia's brother? How did he find you?'

Marcus grunted. 'Easy! The reviews in the papers. It was all there, wasn't it?'

'Not this address. How did he get that?'

'Seems he went to the theatre last night; asked Harry. Harry didn't have a precise address, but he knew vaguely. The rest he wheedled out of the neighbours.'

Juliet's heart plummeted. 'What did he want?'

Marcus looked at her. 'What do you think he wanted? Cash, of course.'

'You didn't give him any?'

'I just wanted him to go away.'

'Is that a yes?'

Marcus was pacing up and down the room now. 'He said that Libby was out of work and too proud to ask,' he said over his shoulder. 'He said she was living in shabby digs without a rag to her name and—'

'*Dad*! You surely didn't fall for that? Even if it were true, which it almost certainly isn't, you don't owe Olivia anything – quite the reverse.'

'Well, never mind. It doesn't matter. He's gone now.'

'For how long though? Now that he knows where you are do you really think he's going to leave you alone?' She got up and went to the telephone. 'I'm going to ring the police.'

Instantly Marcus was on his feet, his face flooded with colour. '*No*! Not the police, Juliet.'

'Why not? He deserves to be punished, demanding money from people. It's against the law.' Her hand hovered over the telephone.

'*Don't*!' he said. 'It'd get out and think what it would do to the show – to my standing in the business. I can't risk the publicity.'

She sighed, letting her hand fall to her side. 'How much did you give him?'

'Not much.' He shook his head dismissively. 'He's just a petty crook, living from hand to mouth. Look, forget it, Juliet. We won't see him again.' He rubbed his hands together and forced a smile. 'Good God, look at the time! Don't know about you, but I'm starving. What's for supper?'

In spite of his insistence that he was starving Marcus ate hardly anything and rose from the supper table pleading a headache.

'I think I'll have an early night, darling, if you don't mind,' he said. 'It's been quite a day one way and another.'

Juliet knew he was far more worried than he'd admit. He'd been badly shaken by Adam Kent's visit. He was clearly afraid of Olivia's brother, but why? What kind of hold did the man have on him? In an attempt to clear her head and try to make sense of what was happening, Juliet decided to take a walk across the heath. The sun was setting, a fiery golden ball in the western sky and the air was cool and fresh on her face. She was close to the gypsy encampment and deep in thought when a voice hailed her.

'Evenin', Miss Juliet!' She turned to see Danny Lee walking towards her.

'Good evening, Danny. Is everyone all right?'

'We're all fine, thank you,' Danny said. 'I was up at yours this afternoon. I wanted to see if the fruit was setting on the fruit trees.'

'That was good of you. The blossom has been wonderful this year.'

'I know, but after them winds we had last week I were worried the fruit might have dropped.'

'And has it?'

'No. It's hung on fine. Should get a good crop of apples and plums come the back end.' He looked sad. 'Trouble is, miss, I shan't be here to see it.'

Juliet guessed what was coming. 'You've been called up for your National Service?'

He nodded. 'What worries me is that the council might make my folk move on if they won't give up the camp and move into them new houses they're building. I might come home and find them all gone.'

'That won't happen, Danny,' Juliet assured him. 'Look, don't worry. I'll keep an eye on Imelda and the children and I'll find out what I can from the council about the houses.'

He nodded and smiled, but seemed reluctant to move away, shuffling his feet as though there was something he wanted to say but couldn't find the words.

'Is everything all right, Danny?' Juliet asked. 'You look worried.'

He looked up at her, his dark eyes wary. 'You and yours've always been good to us, miss,' he said, reaching out a tentative hand to touch Juliet's arm. 'Looking out for us when there was them as'd have us seen off. If I didn't say nuthin' I'd have it on my conscience like.'

'Say something about what, Danny?' Juliet looked at his troubled face.

'I were on me way to come and see you about something this evenin' – something that ain't right.'

'What is it, Danny?'

'I wanted to warn you.' His dark eyes looked into hers gravely. 'When I was up at yours this afternoon your dad had a visitor.'

'I know.'

'I recognized him.'

Juliet looked at him, puzzled. 'Are you sure? He's not from round here.'

'I know that, miss. He's someone I shan't never forget – not if I lives to be a hundred.'

'How do you know him, Danny?'

'It were a long time ago – the year I were seven-year-old. Every summer I can remember we've all gone off to Kent for the hop pickin'.'

'I know.'

'Aye, well, one year that man I saw today was employed as overseer.'

Juliet shook her head. 'I don't think that's very likely, Danny.'

'Oh yes, miss. It were him all right. I ain't never likely to forget. I remember his name were Kent – Adam Kent.' He shook his head. 'I'll never forget him, believe me.'

Juliet gasped. It seemed that unlikely as it was, it was true. 'Go on,' she said.

'Nasty piece of work he was – the worst kind.'

'So what did he do.'

'One evening my dad sent me to the manager's office with a message. Kent were in there. I saw him, plain as plain, stealin' from the cash box. He saw me and grabbed hold of me – half strangled me, said he'd kill me if I split on him.'

'So you never told anyone?'

'I were only a chavvie and I didn't know what to do, but next day, afore I could make up my mind whether to tell on Kent or not, some money were found hidden at the bottom of my hop basket. Kent gave the alarm – said he'd seen me hide it there – said he'd seen me take it from the office the night before. Reckoned my dad had told me to take it.'

'What happened?' Juliet asked.

'We got thrown out,' Danny told her. 'My whole family, Mam, Dad and six of us kids. We relied on the money we would've earned there that summer. Word went round and no one else wouldn't give us no work. No one believed me. They all took Kent's word against mine, even my family. My dad took his belt to me – buckle end – couldn't sit down for a fortnight.' He shook his head. 'We went hungry that winter because of him, Miss Juliet. I'll never forget that man. I dunno what he wanted with you or your dad, but if you take my advice you won't have nuthin' to do with him.'

Juliet walked home deep in thought. Working as a hop-picking overseer in Kent? So much for Olivia's claim to an aristocratic background. And Marcus was giving in to him – giving him his hard-earned money. Her blood boiled. If he came around again she fervently hoped she'd be there to give him short shrift.

'You're sure you'll be all right, aren't you, Dad?' Juliet said at the breakfast table. 'It's only for the weekend.'

Marcus looked far from all right as he stirred his coffee. 'I'm still not all that keen on you going away for the weekend with Max,' he said. 'He's a good chap and all that, but he's a lot older and more experienced than you. I hope his—'

'Intentions are honourable?' Juliet laughed.

Marcus looked annoyed. 'Don't make fun of me. You're my only child. It's a father's right to protect his daughter.'

Juliet stared at her father. 'I can't believe I'm hearing correctly,' she said. 'This is 1947, not 1847. You lived with Olivia – a woman ten years younger than yourself – for years. What right have you to preach morals at me? In any case, Max and I are staying at a hotel where he has booked *single rooms* for two nights. We're hardly eloping!'

'That means nothing. You forget, I'm a man,' Marcus said enigmatically. 'And I know that men have their own agendas.'

'Don't judge all men by yourself,' Juliet said. She got up and went round the table to kiss his forehead. 'Dad, give me some credit. I'm not a wilting Victorian maiden. I'm a child of the twentieth century and I certainly won't be talked, or charmed, into doing anything I don't want to.'

He looked up at her with one eyebrow raised cynically. 'That's what I'm afraid of.'

She sat down and took his hand. 'Dad, seriously, if Adam Kent comes round again you won't give him any more money, will you?'

'What do you take me for?'

'That's not the answer I wanted,' Juliet insisted. 'Promise me you won't.

'Promise. There, that do?'

'It'll have to.' She stood up and pulled on her coat. 'Max will be here any minute now so I'll go down to the gate. Bye, Dad. Look after yourself. Maggie is coming to take you out to lunch on Sunday.' She grinned at him. 'I hope I can trust the pair of you.'

Marcus reached out to grasp her hand as she passed. 'Juliet, seriously, darling, be careful. I know you think I'm an old fusspot, but you're all I've got and I couldn't bear to see you get hurt.'

She smiled. 'I know and I promise you I'll take great care. Bye, Dad.'

The drive to London was uneventful and they reached the Kensmere Hotel by 11.30. As it was Saturday Max had arranged to have lunch with his agent at his home in Richmond so they went their separate ways, arranging to meet back at the hotel later that afternoon.

Armed with Tina Moore's last known address in the East End, Juliet went off on her quest. The address turned out to be a terraced Georgian house on Hackney Road. Once a prosperous three-storeyed residence, it was now a crumbling, run-down house split crudely into bed-sits and flatlets. Juliet picked her way round the dustbins behind the front railings and pushed open the peeling street door. The hallway was littered with assorted prams and bicycles propped up against the staircase.

The number of the room Fliss had given her was on the first floor. Juliet rang the bell, holding her breath. After several minutes the door was opened by a young man wearing jeans and a grubby string vest. He was unshaven and looked heavy-eyed.

'Whatcher want?' he demanded, pushing a hand through his dishevelled hair. 'I'm on nights an' I was tryin' to get some kip, for gawd's sake.'

'I'm sorry to disturb you,' Juliet said. 'I'm looking for a Miss Tina Moore. This is the last address I have for her.'

'Never 'eard of 'er.' The door began to close and Juliet said quickly, '*Please*, haven't you any idea where she went? I've come a long way to see her.'

Through the crack the man muttered, 'Try the landlord. Ground floor.' And the door closed sharply in her face.

There were two doors on the ground floor. Juliet knocked on the one nearest the front of the building, hoping she wouldn't draw another blank. It was opened by a middle-aged man with long greasy grey hair. He looked her up and down.

'Yeah?'

'I'm sorry to trouble you, but I'm trying to locate a Miss Tina Moore. This is the last address I have for her.'

The man scratched his head. 'Yeah, I remember her, long gone though.'

'Would you have a forwarding address for her?'

He shook his head. 'Did have, but it was ages ago,' he said. 'Can't hang on to things for ever.' He leered at her. 'And my memory ain't always what it might be.'

Something about his demeanour told Juliet that he was probably open to persuasion. She opened her handbag and took out a ten shilling note. 'Would this help your memory?'

The man hesitated. 'That the best you can do?' he asked scornfully.

Juliet took out a pound note, but before she could replace the ten shillings the man grabbed both notes.

'That's more like it.' He took a step backwards. 'I'll have to have a look in my address book,' he said, and before she could protest he slammed the door shut. She could hear his muffled laughing.

Juliet banged on the door as hard as she could, shouting for the man to open up, but to no avail.

'What's up, duckie?'

She turned to see an elderly woman laden with bags of shopping standing at the bottom of the stairs. 'I just gave that man money for the address of someone I want to find,' Juliet said, her face red with anger. 'He's tricked me.'

The woman shook her head. 'You're not from round here are you, duck?' she said. 'Or you'd know not to be so trusting. Who were you looking for?'

'Tina Moore,' Juliet said. 'This is the last address I have for her.'

'Tina?' The woman smiled. 'Yes, she was here – moved on about a year ago.'

'You wouldn't have her address, would you?'

'Why do you want to find her?' the woman asked warily.

'I'm a friend of Dr Galbraith who Tina used to work with during the blitz,' Juliet said. 'The doctor was worried as she hadn't heard from Tina for some time.'

'Dr Galbraith? Yes, I heard Tina speak of her lots of times,' the woman said. 'Look, I live upstairs; come up with me and I'll look out Tina's new address for you.'

It turned out that Tina was still working for the ambulance service, but had been moved to another branch. Her new address was in Notting Hill Gate. It took Juliet some time to cross from one side of London to the other, despite the fact that it was Saturday and therefore not as busy as a weekday. The new address was in a back street lined with neat Victorian villas. Once more they were divided into flats and Tina's was in the basement, accessed by stone steps descending into an area. But in contrast to the Hackney house with its jumble of rusty bikes and dustbins this area was swept clean and adorned with tubs of flowers. Under the window was a box planted with tulips opening their crimson heads to the sun. The door was painted a bright green and sported a knocker in the shape of a lion's head. Tina's fortunes had obviously improved. Feeling more optimistic Juliet knocked.

The woman who answered the door was slightly built with dark hair and blue eyes. She was wearing a coat and appeared to be about to go out. She smiled tentatively. 'Can I help you?'

'Are you Miss Moore?' Juliet asked. 'Miss Tina Moore?'

'That's right.'

'I'm a journalist,' Juliet told her. 'I'm hoping to write an article about the valuable work done by ordinary people during the war. I believe you were in the ambulance service.'

'That's right.' She frowned. 'But how did you—?'

'I recently interviewed Dr Galbraith,' Juliet said quickly. 'You'll know, of course that she was awarded the George Cross for her work during the blitz.'

Tina smiled. 'I did know. I went to the palace to see her come out

173

with her medal.'

'Oh, she'll be so disappointed that you didn't let her know you were there.'

'So, what can I do for you?'

'I was hoping you might tell me something about yourself – your experiences.'

The smile left Tina's face. 'I did what had to be done,' she said. 'I wish I could have done more. Now all I want is to forget it.'

'Oh, but surely you'd like some recognition.'

'You can't possibly imagine the horror of it,' Tina said with passion. 'You are too young to have been involved. If you'd been there – seen what I saw, I think you'd want to forget it too. Now, if there's nothing else, I was just about to go out.'

Standing on the doorstep Juliet was beginning to feel desperate. 'I wonder, could you perhaps put me in touch with some of your colleagues,' she said. 'Maybe they wouldn't mind remembering.'

'I'm sorry. I'm afraid I've lost touch with them all,' Tina said. 'It was quite deliberate I'm afraid, even with Dr Fliss. It's all part of putting it behind me – forgetting.'

Juliet thought about what Fliss had told her about this woman. She seemed to spend her entire life trying to forget her past. She looked so fragile, so vulnerable that somehow she couldn't find it in her heart to press her as she would normally have done with a reluctant interviewee.

'Oh well, never mind,' she said. Opening her bag she rummaged for one of the cards the *Clarion* had provided her with. 'If you should change your mind I'd be so pleased if you would get in touch,' she said passing Tina the card. 'I live down in Warnecliff but I could easily come up to Town again.' She moved away towards the area steps and she was almost halfway up when Tina called out to her.

'Wait! Could you come back – perhaps tomorrow?'

Juliet's heart leapt. 'Yes, of course. I wasn't planning to leave until tomorrow evening.'

'About eleven,' Tina said. 'I'll be waiting.'

CHAPTER FOURTEEN

'Did you find her?' Max was waiting when Juliet arrived back at the hotel. He was sitting in the lounge and had already ordered tea. Juliet sank gratefully into the chair opposite.

'Yes, eventually, but I have to go back and interview her tomorrow morning. She was just going out.'

'Oh.' He looked disappointed. 'I thought you might like to go somewhere in the morning; Kew perhaps, or even Petticoat Lane.'

'I'd have loved that,' she told him. 'But after the trouble I had finding Tina I can't miss the chance to do what I came for.'

'No, of course you can't.'

'How was your agent? Did you have a nice lunch?'

'Yes, he was fine; full of ideas.'

'What kind of ideas?'

'None that need bother us for the moment. What we need to concentrate on is where to have dinner. And we haven't that much time. I've booked us a couple of seats at Drury Lane to see *Oklahoma*.'

Juliet's eyes lit up. 'Oh, Max! How lovely. I've read so much about it.'

'I'd have liked to see Shakespeare again at the Old Vic,' he said, 'But they're still rebuilding the theatre after the bombing.'

They ate a sumptuous dinner at a little restaurant in Catherine Street, not far from the theatre then went to take their seats for the show. Juliet was enchanted. The American Mid-West background was so colourful and the costumes and music swept her away. As the ending brought tears to her eyes, her hand reached out to find Max's and without a word he handed her his handkerchief.

When they came out of the theatre into the spring night she was still floating. Max slipped an arm round her shoulders.

'Enjoy it?'

'Oh, Max, it was wonderful,' she said. 'Thank you so much for taking me.'

'Shall we go on to a nightclub? We could get a cab.'

She looked at him. 'Would you mind if I said no? I don't want to spoil the mood I'm in.'

'Of course I don't mind. I know you've had a long day. Back to the hotel then?'

'Yes, please.'

When they got out of the lift Juliet took out her key and handed it to Max. He unlocked the door and stood on the threshold as she walked into the room. She turned to look at him.

'Aren't you coming in?'

He came into the room silently and closed the door behind him. Standing with his back against it he said, 'Listen, Juliet, you don't think I had any . . . expectations about this weekend, do you?'

She looked at him with wide, innocent eyes. 'I can't think what you mean.'

'That I took it for granted that we'd – that I was going to—'

'Seduce me?' For a moment she stared at him, wide-eyed, then she dissolved into laughter. 'Max, I'm not as naïve as you seem to think. Did it ever occur to you that *I* might have what you call expectations?'

'Miss King! Now it's my turn to be shocked.' He couldn't keep the smile off his face as he took a step towards her. 'Are you saying that you came with me to London for the weekend assuming that I had seduction in mind?'

She laughed up into his eyes. 'Why else do you think I came?' She took his hand and they sat down together on the bed. Max turned to look at her, his eyes serious.

'Juliet, you're younger than me; quite a bit younger. I feel responsible for you. I don't want you to think I'm taking advantage of your youth. Maybe I should leave now before . . . maybe this isn't such a good idea.'

'Oh *dear*.' She shook her head at him. 'It looks very much as though I might have to seduce *you*.' She leaned across to kiss him, sliding her arms inside his jacket. 'Take this off,' she whispered.

He disengaged her arms from around his waist and stood up. 'You're not being fair.'

She smiled dreamily. 'What do they say? All's fair in love and war.'

He sat down beside her again and took both her hands in his. 'Do you have the faintest idea of the effect you're having on me?'

She frowned. 'What's wrong, Max?'

'What's wrong is that I know you're . . . well, inexperienced and I'm not sure you know what you're doing.'

'All I know is that I love you,' she told him softly. 'I know that I couldn't possibly want this with anyone I didn't love. All right, this will be the first time, but I want so much for it to be special and that means I want it to be with you.'

He drew her close and kissed her. 'Darling Juliet, you'd never say that if you weren't so young and naïve, but it's such an enormous compliment and I'm so proud.' He looked down at her. 'How do you know you can trust me? You know so little about me.'

'There's plenty of time for me to learn,' she said. 'And as for trust, it's a two-way thing, isn't it? Doesn't it go with love?'

'Ideally, yes. And I do love you, Juliet.'

'Then why are we having a discussion about it?'

Juliet was wakened by a sunbeam that crept through a chink in the curtains. It danced on her eyelids until they opened. Immediately she knew that something had changed; something so miraculous that her life was never going to be the same again.

Turning her head she saw that Max was still asleep, his dark hair tousled and his jaw-line dark with early morning shadow. She studied his face, the strong jaw and sensuous mouth. For the first time she noticed how long his eyelashes were as they lay fanned out on his cheeks. She thought about all that had happened to him before they met; the danger he had been in during his time in the RAF; his bravery during the war – all those things he refused to talk about. He could have been killed before she'd had the chance to know him. The fact that he was alive and here with her now made her sure that they were destined to be together. Asleep he looked so vulnerable and suddenly she felt that she was the older and wiser one.

Last night he'd held back, reluctant to make love to her, so conscious of her inexperience. Little did he know that ever since they had declared their love for one another all she had dreamed of was consummating that love; making the ultimate commitment.

He had been so gentle, so tender, but at first it had seemed a failure.

The stars and fireworks she had anticipated were absent. Max had fallen asleep leaving her anxious and tearful. Had she disappointed him? Were they really so unsuited? Had it been somehow her fault? But in the early hours they had both wakened and Max had reached for her again. This time everything was different, sensuous, languid and beautiful. Together they had reached a place that felt close to heaven, and when they fell asleep in each other's arms her tears this time were for joy.

Sensing her gaze on him Max opened his eyes and smiled at her sleepily.

'Good morning, my Juliet.'

'Hello.'

He reached up to pull her down to him but she resisted. 'It's almost nine o'clock. We should get up.'

He frowned at her with mock reproach. 'Oh that's nice, I must say. You have your wicked way with me and next morning you can hardly remember my name.'

She laughed. 'I remember your name all right, Max Goddard. I remember how much I love you too, and last night is something I'll remember all my life. But I also remember that I have an eleven o'clock appointment.'

He groaned. 'I thought we might spend the rest of the morning right here.'

'Oh, really?' Juliet was out of bed and pulling on her dressing-gown. 'What happened to Kew and Petticoat Lane then?'

'Who on earth would care about Kew or Petticoat Lane when they'd got what we've got?'

She bent across to kiss him. 'We have all the time in the world.'

'No, we haven't. We'll be back in Warnecliff this evening, you with your father at Wycombe and me in my lonely bachelor flat.' He began to get out of bed. 'Seriously, Juliet, do you really have to go and meet this woman? After all, she doesn't really want to talk about her experiences of the blitz, does she? And who can blame her?' He put his arms round her and nuzzled her neck. 'Stay with me – please, darling.'

Juliet sighed. There was nothing she wanted more, especially as they had so little time left. Then she caught sight of the printed notice on the dressing-table.

'We're supposed to be out of the rooms by twelve anyway, look,' she said, pointing.

He looked at his watch. 'That's three hours away.'

'We haven't had breakfast yet.'

'Breakfast!' He stared at her. 'Are you *serious*?'

She laughed. 'Well, I'm starving, aren't you?'

'Well, now that you mention it, I suppose I am. Come on, let's get a move on.'

But as they were eating downstairs in the dining-room a waiter came to tell Max that there was a call for him at the reception desk. He came back a few minutes later to say that his agent wanted another meeting with him before they left for home.

'He's asked me to meet him in a pub in Charing Cross Road.'

'Do you really have to meet this man?' Juliet asked, imitating his voice.

He laughed. 'OK, you win. See you back here at about one then.'

As Juliet was knocking on the door of Tina Moore's flat she heard a church clock somewhere chiming the hour. She congratulated herself on being punctual. Tina opened the door and asked her in. The front door led immediately into a fairly large living-room, comfortably furnished. An open door off led to a tiny kitchen.

'Do sit down. Would you like a coffee?' Tina offered.

'Thank you. That would be lovely.'

Juliet sat down in one of the armchairs and took out her notebook and pencil. Tina returned with a tray and poured coffee. They made small talk about the weather. Juliet mentioned that she had seen *Oklahoma* the previous evening and Tina seemed interested.

'Drury Lane is lovely,' she remarked. 'Such an historic theatre.'

Juliet tried hard to get her to talk about her work during the blitz, but Tina was frustratingly evasive. Instead she seemed to want to speak about herself. In the end Juliet decided to let her, deciding that she could always pick out the relevant bits later.

'Did Fliss tell you that I'd been to prison?' Tina asked suddenly.

Juliet looked up in surprise. Not wanting to let the doctor down she shrugged noncommittally. 'Well, she—'

'It doesn't matter,' Tina said. 'It was a long time ago now and there's nothing anyone can do to alter it.' She leaned forward. 'Would you mind if I told you the story?'

Juliet was at a loss. Fliss had insisted that Tina hated to talk about her past. 'Of course I don't mind,' she said. 'Though if it's painful for you to remember. . . .'

'It isn't – not any more.' Tina poured more coffee and passed Juliet her cup. 'The man I loved – the father of my child – worked away from home a lot,' she began. 'He was always promising to marry me, but somehow he never got round to it, even after our child was born.' She took a sip of her coffee. 'It was very hard being pregnant and bringing up a baby on my own. He never even managed to get home for the birth, though I have to say that he was utterly enchanted by her.'

'You had a little girl then?'

'Yes.' Tina's eyes grew reminiscent. 'Such a sweet little girl. When she was almost two years old – and I was still waiting for her father to make a firm commitment to us – I met a man. It was quite by chance. He called at the flat by mistake one day. He had the wrong address. We talked and the next day he came back. To cut a long story short we began seeing each other. He was good to us. I'd been lonely for so long. It was nice – flattering to have a considerate man around. He used to bring food and make special suppers for us – buy me flowers – take us to the park on Sundays. It went on for several months. Then one evening – it was my birthday – he arrived with a young girl who he said was his sister. He said she would sit with the baby while he took me out. A special surprise, he said. He took me to this club – I don't remember the name, or where it was, but I didn't like the place from the first; dark and noisy and crowded. I'd been asking to go home and then suddenly he wasn't there any more and the place was full of policemen. It was very frightening. A lot of us were arrested and bundled into a van. At the police station we were searched. I was terrified, especially when they found stolen jewellery in my handbag and refused to believe that I knew nothing about it.'

Juliet had heard the story before from Fliss, but she said nothing. Tina seemed to need to get it all off her chest. 'So what happened next?' she asked politely.

'I told them I had to get home,' Tina said. 'I said I had a child and that the sitter would be wondering where I was. Someone must have gone to my flat. When they returned to my horror they charged me with neglect – said there was no sitter there and that my baby was crying and distressed.'

'Did they bring her to you?'

'No. They wouldn't tell me where she was. I was formally charged and refused bail. They sent me to a remand prison and I heard later that her father had taken her away. He sent a letter to the solicitor representing me to say that if I was found guilty I was never to see her again.'

'How cruel! Surely he knew you were innocent and that you'd never have left the baby alone.'

Tina shook her head. 'I don't think he ever really knew me at all,' she said sadly.

'And the girl who baby-sat for you and your man friend – they never came forward?'

'No. And the address he'd given me turned out to be false, which made the police believe even more strongly that I was lying. They refused to believe he even existed. I knew then I'd been set up. There was no one I could go to; no family or friends. There was no one to speak up for me, no way to prove my innocence, so I went down for seven years.'

There was a pause. Juliet said, 'And when you came out you joined the ambulance service.' She took a surreptitious peep at her watch. This was taking longer than she had anticipated and she still hadn't got anything that would be useful for her proposed article.

'Yes, eventually,' Tina said. 'I tried to change my life – my identity. I tried to find Adam again but he must have left town, the country even. I never heard from him again.'

Juliet stood up. 'I think it's time I was going, Miss Moore.'

'No!' Tina got quickly to her feet. 'Not yet,' she said abruptly. 'There's a reason I've told you all this. There's something you should know.'

'Is there?' Juliet was beginning to feel distinctly uncomfortable. There was something almost desperate about the other woman's expression. She noticed that her eyes were filling with tears and her hands were shaking as she reached out to touch her arm.

'When I came out of prison I was determined to start again – make a success of my life. I even called myself Tina instead of Christine, the name everyone knew me by before.'

Juliet waited, wondering what she was about to hear. Somewhere deep inside warning bells had begun to ring.

'I know it will be a shock,' Tina went on. 'Ever since yesterday I've struggled with my conscience. Everything is telling me what's past is past – to let sleeping dogs lie but I can't let the opportunity go by. It's as though fate has sent you to me.'

'*Oh my God!*' Juliet's heart was beating so fast she felt dizzy. She sat down suddenly, her hand to her mouth.

'My child's father was an actor. I hero worshipped him – used to buy a ticket whenever I could afford it and sit in the gallery to watch him act. Afterwards I'd wait at the stage door just to get a peep at him close-up. Eventually he noticed me and asked me out for a drink. We began to see each other regularly. I was so happy. I thought I was the luckiest girl in the world.' She sighed. 'I've told you the rest.' She paused to look at Juliet. 'You'll have guessed by now – his name was Marcus King and his family came from Warnecliff. When you gave me your card yesterday I knew it had to be more than just coincidence.'

The silence that hung between them was almost tangible. Then Tina asked in a small voice, 'I'm right, aren't I – Juliet?'

Hardy able to believe she was hearing correctly, Juliet nodded silently.

'Did – did he ever marry again – have any more children?'

Juliet's head was reeling. It all felt so unreal. 'No, there's only me. My grandmother and aunt brought me up.'

'Marion?'

'Yes. She married a Canadian and went to live in Canada.'

'And your grandmother?'

'She died – two years ago.' Juliet frowned trying to make sense of the tangled threads inside her head. 'So, you're saying that you and Dad were never married?'

Tina shook her head. 'We were to have been. He was always promising. In fact, his mother and Marion thought we were. Marcus thought they'd be shocked so he told them we'd had a quiet register office wedding and I went along with it, feeling sure that it was only a matter of time before it was the truth.' She looked at Juliet. 'How is he?'

Juliet could hardly believe what she was hearing. Marcus had disowned this woman. Without waiting to hear her side of it he had believed her guilty of theft and child neglect. He had refused her access to her child and yet here she was asking after him. 'He's fine,' she said.

'He's still acting – a summer season. I saw the review in the paper.'

'Yes, he's still acting.' Juliet looked at her. Something Tina had said earlier suddenly surfaced and the scattered pieces of the puzzle began to fit together.

'Did you say the man who betrayed you was called Adam?' she asked.

Tina nodded. 'Yes, Adam Kent. But for all I know the name could have been false too.'

'Did he ever mention a sister?'

'Only the young girl he brought to baby-sit and that was obviously a lie.'

Juliet was beginning to form her own idea of Adam's motives for framing Tina but for now she could say nothing. 'What do you want to do?' she asked. 'Do you want to get in touch with Dad again?'

Tina shook her head adamantly. 'No. Nothing could ever make up for what he did. I've managed to rebuild my life. It's taken a long time but I've survived.' She smiled. 'I've even met someone – a man – a lovely man. Someone I feel I can trust and at last I feel I have a future. I'm so happy to have met you though, Juliet. You've grown up to be a beautiful young woman. At least you had Marion and your grandmother to bring you up. I couldn't have chosen two better people. I hope you've been happy and that you'll have a good life.'

A huge lump in her throat, Juliet crossed the room and put her arms round the mother she had never known. 'I'm glad to have found you too. It would be nice to stay in touch, if that's what you'd like.'

Tina nodded, her eyes full of tears. 'I was hoping so much that you'd say that. But please don't give your father my address.'

'I won't. I'll write to you. And I'll come and see you again...' She stood back and looked at the woman standing before her. 'I don't know what to call you.'

'Call me Tina. That's who I am now.'

Juliet hugged her again. 'Goodbye for now, Tina. I'm so glad you've survived the awful things that happened to you. It tells me that Fliss was right when she said you were one of the bravest women she'd ever met. I promise to stay in touch.'

Juliet left the house and walked along the street in a daze. On the corner was a café, just opening its doors for lunch. She went inside and ordered a coffee. She had to have time to work out just what had happened.

She strongly suspected that her mother had been set up by Olivia. The fiercely ambitious young actress Marcus had met and become besotted with at around that time. Olivia and her twisted, money-grabbing brother had hatched a plan – Adam was to set Christine up as a criminal leaving Marcus free for Olivia, who had been determined to pursue her career by hanging on to Marcus's coat-tails. Juliet reminded herself that she herself was illegitimate. Something she had never known till now. Glancing at her watch she saw that it was already after one o'clock. Max would be waiting for her back at the hotel. What should she tell him? That she was Marcus's illegitimate daughter? That her mother had spent seven years in prison, convicted of theft and child neglect? It was as though she had suddenly become a different person – as though all these years she had been living a lie.

She decided she must face Marcus with the truth before she told Max. How could her father have deceived her all these years? Why had he never told her that he and her mother were never married? Suddenly another mystery became clear: Adam Kent had been blackmailing Marcus; probably threatening to tell her the truth about her mother if he wasn't paid for his silence. Perhaps that was where her grandmother's legacy had gone. He was probably blackmailing Olivia too – threatening to spill the beans about the plot they had hatched between them all those years ago.

At the hotel Max was relieved to see her. 'I was about to send out a search party,' he joked. 'Let's have lunch and then we should make tracks for home.' He looked at her. 'Are you all right, darling? You look pale.'

She shook her head. 'I got a bit lost on the Underground,' she lied. 'I knew you'd be waiting. I got into a bit of a panic.'

He slipped an arm round her shoulders. 'Silly girl. Did you think I'd go without you? Come and have lunch. I've got some news.'

They went into the restaurant and ordered lunch, but Juliet found she had no appetite. Her mind was still trying to assimilate all she had discovered during the past two hours. She realized that Max was talking about his meeting with his agent and forced herself to pay attention.

'The Old Vic Theatre won't be ready for opening for a couple of years yet,' he said. 'But the company is taking a new Shakespeare season on tour, coming back into the New Theatre where they'll stay until the move into the newly restored Vic.'

'That sounds exciting,' Juliet said. 'But why did he need you to meet him again to tell you that?'

'Because I've been offered a place in the company!' Max told her. 'The director is David Everett, someone I worked with on the documentary films and he's asked for me specially.'

She looked up. His face was wreathed in smiles and she could see how excited he was at the prospect. 'What about your job at the Royal?' she asked.

'Rehearsals don't begin until September,' he told her. 'And the tour doesn't go out until the New Year so I'll have plenty of time to find a replacement.' He leaned forward. 'As a matter of fact I've been wondering if Marcus would like to take over from me. Of course I'll have to put his name forward to the committee but I'm pretty confident that they'll trust my judgement.' He looked at her, trying to interpret her expression. 'What's wrong – aren't you pleased?'

'How long will you be away?'

He laughed. 'I *won't*! Not from you. You'll be coming with me.'

She stared at him.

He reached across the table to take her hand. 'I meant to make this special, but I want us to be married, darling. First stop on the tour is Canada. Toronto is the first date. Just think you'll be able to see your Aunt Marion.'

When she still didn't respond he frowned. 'Darling, what is it? I thought you'd be as excited as me.'

'There's – there's my job,' she said, clutching at straws. 'And Dad. How could I leave him to cope alone?'

Max gave an exasperated little laugh. 'Your father is a middle-aged man, Juliet. He'll have a job and a home falling into his lap. Of course he'll cope. As for your job – well. . . .' He spread his hands.

Juliet looked up at him, colour flooding her cheeks. 'It might not seem much to you,' she said. 'Junior reporter on a provincial paper, but it's just the beginning as far as I'm concerned; a good beginning too. I've already got my own column.'

'Ah yes, *Juliet's Jottings*. I'd forgotten that!'

His tone made her smart with indignation. 'That's right – laugh at me and my trifling little career,' she said.

'I'm not laughing; far from it when you're choosing it over me?' he said.

'That's just it though, isn't it? I haven't been given the chance to choose. I don't like being taken for granted, Max.'

He looked at her for a long moment. 'Are you asking me to turn the job down?'

Suddenly she wanted to burst into tears. Of *course* it was a marvellous chance for Max. Ordinarily she'd have been as excited as he was, and as for his proposal of marriage! But so much was happening to her all at once. Max was yet to hear about the doubtful background that she herself had only just discovered. He would probably have second thoughts about her anyway once he knew about her shady start in life. He might even have a poorer opinion of Marcus too, and whatever happened, however betrayed she felt, Marcus was still her father. She'd worked hard to bring him back from the brink of self-destruction. She couldn't let him lose out on an opportunity like becoming producer/director of the Theatre Royal.

'Of course I'm not asking you to turn the job down,' she said. 'It's none of my business.' She looked at her watch. 'We'd better go.'

They drove back to Warnecliff in near silence. Juliet felt sick with misery. Last night she'd been so sure that her future was with Max. She loved him now more than ever and the hurt look on his face had cut her to the quick. But how would he react when he knew about her? Perhaps one day things like illegitimacy wouldn't hold the stigma it did today. Perhaps Max would see things differently. She had no idea. She remembered that there had been a girl at school whose parents turned out not to be married. When the truth came out many of the other girls shunned her, talked in corners; made her life miserable. And for her to have to tell Max that her mother had been in prison. Even though she was innocent of the crime there was always a doubt once the accused had been convicted. The thought of it made her heart sink. Perhaps it was better to let him go without telling him any of it. He'd soon forget her in all the excitement of the tour and his longed-for ambition to appear at the Old Vic.

As they drew up outside Heathlands Cottage he turned to her. 'Juliet – what's wrong, darling? I'm sorry if you think I took you for granted, but last night you convinced me that you wanted us to be together.'

Her heart twisted inside her and she swallowed hard at the lump in her throat. 'I am pleased for you about the tour,' she said. 'I know it's your dream come true. You should grasp it with all your heart. I know you'll be successful.' She turned and gave him a quick kiss on the cheek. 'I have to go now, Max. Goodbye.'

She got out of the car quickly and hurried through the gate before he could say anything else, pausing behind the hedge until she heard the car drive away, choking back the tears, dreading the confrontation she was about to have with Marcus.

CHAPTER FIFTEEN

Juliet walked in to find Marcus sitting with a supper tray on his lap, listening to a concert on the radio. He looked up.

'Hello, darling. I didn't hear the car. Nice weekend?'

'Fine thanks.' She threw her coat and bag down on the settee.

'Manage to find the woman you were looking for?'

'Yes.'

'Get some good material for your article?'

'No. What I did get was a devastating shock.'

'Really?' Marcus laughed. 'I thought my daughter was unshockable.'

'Did you?' She went across and switched off the radio. 'I've learned things today that have shaken me to the core, Dad. Things I should have been told about long ago.'

The smile left Marcus's face and he sat forward on his chair, putting his tray aside. 'What are you talking about?'

'I'm talking about Christine Moore; my mother,' Juliet told him. 'Remember her? She was the woman who had your child – *me*; the woman you promised to marry but let down; the woman who was framed for theft and child neglect so that Olivia Kent could get her claws into you.'

Marcus's face was ashen. 'Who's been filling your head with all these lies?'

'Who do you think? The victim herself; my mother told me. And they're not lies, Dad, you know they're not. You are the one who lied – even to your own mother and sister.'

He turned suddenly, knocking the tray with his elbow and sending the contents crashing to the floor. 'I don't understand,' he said weakly. 'How did you find her?'

'She turned out to be the woman Dr Galbraith told me about; the ambulance driver who made so many brave rescues during the blitz but couldn't be decorated because she'd been in prison. She calls herself Tina Moore now to try to block out the past. Why couldn't you believe her, Dad? She loved and trusted you, gave birth to your child.' He stared at her wordlessly, his mouth agape. 'It was Olivia's brother who set her up and he's been blackmailing you, hasn't he?' Juliet said. 'Not just asking for money, but *blackmailing* you.'

Marcus muttered something unintelligible, his head in his hands.

'If only you'd told me what had happened to my mother none of this would have happened,' she said. 'Why didn't you believe her, Dad? How could you do it to her – to all . . . *all* of us?'

Her voice broke on a sob. Tears were streaming down her cheeks now; all the traumatic events of the day culminating in a flood of emotion. Marcus stood up and tried to put his arms around her. She pushed him away. 'Don't touch me. Leave me alone.'

'It was a shock at the time,' he said thickly. 'You can't imagine how horrified I was when I heard she'd been arrested and charged.' He reached out his hands to her. 'All I could think about was my little daughter – my baby. As soon as I heard Christine was in custody I collected you from the foster home where they'd taken you and brought you here to Wycombe, to Mother and Marion. Then I applied for sole custody.'

'And you sent her a letter telling her she'd never see her child again.'

He lifted his shoulders helplessly. 'Yes, I did that. I didn't want the stigma to rub off on you.'

She shook her head. 'I still can't imagine how you could have been so cruel.'

'I was young; my career was blooming.' Marcus sighed. 'I was making a name for myself back then and I was afraid it might get into the papers. It never made the nationals but the London papers reported it. Somehow it got out that Christine and I were . . . connected . . . had a child together, and the fact that we weren't married didn't help. Word got round in the business and I began to get dropped by agents, managements. I'd even had a tentative offer from Hollywood, but that sank without trace. I even began to fail auditions for supporting parts. No one ever mentioned why, but I knew the real reason and I was angry.'

'With Christine – and that's why you abandoned her?'

'I was young, conceited and self-centred – immature, I suppose.'

'Yes you were all of that and more, but *she* was the one going to prison. Her *life* was in shreds, not just her career. And the worst part is, she was *innocent*, Dad. It was all set up by that evil monster, Adam Kent, but you never gave her the chance to prove it. You never visited her in prison, never appeared in court in her defence even though you knew she had no one to speak for her.'

'I wasn't called. We hadn't been living together at the time.'

'You were with Olivia?'

'Not then.' He couldn't look at her. 'Not until after—'

'After she'd carefully arranged to clear the way by having my mother locked away. Couldn't you see that she only wanted you so that she could benefit from your rising fame?' She smiled wryly. 'Little did she know that it would wreck your career too and defeat her own aspirations.'

'The war came,' Marcus muttered. 'We got into ENSA together. It was the best we could get.'

'And she's never forgiven you – she's been making you suffer ever since.' She stood over him. 'And in the end she was *your* crutch instead of the other way round. How ironic!' She looked down at him. 'Tell me one thing, Dad, and tell me the truth this time. Did you know about the plot she and her brother hatched to disgrace Christine? Did you know she was deliberately set up to clear the way for Olivia?' Marcus buried his face in his hands, unable to look at her. 'I'm *waiting*, Dad,' she insisted. 'I want the truth from you now. It's long overdue.'

The face he turned up to her said it all. Suddenly he looked ten years older. Slowly he nodded. 'Yes, but not at the time – not until much later. You must believe that, Juliet. I swear it's the truth.'

'So how did you find out?'

'Libby let it slip once during a row. She laughed in my face about it. Naturally I was appalled. But it was too late by then to do anything about it. Christine had already served her sentence. It was during the war, when we were with ENSA. I would have walked out on her there and then but we were touring Egypt at the time and it was impossible.'

'But you still stayed together?'

Marcus nodded. 'By then we were tied together – by her wickedness and my weakness, I suppose. But I did love her, Juliet, even though I always knew she didn't really love me. I suppose I deserved to be hurt. But this – you stumbling across Christine, discovering what I hoped you never would; that is my ultimate punishment.'

Juliet laughed. '*Your* ultimate punishment! It's still all about you, isn't it, Dad? You have no idea what this has done to me.' She sank into a chair and turned her head away from him. Marcus crossed the room and touched her shoulder.

'We'll get over this, darling. I admit I should have told you but now that it's out in the open I'll do all I can to make amends.'

'You can't!' She rounded on him. 'Max asked me to marry him this afternoon. He's been offered a place in the new Old Vic company. They're going on tour abroad and he wanted me to go with him.'

'Juliet! Darling, that's wonderful!'

'*Wonderful*! How is he going to feel when I tell him my mother served a term in prison for theft and child neglect? Even though she's innocent it's still a fact. Mud sticks. Then there's the fact that you never married her. What does that make me? Let me think – there's a word for it, isn't there? I'm sure Max's family would be delighted to hear that their son intended to get himself involved with the bastard daughter of a jailbird!'

'*Juliet*!' Marcus shook his head, tears brimming over to run down his cheeks. 'Please, darling, don't! You're not. I made sure you had my name. I had it changed by deed poll while you were still a baby and applied for a new birth certificate. You're not illegitimate.'

She laughed bitterly. 'And how did Olivia feel about that?'

'Never mind Libby.' Marcus looked at her. 'What about Max? Will you tell him?'

'I can't tell him about the despicable thing you did. You're still my father in spite of everything. I probably shouldn't be telling you this, but when he gives in his notice he's going to recommend you to the committee as his replacement. I can't let anything stand in the way of that, Dad, because, God help me, I still feel responsible for you. I'll just tell him I've thought it over and I don't want to marry him.'

'You can't do that. You love him, don't you?'

'I'll get over it. I'd rather have it this way than see the look of horror on his face when he hears about my background.'

Marcus knelt beside her chair and took both her hands, his eyes pleading. 'Juliet – darling, can you ever find it in your heart to forgive me?'

She couldn't meet his eyes. 'I don't know, Dad. It's going to take time for me to come to terms with what I've learned today. But I'll tell you one thing: Christine will never forgive you. She doesn't want to see you or speak to you. But that didn't stop her asking how you were; it didn't stop her reading your reviews in the London papers. Maybe loyalty is the best you're going to get from either of us.'

That evening as the sun was setting Juliet walked across to the gypsy encampment. There was always work, she told herself. From now on she would throw herself wholeheartedly into her job. And she had already decided what her next crusade would be.

She tapped gently on the open door of the Lees' caravan. Inside Imelda was making tea. She looked up with a smile.

'Juliet. Please come in. How nice to see you. Celina's here. Danny's out walking with baby. Her teeth are coming through and she can't settle. Billy begged to go too so he's taken him.'

Inside the caravan Juliet sat down on one of the padded benches and Imelda poured her a cup of strong tea from a big blue enamelled teapot decorated with birds and flowers.

Celina sat in the corner, her pillow on her lap as she worked on her lace. She observed Juliet silently with her dark perceptive eyes. 'You're troubled, my pet,' she said at last. 'Maybe you should have some camomile to calm you.'

Juliet shook her head, watching in fascination as Celina made the beaded bobbins fly with her nimble brown fingers. 'No, thank you. Tea is fine.' She looked at Imelda. 'When does Danny have to join up?'

The girl shook her head. 'Week after next. I don't know what we'll do without him. He'll send me some money of course, but it won't be the same.'

'You know you'n the chavvies'll be well looked after,' Celina put in. 'We don't never let one of our own go without. We've got the lace to sell an' the pegs and my lucky charms.'

'I know that, but my Danny's worried the council might make us move if we don't agree to live in them houses.' Imelda said. 'I heard tell that the council's still waitin' for plannin' permission an' the buildin' grant to start them.'

'Maybe they won't get it.' Celina shook her head. 'They can't *make* us do nuthin. We've been here on Wycombe Heath for three generations and we got squatters' rights.'

'But they're not trying to make you move,' Juliet said. 'They think they're making a concession by providing you with houses.'

'And they'll charge us rent for 'em!' Celina's eyes flashed. 'But we're Romany!' she said. 'We don't live like Gorjers. We don't want no houses. Why can't they understand? This be common land, free for all.'

'That's why I'm here,' Juliet told her. 'I work for the *Clarion*, the local paper. I'll try to help make your problem clearer. Maybe we could get up a petition.'

Celina gave a short laugh. 'There's folks round these parts as'll be only too glad to see us go,' she said. 'Even though we means nuthin' but good. They still thinks we puts the evil eye on 'em an' rubbish like that.'

'That's just ignorance,' Juliet said. 'If they knew better. . . . What I need is for someone from your community to tell the readers exactly what the Romany community stands for and how you feel.'

Imelda was looking at her with admiration. 'You'd really help us, Juliet?'

'Of course.' She looked at Celina. 'If I come across with my notebook would you tell me what Romany life is all about?'

'I will that and gladly,' the older woman said. She reached out a hand to touch Juliet's arm. 'Drink your tea, my pretty. You've had a bad day if I know right.'

Juliet nodded. 'It has been a bit fraught.' She looked out of the caravan window at the gathering dusk. A fine mist was rising off the heath. 'I'd better be getting back,' she said.

Celina stood up and put down her pillow and bobbins. 'I'll walk with you.'

As Juliet was leaving, Danny returned; his young son riding piggy-back and a peacefully sleeping baby Clover wrapped in a shawl tied securely round him. Imelda lifted Billy from his father's shoulders and set him on the floor.

'Time you was in bed, my man,' she said, ruffling his curly hair.

Juliet touched one of the baby's rosy cheeks. 'She's so beautiful.' She looked at Imelda. 'You're very lucky.'

Sleepy-eyed Billy put his thumb in his mouth and clung to his mother's skirt. Imelda smiled at her young husband, her dark eyes bright with love. 'I know. I'm three times blessed.'

Juliet walked for a moment in silence, the older gypsy woman beside her. At last Celina said, 'Mebbe you'd like a husband and chavvies of your own.'

'Some day, perhaps.'

'I'm guessing it's your ma you're thinkin' about tonight though. Am I right, child?'

Juliet turned to smile at her. 'How do you do it, Celina? Yes, I'm thinking of her. You were right; she has been unhappy. I talked to her this morning. Until today I hadn't even known if she was alive.'

Celina nodded. 'I saw it all in your eyes, child. Mebbe she won't grieve s'much now she knows you growed up fine and beautiful.' She peered into Juliet's eyes. 'But there's more, ain't there? To do with someone you love – maybe your da, maybe a lover, both even. You been hurt real bad, my lovely.'

They'd reached the end of the cottage garden now and Juliet turned to her. 'I don't know what to do, Celina,' she said. 'This morning I was so happy – now. . . .'

The gypsy took both her hands and held them warmly. 'You come and talk to old Celina if you lose your way,' she said. 'A trouble shared is a trouble halved. You must listen to your heart. Love won't be denied, you know, no matter what. It's a gaoler an' the chains are strong. It won't set you free just because you turn your back.' The next moment she was gone, disappearing into the drifting wraiths of mist.

Juliet stood for a moment, reluctant to go in. If only it were that simple, she told herself.

Juliet hardly slept at all that night. Her head swam with thoughts of Tina, of Marcus, and the blinkered ego that had led to the wrecking of three lives. She struggled with the pain of parting with Max. Part of her wanted to tell him everything and throw herself on the strength of his love for her whilst the other half was afraid – partly of shocking and disappointing him, partly of testing the love she wanted so much to believe in. When she slept it was to toss and turn, restless with dreams of her childhood – of a dark fearful place and someone telling her that her mother wasn't coming back.

She was up as soon as it was light. Out of the house, on the bus and in the office early, determined to fill her mind with more immediate things.

First of all she sounded Bill Martin out about her idea. 'The gypsies have made their permanent home on the heath for three generations,' she told him. 'And now the council wants to make them live in some houses they'll build and rent out to them. It won't work. They're true Romany; being shut up in bricks and mortar is totally against their culture. Do you think I could start a campaign for them? Do you think Gerry will let me?'

Bill stroked his chin. 'You can ask him. You seem to be able to wind him round your little finger so I don't see any reason why you won't get your way.'

She looked at him in surprise. 'Wind him round my finger? I don't think so. He terrifies me!'

Bill laughed. 'He might be an old grump, but he's got a soft heart underneath it all. He admires you for standing up to him. Why don't you go in and ask him now, before Monday morning starts to eat away at his patience?'

'So how do you intend to go about it?' Gerry asked, after she'd explained briefly what she wanted to do. 'As far as I know most people think gypos are a bunch of no-good scroungers with their peg-selling and bogus fortune-telling. Most people want them off their land.'

'These are real Romany,' Juliet told him. 'They've lived on the heath for many years and they work hard and do no harm to anyone. All they ask is to be left in peace to live as they always have.'

'We all have to move on. If we didn't we'd still be living in caves and hunting wild animals,' Gerry said. 'I can't see why they can't live in proper houses like the rest of us.'

'Because they have to be free to go where the work is,' Juliet pointed out. 'And take their homes with them. East Anglia in summer for the fruit picking, Kent later for the hops. They couldn't do that if they had to pay rent for houses and find money for accommodation too. They'd have to change their whole way of living.'

'So what makes you think we can do anything about it?' Gerry leaned back in his chair and began to pack his pipe.

'A lot of people are ignorant. They don't understand what Romany life really is,' she said. 'We could explain what their life is all about,' Juliet told him. 'If the general public knew more. . . .'

'And you'd tell them, write about it?'

'Well, yes. And maybe start some sort of campaign.'

'Mmm, don't know about that.' Gerry applied his lighter to the pipe and sucked thoughtfully. 'Let me have a think about it. I'll let you know.'

'When?'

'*When?*' He glared at her. 'When I'm good and bloody ready, that's when. Now get out of here and let me get some proper work done.' As she scuttled across the office he called after her, 'And don't forget you've got a weekly column to write, girl. I don't know! What will you fill that head of yours with next?'

Juliet worked hard all morning gathering material for her *Juliet's Jottings* page. Now that Warnecliff's first real summer season since the war was getting into full swing there was a lively, optimistic feel about the town. The beach kiosks were displaying new striped blinds and little tables outside with gaily coloured umbrellas; the little shops were full of buckets and spades and saucy postcards, and Brightwell's department store was full of beach and holiday clothes. There was plenty to write about. She was trying hard to keep her mind from wandering back to the weekend: to the blissful high of her time with Max and the devastating lows of her conversations with both parents. She thought about Celina's offer to talk and felt tempted to pour out all her troubles to the gypsy woman. *A trouble shared is a trouble halved*, she had said, and Juliet certainly felt heavily laden. She worked all through her lunch break, sending out for a sandwich and making herself a cup of strong coffee in the grubby little cubby-hole that passed for a kitchen.

When she arrived home that evening, reeling with exhaustion from hard work and lack of sleep she was surprised to find Marcus in the kitchen. He was unshaven and wearing his dressing-gown. She guessed that he hadn't been up all that long.

'Shouldn't you have left for the theatre by now?' she asked, standing just inside the kitchen door.

'I'm not going,' he said. 'I can't go on tonight. I hardly slept last night and I'm just not up to it. I was just about to ring Max.'

'*Oh no you don't!*' She threw down her bag and coat and grabbed him by the arm. 'Don't you even *think* about letting everyone down,' she said. 'How dare you, Dad, after I've given up so much for you? Get upstairs and have a shave – get yourself dressed. I'll ring for a taxi for you. I warn you, if you don't get yourself to the theatre in the next half-hour I'll walk out of here and you'll never see me again. *I mean it*! On top of everything that's happened I've had just about enough of you!'

He looked at her as she stood there trembling with fury, her eyes glinting with angry tears, and he knew that she meant every word.

'Have you been drinking?' she demanded, sniffing at him. He shook his head. 'Well that's something at least. Face it, Dad, you wouldn't have this job if it wasn't for me, so you're going on tonight if it kills you and you're going to give the performance of your life or lose me for ever. To make sure you do I'm coming with you. I'll be at the back of the stalls so there's no getting out of it. Now go – *go!*' She gave him a push towards the door.

When he'd gone upstairs and she could hear the bath water running she sank onto a chair with a sigh. So much for falling into bed and sleeping. She went into the hall and telephoned for a taxi.

When the curtain came down on the first act to tumultuous applause Juliet crept out of the auditorium. Marcus would be all right now and she wanted nothing more than to fall into bed and sleep for a week. She was crossing the theatre foyer when the front-of-house office door opened and Max came out. For a moment they stood looking at each other then Max spoke.

'Juliet! I wasn't expecting to see you this evening.'

'No, I. . . .' She stumbled, lost for words. 'Dad seemed to be a bit under the weather so I thought I'd pop in and make sure he was all right.'

'He seems on top of his form,' he said. 'I've never heard so many laughs from the audience.'

She shook her head. 'Yes, he's obviously fine. Probably just a bit of a sniffle. You know what a worrier I am. Sorry, Max, I'll have to go. There's a bus in five minutes.' As she made to pass him he took her arm.

'Juliet, wait. Don't run off like that, come and have a drink – a coffee or something.'

'I would, but I'm really tired,' she said. 'I'm frantically busy at work and I could do with an early night.'

'Then let me drive you home.'

'It's all right. I'll get the bus.'

'Juliet, please.' His grip on her arm tightened. 'We really need to talk.'

Looking into his eyes she knew she'd lost. She was going to have to tell him now. There was no putting it off. 'All right,' she said.

Once seated beside her in the car Max looked at her. 'Are you going to tell me what's really wrong?'

She couldn't look at him. 'It's just— I was so . . . so flattered when you asked me to marry you, Max. But I know now that I can't.'

'But why? We love each other. Everything seemed to be going so well – we have a great future ahead of us. So why?'

197

She shrugged. 'I told you, there's Dad, my job. . . .'

'Oh, come *on*. Those aren't reasons. You know damn well that Marcus will be fine. I'm pretty sure the committee will agree to his appointment here and I'm confident that he'll make a magnificent director. As for your job—'

'Yes, I know. You laughed at *Juliet's Jottings*. It might all seem trivial to you,' she said. 'But I'm young. It's the first step on the ladder for me.'

'And clearly more important than I am on the scale of things.' The hurt in his voice was all too tangible.

'It's not that.' Juliet felt her eyes filling with tears and tried to blink them away. It was so hard, making him believe she didn't want him when she did – so much. 'Maybe – maybe after the tour. Canada is such a long way away.'

'Oh, well, if that's the only problem, it's easy: I'll turn it down.'

'*No!*' She turned to him, appalled. 'You can't do that. It's such a big opportunity for you – your dream job.'

'So, if I'm willing to give it up for you doesn't that tell you anything?' He spread his hands helplessly. 'What else can I do?'

She sighed. 'Nothing. There's nothing you can do. Just go to Canada and have a successful tour. Forget all about me.'

He stared at her. 'I can't believe you're saying these things, Juliet, especially after . . .' He turned to her. 'Look, I'll ask you just this once. Leaving Canada out of it – do you love me enough to marry me?'

Her eyes downcast, she said, 'I-I don't know.'

'You must *know*, damn it!' he said roughly. 'We're not leaving here till I get an answer: *do you love me?*'

She took a deep breath and forced the words past the lump in her throat. 'No, Max. I don't think I do – not enough.'

'You don't *think?*'

'All right then. *No, I don't!*' A thought occurred to her and she made herself look up at him. 'You won't let it stop you putting Dad's name forward for your job?'

He drew in his breath sharply as though she had struck him. 'My God! Do you really think I'd be that spiteful? You haven't a very high opinion of me, have you, Juliet?'

She turned, grasping the door handle. 'I think we'd better not see each other again, Max. It'll be easier that way. Look, I'll get the bus home. I'd rather.' Before he could stop her she scrambled out of the car and made off down the street.

There was a bus waiting when she reached the bus stop and she boarded it blinded by tears. This was the worst, the hardest thing she had ever had to do. Sending away the man she loved, telling him she didn't love him when her heart ached so much that she thought she must surely die. And all for something she had absolutely no control over.

CHAPTER SIXTEEN

Juliet sat in Celina's caravan, her notebook on her knee as the gypsy woman made the inevitable pot of tea. Celina's caravan was very similar to the one shared by Imelda and Danny and their children; spotlessly clean and everything neatly in its own place. Juliet admired the delicate, brightly coloured china cups into which Celina poured the tea.

'Colour is part of a Romany's life,' Celina said. 'Just like being clean and following strict morals. Folks thinks we're dirty and loose livin' an' that ain't true. Respect is our way of life,' she went on. 'Respect for our homes, for each other and our animals.'

'Your horses are beautiful,' Juliet observed, looking out of the window. 'They certainly look well cared for.' She looked across to where the little group of tethered piebald ponies were grazing on the edge of the camp. 'Especially that black and white one. He's a real beauty.'

'She,' Celina corrected. 'She's a mare. She belongs to my lad Tom. His pride and joy, she is. Bred her himself an' named her Toria.' She nodded. 'A black and white gry – that's what we calls a horse – is a prized animal to a Romany.'

Juliet looked around. 'And does Tom live here with you?'

Celina shook her head. 'Bless you no, lovey. When our lads gets to be twelve years old they can't sleep with the family no more. I still cooks and washes for him of course, till he finds himself a wife, but he's got his own vardo now.'

'That's the word for caravan, I know. Where does it come from?'

Celina shrugged. 'Who knows? Our language is a mix-up of all kinds of lingos, Indian, Italian – wherever Romanies have come from in years gone by.' She smiled. 'We're a very old, very proud race o'people,' she said with a lift of her head. 'And as you know, travellin' is our way of life.'

Juliet learned from Celina about Romany cooking, done inside the vardos in winter on the little built-in stoves but in summer carried out barbeque fashion on a fire outside. Celina also told her solemnly that a Romany's handshake is his word – never to be broken.

'So why do you think people are so suspicious and afraid of you?' she asked at last.

Celina sighed. 'Folks is afraid of what they don't understand,' she said. 'An' o'course we'm not all angels. One bad apple rots the whole barrel as they say. It only takes one lad to get labelled a wrong-un for us all to get tarred with the same brush.'

Juliet remembered the story Danny had told her about Adam Kent and the despicable hop-picking incident. 'And that's why I want people to know all the things you've told me this evening,' she said. She closed her notebook and lifted her teacup to finish the last of her tea. As she did so an idea occurred to her. She looked speculatively at the gypsy woman sitting among her brightly coloured treasures.

'Celina, would you be willing to let people come and see all this for themselves?' she asked. 'Just for the summer. We could call it the Romany Museum.'

Celina looked doubtful. 'A lot of Gorjas gawpin' at us – like animals in the zoo?'

'No! It wouldn't be like that,' Juliet said. 'We could limit it to small groups – get them to book in advance. You'd be treated with the respect you deserve. You could show them your beautiful vardos and tell them some of your stories. I could arrange all the booking and organization for you. It would all be done properly in a businesslike way. We could have some leaflets printed and put them in the tourist office. We'd advertise it in the paper as well. There'd be an admission charge and you could sell your lace and the other pretty things you make.'

'I dunno. It'll soon be fruit pickin' and hops and such,' Celina said. 'Half of us'll be gone.'

'But those of you who stay to look after the camp could be earning money back here showing people round and educating them about your real ways. Surely that would make it twice as worthwhile' Juliet laid a hand on Celina's arm. 'Will you think about it?'

'I'd have to call a meetin',' Celina said. 'I'll put it to them and see what they thinks.'

'And you'll let me know?'

'I will, soon's I can.'

'Of course, I'll have to get permission from the local council before we could go ahead,' Juliet told her. 'It will all be part of getting them to drop their plan to move you into the houses.'

Celina began to see Juliet's point and she began to look more cheerful, then suddenly her face dropped and she said, 'You don't think they'll expect me to tell fortunes, do you?'

'Would that be so bad?'

'I can't do it for just anyone,' Celina said. 'I has to *feel* somethin' in a person to be able to see for them. It ain't a thing as can be turned on at will.'

'I understand, so we won't mention it.'

'But I can see for you, my love.' Celina's dark eyes seemed to bore right through to Juliet's innermost emotions as she looked at her. 'I know you're unhappy – afraid you've thrown away the most important thing in your young life. Am I right?'

A lump rose in Juliet's throat. 'Yes, you are as usual, Celina. But there's nothing anyone can do about it.'

'Ah, don't say that.' Celina reached for the teapot that stood warming on the stove and refilled their cups. 'Just you tell old Celina all about it. It won't go no further, I promise, and even if I can't help you'll feel better.'

Juliet began to talk. She meant to tell just her own story but it was so inextricably linked with Marcus and Christine, Olivia and Adam Kent that it was impossible to leave anything out. Twice she had to stop and begin all over again but at last when it was all out she looked up into Celina's dark eyes.

'And so you must surely understand why I can't marry Max,' she said. 'You of all people. After what you've just told me about Romany ways, your people would never accept someone whose mother and father were never properly married, whose mother had been to prison.'

Celina sighed. 'You think them things never happened to a Romany?' she said. 'We'm got our own special values that's true, but we don't never turn our backs on one of our own. No young girl who finds herself in the family way 'ould ever be turned out. An' if you think no gypsy has ever been to prison you'd be very wrong, my love. It might be that he's been locked up for a crime he never done – just like your ma. But if you think that stain can never be cleaned pure again, you're wrong. If your young man really loves you nuthin in your past is gonna change that.' She reached out a strong brown hand to grasp Juliet's. 'But you'm very wrong not to give him the choice, love. You should tell 'im the truth.'

'I can't, Celina. Suppose he doesn't feel as you say? I can't risk seeing the look on his face. I can't risk his disappointment – his rejection.'

'Ain't keepin' his love worth the risk?' When Juliet didn't reply Celina said, 'It's in your hands, my love. But what does he think of you now – that you're fickle-hearted and not to be trusted. Is that worse than somethin' you can't help that happened when you was still a chavvie?' She stood up and held out her hand. 'Come on my pretty. I'll walk across the heath with you. Just think about what I've said. I haven't lived all these years without knowin' a bit about folks an' I reckon you deserve the best.'

Juliet stood up and put her notebook away in her bag. 'We don't all get what we deserve, Celina,' she said.

'No, but it's worth fightin' for. That I do know.' She reached out to touch Juliet's hand. 'And make your peace with your da, my love. What happened was a long time ago. We all makes mistakes when we'm young, an' I'm sure he's paid the price by now. I know you'n him are close to one another. Don't turn your back on the father who loves you.'

The following day Juliet made enquiries into who was responsible for the common land on the heath and the proposed building of the new houses. She discovered that the man in charge was called Dennis Maybury. Most of the copy for *Juliet's Jottings* was complete and she hadn't been given another assignment so she rang and made an appointment to see Mr Maybury early that afternoon in his office at the Town Hall.

Dennis Maybury was thirty-five and had been invalided out of the armed forces in 1942 because of a weak chest. Although he often boasted about his 'war record' he'd never actually been any further than Aldershot where he'd had a desk job in the Pay Corps. He wore steel-rimmed spectacles, had thinning hair and his wife had just given birth to their fourth child. He was exhausted from overwork and lack of sleep and when Juliet was ushered into his office that afternoon the day felt tedious and endless. He peered at the girl in front of him over the tops of his glasses, deciding to make the interview as brief as possible. 'Yes?'

Juliet's request was made to the bald spot on top of his head as he studied the papers on his desk. When she had finished he was curt and dismissive, barely looking up at her as he barked, 'The matter is already in hand.'

Clearly he was of the same cynical opinion of gypsies as so many others. But his attitude merely made Juliet all the more determined.

'Mr Maybury,' she said, with all the dignity she could muster, 'I suppose you realize that these people are bound by the same laws and regulations as the rest of us. Their men fought in the war and their younger men are still doing their National Service, so I don't see why they shouldn't be allowed the same rights as anyone else.'

'No one is denying them their rights,' Dennis Maybury said wearily. 'Miss – er – King,' he glanced at the note on his memo pad. 'I'm very busy, so may I ask you what the actual purpose of your visit is?'

Juliet raised her eyebrows. 'I thought I'd made that clear,' she said. 'These people are true Romanies. They have occupied the common land on Wycombe Heath for three generations and now the council wants to build houses to be rented out to them. It is totally against their culture and they wish to remain where they are. If you insist on trying to make them move they will leave the area.'

Dennis Maybury sighed. Leaning back in his chair he looked up at her and asked with a sneer, 'And would that be *emotionally crippling* to anyone?'

Juliet felt her colour rising. 'I believe it would be a great shame,' she told him. 'I am writing an article for the *Clarion* about Romany life because I believe most people – like yourself – are suffering from ignorance. I happen to believe they are an asset to our community and in addition to my article I shall shortly be applying to the Entertainments Committee for a licence to open the site as a museum.'

He blinked at her. 'Museum? I don't quite . . .'

'Parties of holidaymakers can be shown round the camp and told about Romany life by some of the colourful characters who live there. Believe me, it will be vibrant and fascinating. Small groups can be booked in on certain days of the week.' She cleared her throat. 'The scheme is to be fully backed by the *Clarion* of course.' Under cover of the desk she crossed her fingers in her lap, praying that Gerry Bates would OK her idea before he found out that she had already involved him.

'Really?'

'But, of course, if you are going to veto it before it even gets off the ground, I shall have to tell the committee that you are against the idea of offering an extra and inexpensive incentive to attract summer visitors.'

'No, no! Not at all,' Dennis said, pushing his spectacles over the bridge of his nose and staring at her through them. Really, she might look young and fragile, but she was quite tenacious; the most persistent young woman he had met by a long chalk. 'By all means tell them that I feel the idea has possibilities.'

'Possibilities?'

Juliet gave him a steady look and he added, 'Yes, quite. *Distinct* possibilities.'

Juliet stood up and smiled at him. 'So, I have your assurance that the Romany families on Wycombe Heath will be allowed to stay and continue to live as they do now?'

He frowned. 'I didn't say that.'

'If I might warn you, Mr Maybury, try to make them move and Warnecliff will lose its Romany Museum.'

Dennis leaned forward. 'Miss King, you are jumping the gun. The museum does not as yet exist.'

'But it will, just as long as those houses don't get built.'

He stared at her for a long moment, his eyes glinting with the knowledge that he held the trump card, then he leaned across the desk and said in a low voice, 'I'll probably get shot for telling you this, Miss King, but planning permission for the gypsy housing scheme has just been turned down.' As her face dropped in surprise he added, '*Indefinitely*. Good afternoon, Miss King.'

To Juliet's surprise, Gerry was pleased with her Romany article.

'Yes, very entertaining and educational,' he said, removing his pipe from his mouth. 'Ask Bill to find a space for it next week sometime.'

'Can we have a photo to go with it?' Juliet asked.

Gerry removed his pipe. 'Depends how much space Bill can spare. See him about it.' He looked at her thoughtfully. When she hesitated he asked abruptly, 'Well?'

'I – er – wanted to talk to you about something else.'

'Thought as much.' He sighed and laid the pipe down on the over-full ashtray. 'I'm getting to know that look. Right, what is it?'

'Since I spoke to you about the rehousing scheme I've found out that planning permission has been withdrawn,' she said. 'Indefinitely.'

'Huh!' He leaned back in his chair. 'I see, so there's no problem with the gypos now? No need for this article in other words?'

'Well, not quite.' She outlined her plan for the gypsy museum and revealed that she'd already drafted a letter to the Entertainments Committee with the idea. 'But if I could add that the *Clarion* is backing the idea and is prepared to give it some free publicity. . . .'

'Absolutely not!'

Juliet's heart sank. 'But it's a very good idea. And it would be an asset to the holiday programme.'

'A good idea? *Whose* idea, may I ask?'

'Well, mi—'

'*Yours* – exactly!' He picked up the article and waved it at her. 'And I suppose this is by way of being your opening gambit.'

'Please, won't you think about it, Mr Bates?' She half closed her eyes. 'I can already see colourful posters all over town advertising the Romany Museum. We could even be the first in the country. It could be a big talking point.'

'It could indeed! And who, may I ask, are you going to persuade to print and distribute your colourful posters?' he asked.

'I'll find someone,' she told him defiantly. 'If not I'll do it myself.'

'I don't doubt it.' Gerry bristled. 'But this time the answer's a definite no. As usual you're getting much too far ahead of yourself, Juliet. It's my neck on the line at the end of the day; me who has to answer to the newspaper's owner and in my opinion, this is far too prejudiced to run. I'll publish your article but that's where I draw the line. Right?' He pointed the stem of his pipe at her.

'Yes, Mr Bates.'

As she turned to the door, a downcast expression on her face he shouted, 'And I want fifty words cutting out of that article before it goes to press, miss. It's too flowery – too flowery by halves! This is the Warnecliff *Clarion*, not *The Times*!'

It was ten minutes later that Bill Martin caught Juliet in the kitchen, tears trickling down her cheeks as she made the afternoon tea.

'Juliet?' He took her by the shoulders and turned her to face him. 'This isn't like you. What's wrong? Gerry been barking at you again?'

'It's not that,' she sniffed, glad that she hadn't confided her idea about the museum to Bill. 'I'm just a bit . . . bit tired, that's all.'

He handed her a large clean handkerchief. 'Here, take this. I'll make the tea, you sit down.' As he poured boiling water into the teapot he glanced at her out of the corner of his eye. 'You haven't been looking yourself for some days now. Not coming down with something, are you?'

She shook her head. 'No, I'll be fine. Just had a few personal problems lately.' She blew her nose on Bill's hanky and dabbed her eyes. 'By the way, Gerry wants me to cut fifty words off the gypsy article. I'll do it tonight.'

He smiled. 'Fifty words? Rubbish. It's fine as it is. We'll get Fred to pop out and take a couple of shots of the camp tomorrow evening and it can go in next Tuesday. It'll make a nice spread.'

'Oh, Bill, you are a dear. Are you sure?'

He winked. 'You bet. Gerry'll never know the difference. He just likes to have the last word, that's all.'

Juliet didn't feel like going straight home that evening. Instead she walked along the promenade. Most of the visitors had gone back to their hotels for their evening meals, but there were still a few holidaymakers on the beach. She watched as a young couple ran down the beach hand in hand and into the sea together, laughing and screaming as the water chilled their sun-warmed skin. For a few minutes they swam together then stopped to tread water, the girl's arms round the boy's neck as they kissed. She turned away, ashamed of watching, so envious of their carefree happiness.

Marcus had already left for the theatre when she arrived home and she was relieved. Relations between them were still strained. They spoke to each other only when it was necessary. She was all too aware that something must be done about it soon. They could not go on like this, but she was not yet ready to forgive her father for the lies and duplicity he had kept up over so many years – her whole lifetime.

She was making herself some supper when there was a knock at the back door. She opened it and gasped with shocked surprise to find herself looking into Adam Kent's face. He was quick to pick up on her revulsion. His darting brown eyes glittered with amusement.

'Well, well, if it isn't the lovely Juliet herself.'

'What do you want?' she demanded.

'Your dad in, is he?'

'No, he isn't. And if you know what's good for you you'll leave now and never come back.'

He shook his head assuming a look of disappointment. 'Ah, now, is that a nice way to treat an old friend who's come a long way to see you?'

'Let's not beat about the bush,' Juliet said. 'You're here to try to extract more money out of my father. It's called extortion – blackmail to you.'

He stepped back, his eyes widening in mock horror. 'Are you suggesting that I'd stoop to blackmail?'

'I'm not suggesting anything; I'm accusing you. But it's over. You've had your last payment. I know everything that you could possibly hold against him,' she told him. 'I've met Christine, my mother, and I know the whole story. I know what you did all those years ago – you and your devious sister.'

'You mean you know *her* version of it. Are you telling me you'd take the word of a jailbird?'

He was blustering, but she knew she'd got through to him now by the change of expression on his face.

'I'm closing this door now,' she told him. 'And then I'm going to telephone the police and tell them everything.'

His foot shot out and planted itself in the gap. He leaned forward and thrust his face close to hers. 'Call the police, eh? You want it to get into all the papers again, do you? Want to take me to court? If you do, Marcus King's acting career will be well and truly up the creek.'

'D'you know, I don't think he'll care,' she said. 'You and your sister ruined his career long ago and since then you've been bleeding him dry. It'll be worth a smashed career to see you go down. You saw my mother sent to prison for something she didn't do. You ruined three lives and you're still expecting to be *paid* for it? Well now it's your turn for a prison cell, Adam Kent. You think I won't go to the police? Just try me.' She looked down at his foot. 'What are you going to do, force your way in? Give me something else to charge you with?'

There was a pause during which Juliet's heart thumped so loudly that she was afraid she might faint. Then to her relief he stepped back. His face had turned a sickly yellow and his eyes looked wild. 'You haven't heard the last of me,' he muttered.

'No, next time I'll be reading about you in the papers! And I hope they give you a good long sentence.' She slammed the door and locked it, leaning against it as she waited for her heartbeat to slow. She heard his feet going down the drive and watched from the kitchen window as he climbed into a battered car and drove off. Going into the hall she lifted the telephone receiver then she stopped. Adam had been right in one thing. If he were to be charged Marcus would never get the job Max had promised. He would never get another job at all if the whole miserable scandal were to be resurrected. She longed to see Adam and Olivia get their just deserts but she couldn't do it to Marcus. It told her one thing: that whatever he had done she couldn't stop loving her father. She was going to have to put the past behind her and forgive him – and regrettably Adam Kent was going to get away with it all.

CHAPTER SEVENTEEN

Juliet woke at first light on Sunday morning and found it impossible to get back to sleep. Finally she got up and dressed. From her window she could see that the gypsies were already preparing for the day. The younger members of the group would be leaving for East Anglia for the soft fruit picking. Only the older women and men would remain to keep an eye on the camp and make supplies of goods to sell when the fruit and hop seasons were over. Juliet decided to go across and break the news to Celina that Gerry had refused to back the proposed museum.

As she approached the camp a thin column of smoke arose from where Celina was frying breakfast on a grid placed over the fire. She looked up as Juliet approached.

'Good morning, my lovey. You'm up bright an' early. Take a bite o'breakfast with us?'

Juliet's mouth was already watering at the smell of frying bacon, but she shook her head. 'I can't eat your rations.'

Celina shook her head. 'The farmers our lads work for never lets us go short,' she said. 'Always generous with their eggs an' bacon.'

They ate their breakfast inside the vardo with Tom who would be off with his friends shortly. He was a strapping lad of sixteen with his mother's dark eyes and glossy black hair. He wore a check shirt with a red kerchief tied round his neck and Juliet thought he looked every inch a Romany, as she tucked into her bacon and eggs.

'The man from your paper come and took photographs of us yesterday,' Celina said. 'Some of our folks weren't keen but when I told them you'd written a nice piece about us that was goin' to be in the paper they calmed down.' She popped a large piece of fried bread into her mouth and chewed thoughtfully. 'But I'm afraid to say, my lovey, that they'm not happy with your idea of showing folks round – what d'you call it – a museum? No, when I put it to them they weren't for it at all. They all say the same – that we'm human-bein's not curiosities to be put on show.'

'I understand.' Juliet nodded, wondering briefly why everything she'd tried lately had turned to ashes. 'It's all right, Celina. It was just an idea.' She laid down her knife and fork. 'But I hope my article will explain to people that you're to be respected. And I do have some good news for you.'

'What might that be?'

'They're not going to build the houses after all. The Ministry of Works has refused planning permission. I imagine there are too many people who *do* want houses.'

Tom let out a whoop of joy and ran off to tell the others whilst Celina took the news more philosophically.

'Well now. That's a relief and no mistake. We got you to thank for that my pretty.'

Juliet shook her head. 'No. I didn't do anything.'

'You do more for folk than you know,' Celina said. 'A good heart, that's what you got, child. Just like your auntie.' She smiled. 'An' I knows that today's special for you. Ain't I right?'

'Special?'

'Unless I'm mistaken this is your birthday.'

Juliet gasped. She had completely forgotten. 'So it is. But how did you know?'

'I got everybody's birthdays written down,' Celina said. 'Your auntie told me back when you was a chavvie, an' it went in my book along with all the others.' She got up and went to a box in the corner. 'I got a little somethin' for you.'

She took out a tiny package of tissue paper tied with ribbon. When Juliet opened it she found a silver ring with a curious Celtic looking knot fashioned into the silver. She slipped it onto her middle finger and found that it fitted perfectly.

'Oh, Celina, it's lovely,' she said. 'So unusual.'

'That's a Romany love knot,' Celina told her. 'Our Petulengro makes 'em. He's our blacksmith. He shoes the horses; makes wheels and mends the vardos and such. You'd never think them big hands of his could make anything so delicate, would you?'

'No. It's lovely,' Juliet turned her hand this way and that, admiring the ring.

'It's to bring you luck,' Celia told her. 'An' it makes you one of us.

210

Any Romany what sees you wearin' that'll know you'm a friend.' She touched Juliet's cheek. 'I hopes it'll bring you what you deserve, my pretty.'

Juliet kissed Celina's cheek. 'Thank you so much. I'll wear it always. It's a great honour.'

As she walked back across the heath the sun was climbing in a cloudless blue sky. The gypsies would have a good day for their travelling. As she let herself in at the back door she saw that the kettle was already boiling. Marcus must be up already, surprising for him, especially on a Sunday. Then she saw the tray on the kitchen table. It was laid with one of Granny's daintily embroidered tray cloths and a little vase held a single rosebud from the garden. A plate, cup and saucer were from Granny's prized Derby tea set. She was still looking at them when the door opened and Marcus walked in. His face fell when he saw her.

'Oh! I thought you were still asleep. I was going to bring you breakfast in bed.'

'I've been up ages, Dad. I've been down to have breakfast with Celina.'

'You've had breakfast? Oh.'

He looked so crestfallen that she laughed. 'It's all right. I've got room for a slice of toast and a cup of tea.'

'It's your birthday,' he said. 'I wanted to surprise you. I wanted – *hoped* – to make up to you a bit for . . . well, you know.'

'Oh, Dad.' Her heart full she went to him and put her arms around his neck. 'We can't go on like this, can we?'

He rested his chin on top of her head. 'I've been so miserable. You're my life, Ju. You mean so much to me. You always have. If it takes me the rest of my life I'll make up to you for what I did – for keeping you in the dark. I promise you I thought it was for your own good.'

'I know.'

He reached into his dressing-gown pocket and handed her a small package. Inside she found a single pearl on a fine gold chain.

'Oh, Dad, it's lovely. Thank you.'

He looked down at her. 'It's far less than you deserve. This is your twenty-first and I'd like to have bought you something special – a car, or a mink coat or something.' He kissed her forehead. 'Maybe next year eh?'

She reached up to kiss him. 'This is fine, Dad. I love it.'

'I've arranged another little treat too,' he said. 'I've booked a table for lunch at the Feathers.' He hesitated. 'I hope you don't mind but I've invited Maggie to join us.'

She smiled. 'Of course not. I like Maggie.'

'I know you do and to tell the truth I didn't quite know if we'd have made up by today and I thought. . . .'

She laughed. 'No need to draw me a picture.'

As they sat over their toast and tea Marcus glanced at her. 'Ju, what about Max?'

She shook her head. 'Shall we not talk about him today, please?'

'You can't give him up because of—'

'Dad! Not *today*.'

'OK. You're the boss; not today.'

As the three of them sat in the restaurant over lunch it became clear to Juliet that Marcus and Maggie had become quite close. She was pleased. Maggie had the right down-to-earth, practical nature needed to keep Marcus's feet firmly on the ground. When the meal was over and they sat in the lounge with their coffee Marcus leaned towards her.

'Ju, I hope you don't mind, but I've told Maggie what you might call our family secret. She knows what happened to us – to Christine and you – because of me.'

Juliet swallowed hard and looked across the table at Maggie. They must indeed have become close if Marcus had entrusted that much of his past to her.

Maggie said, 'Don't worry, it's strictly between ourselves and I'm not one to judge. What's past is past as far as I'm concerned and I've always believed that we pay the price for what we do, as Marcus certainly has.' She reached across to touch Juliet's hand. 'You are who you are, darling; a fine girl. Marcus doesn't deserve you but he does love you nevertheless.'

'I know he does,' Juliet said. 'And now can we lay it all to rest? No need for any of us to bring it up again.'

The others agreed, but Juliet knew that it would never be forgotten as far as she was concerned. She was still 'paying the price' as Maggie put it. And would go on paying it for a very long time.

Later that evening Marcus and Maggie decided to go out for a drive in Maggie's car. They invited Juliet but she refused, reluctant to play gooseberry. She said that she'd been up early and was tired. Some time later she was listening to a play on the radio when there was a knock on the door. She opened it to find Sylvia outside.

'Sylv! What a surprise, come in.'

'I didn't want you to think I'd forgotten your birthday,' the other girl said. ' 'Specially as it's the big one this year. I've brought you a card and a little present. I did come earlier but you were out.'

'Yes. Dad took me out to lunch.'

'Lovely. Lucky you.' She paused. 'It's mine this year too as you know. Mum and Dad are giving me a party at a restaurant in town.'

'That'll be nice. I didn't want any fuss.'

'No, well you know how many relatives we've got.'

'Yes, I suppose they'll expect it.' Juliet put the kettle on for coffee and they sat opposite each other at the kitchen table as they had so many times in the past. Juliet opened her card and present and found that Sylvia had bought her a pretty scarf. She slipped it round her neck.

'Thanks, Sylv. It's just my colour.'

'Sorry it's not more, but I'm saving up as fast as I can.'

'Really? For something special?'

'I'll say!' Triumphantly, Sylvia held out her left hand, the third finger of which sported an engagement ring. Juliet's eyes opened wide.

'Wow! That's a surprise. Who's the lucky man?'

'What do you mean, *who*?' Sylvia bridled. 'Nigel, of course. Who else? I'm not as fickle as all that.'

'Nigel!' Juliet was taken aback. 'It's very quick.'

'Not really. Actually I think it was love at first sight – for both of us. And it's all thanks to you for introducing us,' Sylvia said. 'We intend to get married as soon as Nigel gets out of the army and some of them are getting out now after eighteen months so it won't be long. I'll want you to be a bridesmaid, of course.'

'Won't he have to get a job first?' Juliet ventured.

'Job?' Sylvia stared at her. 'He'll have one, won't he?'

'Will he? Where?'

'At the *Clarion* of course. You must know you're only filling in for him. They promised to keep his job open for him.' Seeing the shocked

213

look on her friend's face she added, 'Well, it's only fair, isn't it? He didn't *ask* to join the army for two years. Most firms are doing the same.'

'Yes . . . yes of course they are.'

Juliet tried hard not to let Sylvia see how shocked and upset she was by her casual revelation but the other girl was so preoccupied with excitement over her engagement that she doubted she would have noticed anyway.

After she'd gone Juliet sat down to think. She might have known that Nigel would want his job back when he'd finished his National Service. She shouldn't really be surprised and she certainly didn't grudge him the job, but where did that leave her? It was suddenly as though everything was pointing to her leaving Warnecliff. Now that she'd reached her twenty-first birthday Heathlands Cottage would be hers legally. She would be entitled to sell it and move on – try to make a new life for herself – an unimaginable life without Max. But she hated the idea of selling the only family home she had ever known. She decided to sleep on it and say nothing to Marcus until she had come to some kind of decision.

The morning's post brought a card and present – a generous cheque – from Marion and Elliot in Canada. The accompanying letter repeated Marion's invitation to come and visit. Juliet folded the letter with a sigh, reflecting that she would have been able to write with the news that she was coming over very soon if fate hadn't cruelly stepped in to prevent it. When she arrived at the office she decided to go and see Gerry, ask him outright whether she should be looking for another job.

'But I thought you knew the position was only temporary,' Gerry looked genuinely taken aback.

'No one ever actually said so,' Juliet reminded him.

'But you knew young Forbes – knew he was only leaving to do his National Service.'

'That's true. I suppose I should have put two and two together.'

'That's not good enough.' Gerry shook his head. 'You should have been put in the picture. I'm sorry about this, Juliet. You've worked hard since you've been with us. You've got the makings of a very good journalist. Whatever you decide to do you can be sure I'll give you a very good testimonial.'

'Thank you.'

'But there's a while to go yet, isn't there?' he said in an attempt to be positive. 'I mean, no need to start clearing your desk yet.'

'No, of course not.' Juliet didn't tell him that she was already planning to look for a new job as soon as she could. There was no reason to stay on now, and the constant risk of a chance meeting with Max was shredding her nerves. So much for Celina's lucky ring, she told herself bitterly.

Marcus was the only one sitting at the bar in the greenroom. The curtain had come down on the Saturday evening performance almost an hour ago, but he was reluctant to go home until he had done what he knew he must do. He ordered a beer. It wasn't that he needed or wanted a drink. Somehow these days alcohol was neither important nor necessary to him. He'd been happier this summer than he could remember being for a long time and it was all down to Juliet: the wonderful daughter who was eating her heart out, her future in ruins because of his past selfishness. Maggie had never spoken a truer word when she said that he didn't deserve her.

It was only the previous evening that she'd told him about Adam Kent's visit when she was alone last Sunday evening. He winced inwardly when he imagined how afraid she must have been. Nevertheless she had stood up to him, telling him he now had nothing to use as a blackmailing tool and threatening to go to the police. She could and *should* have done it, too. But at the last minute – as usual – her only thoughts had been for him, Marcus, and the effect of a court case on his career and happiness. Still, he assured himself, Kent would be looking over his shoulder for some time to come. That should take the smirk off his nasty little face.

Juliet had also told him that her present job with the *Clarion* was only temporary and that she had asked for a few days off so that she could go up to London and try to find out what chance she had of finding a job there. Clearly, whatever the outcome, she intended to leave Warnecliff.

'Marion's birthday cheque and what I've managed to save will keep me going till I find another job,' she told him.

Trying to hide his dismay, he'd asked, 'What about the cottage? It's yours to sell and I wouldn't blame you if you wanted to benefit from the sale of it.'

'No, Dad. It's always been the family home. I'd like to have somewhere to come home to. And I'll need a caretaker too, won't I? Are you up for the job?' She'd given him a grin and he'd caught a glimpse of the old Juliet – the one he loved, the one who used to sparkle with youth and happiness until recently.

'You can pay me rent though if you like.' She suggested. 'That'd come in useful.'

'Of course I will,' he answered quickly. 'I can afford it now and it's only fair – the least I can do.'

Marcus sighed, regretting the little he'd done for his daughter over the years. He knew that she'd tried hard to throw herself into her work to ease the pain of what she saw as the necessary parting from Max, but nothing she tried seemed to have worked out and now it seemed she was to lose her hard-won job as well. It was so unfair. He knew there was only one way to make her happy again, but even that was far from guaranteed. This time though he must be the one making the sacrifice. He couldn't allow her to ruin her life.

That morning Max had called him into his office and asked him for his permission to put his name forward as a possible replacement for him at the Theatre Royal. Marcus had assured him that it would be a wonderful opportunity. Now he felt guilty. It was going to feel like benefiting from Juliet's misery.

'Hi there! Still here?' Max walked into the empty greenroom. Like Juliet, he looked tired and drawn, and in that second Marcus made a momentous decision. It had to be now – tonight.

'Just having a last drink,' he said.

'Great minds think alike, as they say.' Max ordered a whisky and hoisted himself onto a stool next to Marcus. 'Not in a hurry to get home to Juliet then?' he added with studied nonchalance.

Marcus looked at him. 'Max, have you done anything about the job you mentioned yet?'

'Yours, you mean?'

'Yes.'

'No. Why, having second thoughts?'

'No, but there are some things I feel you should know.'

Max cocked an eyebrow. 'Things? About what, or who?'

'About me – and inadvertently Juliet.'

The smile left Max's face. 'That sounds serious.'

'It is.'

'OK. Fire away then.'

Marcus glanced across to where the barman stood polishing glasses, his ears alert, hoping for a juicy bit of gossip. 'Could we perhaps go to your office?'

'Better than that, come back to the flat with me.' Max tossed back his whisky and stood up. 'The car's round the corner. It won't take a minute. We can relax and be private there.'

'I don't want to intrude; your office will do.'

'No, it's fine. I'm not too keen on my own company tonight anyway.' He gave Marcus a rueful grin. 'Or any other night, come to that.'

At the flat Max offered Marcus the choice of a drink or coffee. Marcus chose coffee. He needed to keep a clear head. When they were seated opposite one another Max looked across enquiringly. 'So, what is it you want to tell me?'

Marcus cleared his throat. 'I hardly know where to begin, but I suppose the beginning is the best place. Success came to me very early in my career,' he said. 'Too early. It made me arrogant and conceited. There were always girls at the stage door. I knew I could have my pick. But there was one in particular. Her name was Christine.' He went on to relate their blossoming love affair and subsequent moving in together – later his neglect and deceit towards Christine who loved him, even to his own family. When he paused and took a long draught of his now cold coffee Max guessed that what was to come was going to be even more difficult.

'I'll make some fresh coffee,' he said, picking up the tray. 'You look as though you could do with some.' He went through to the kitchen, allowing Marcus a few minutes to collect his thoughts.

As he poured the fresh, hot coffee he glanced up at Marcus. 'Go on. I'm still listening.' He passed Marcus a steaming cup. 'But are you really sure you want to tell me? All of this is a very long time ago. I can't really see why I need to know.'

'Please, bear with me.' Marcus took a long drink of his coffee. 'This isn't easy but I have to get it off my chest and I promise you, it does concern you.' He put down his cup and went on, 'Juliet is Christine's daughter; Christine's and mine.'

'I'd already guessed that,' Max said quietly.

'I meant to marry her, I really did, especially after Juliet was born.' Marcus sighed. 'But I'm afraid I neglected her shamefully.' Haltingly he went on to describe what had happened on the night of Christine's arrest and what followed.

'I did what I thought was best at the time,' he said. 'Looking back I realize that I should have trusted her. I should have known her well enough to be sure she wouldn't do anything that would harm our child. The truth is I hadn't given myself the chance to know her at all. All I could think about was myself: my career, my reputation. And – God forgive me – relief that I had escaped being legally tied to her.'

'But you cared about Juliet.'

'Yes, I'd loved her from the first moment I set eyes on her, which was why I was so angry about the alleged neglect. I was determined that she wouldn't be brought up by strangers. But even in that I was selfish. I put all the work, all the responsibility on my mother and sister. I hardly ever saw the little girl I'd deprived of a mother.'

'And Christine?'

'Marcus sighed. 'She went for trial and was found guilty. The evidence was circumstantial and she had no character witnesses. I discovered much later that she was set up. A woman I'd become besotted with and her brother plotted to take her out of the picture, but the plan backfired on all of us.' He sighed. 'I daresay there are people who believe I was implicated in the plot, but I wasn't.' He put down his cup and saucer with an angry clatter. 'I was so self-obsessed, so blinkered, that I couldn't see the wood for the trees.'

Max was silent for a moment. 'I take it Juliet has always known all this,' he said at last.

'No!' Marcus shook his head. 'That's why I'm talking to you now. I refused to tell my family what had really happened to Christine. Fortunately it only ever got into the London newspapers. I let them think that Christine had abandoned Juliet. I thought it would be better all round if no one knew she was actually in prison.' He shook his head. 'Word got around in the business, of course, though. The scandal wrecked my career as a classical actor, abandoning Christine did me no good at all. The war and ENSA saved my bacon in a way. If it hadn't been for that I'd probably be sweeping the streets by now.'

'And all this time Juliet knew nothing?'

'No and I hoped she never would. What I never bargained for was that one day she would find her mother and stumble across the truth – as she did recently – quite by accident.' He glanced at Max. 'It was the weekend you and she spent in London.'

Suddenly everything fell into place for Max. He sat back in his chair with a sigh. 'Ah, the woman who couldn't receive a bravery award because of a prison record. Oh my God, poor Juliet.' Marcus's story explained a lot, but he still couldn't understand why she had sent him away and denied all feeling for him at a time when she needed his love and support most?

Marcus saw the question in his eyes.'Obviously it was a cruel shock for her to find that her mother was an ex-convict,' he said. 'Even though Christine was totally innocent it's still a stigma and, of course, she never had the means or the opportunity to clear her name. The fact that her mother and I were never married was a double blow to Juliet.' He swallowed hard and leaned forward, his head in his hands. 'That and having a liar and a cheat for a father have undermined her confidence – made her feel worthless.' He looked up at Max. 'She feels it isn't fair to impose herself on you, knowing her background.'

'Oh my God!' Max got up and began to pace the room. 'I don't believe this. Why couldn't she have told me the truth? Why couldn't she trust me? I *love* her, damn it! Surely she knows I'd do anything for her.'

'I believe you, which is why I'm here now, telling you all this. And if you want to change your mind about recommending someone as self-obsessed as I am to take your place at the Royal—'

Max stopped pacing to look at him. 'Marcus, all this – all you've just told me happened years – *decades* ago. It's no one's business but your own. Why do you think it would have any bearing on my opinion of you as an actor or director?'

Marcus felt the tension go out of his shoulders. 'Do you mean that?'

'Of course I do. The takings at the Royal have been up fifty per cent since the summer run. You were one of my boyhood heroes. I fashioned my whole future career on your work. And here *work* is the operative word. It's all I'm interested in.' He leaned forward. 'What you've told me tonight is between you and me. No one else needs to know anything about it. As far as I'm concerned there is no one better suited to take over from me than Marcus King and that is what I shall tell the committee.'

Marcus sighed. 'I can't tell you what this means to me. I promise you I won't let you down. You won't regret it.' He looked up. 'And Juliet?'

Max smiled. 'Yes, Juliet.'

'If you're planning to try and see her you're going to have to be quick. She's going up to London first thing tomorrow morning – catching the early train. Her case is packed. She's planning to get a job and move there permanently.'

'Then we shall have to think of a way to make her change her mind, won't we?'

Platform one at Warnecliff Central Station was almost empty. Apart from Juliet there were a few sleepy-looking night shift railway workers waiting for the train. It was chilly; a fine mist drifted along the line to bead all the benches with moisture so that sitting down was out of the question. Juliet would have welcomed a cup of coffee and somewhere warm to wait for the London train but the buffet was not yet open. Turning up the collar of her light summer jacket she perched on her suitcase and looked up at the big round face of the station clock. Another twenty minutes to wait. It was going to seem interminable.

Marcus had wanted to come with her but she had insisted that she would rather leave alone.

'I'm only going for a few days, Dad,' she told him. 'And you know how you hate getting up at the crack of dawn. I'll be back again before you know it.'

But now she wished she had let him come with her. Having someone to talk to would have helped to pass the time and take her mind off the fact that she was about to prepare to change her life – yet again. Marcus had been very late home the previous evening. She'd gone to bed early and wakened as she heard him come in. It must have been well after midnight. Putting her head round the bedroom door she had asked if he was all right and where he had been. He'd been slightly evasive, but she was glad to see that he hadn't been drinking. She guessed that he'd been with Maggie so she hadn't pressed him too hard. She was reminded momentarily of a remark that Max had once made: *'Sometimes I wonder which of you two is the parent'*. Max – she tried hard not to think of him but moments they had shared, things he had done or said were always popping into her mind. What hurt the most was the memory of his face. The way his hair grew and the tiny lines at the corners of his eyes. It was all but impossible to forget any of it and she knew it would be for a very long time.

Above her through the sooty glass roof of the station she saw that the clouds were beginning to clear and a few rays of weak sunshine pierced the gloom. Maybe it wasn't going to be such a bad day after all.

A railway worker passed her pushing a trolley and she asked him, 'Is the London train on time?'

He nodded. 'Better be, miss. This one brings the morning papers.' He looked at her. 'Got your ticket?'

She shook her head. 'The ticket office wasn't open when I arrived.'

'Well, sometimes the train comes in early but there's a bit of unloading to do so there's no hurry to board.' He looked at his watch. 'Office'll be open in another five minutes so you can get your ticket then.' He trundled off down the platform, whistling tunelessly as he went.

Perched on her suitcase Juliet felt cold and tired. She hadn't slept well last night and getting up so early had been hard. She wondered what her chances were of getting a job in London. She planned to go and see the editor who had been kind and encouraging to her before. How long ago that seemed and how much had happened since. She had inherited a house, found work for Marcus and a job for herself – found her mother and learned the shocking truth about her background – fallen in love with Max. She shook her head, quickly dismissing the memory. There she went again, every line of thought seemed to lead her to the same end – a heartbreaking dead end.

The big minute hand of the station clock jerked two minutes nearer her time of departure and Juliet stood up. The ticket office should be open now. She'd go and buy her ticket. That would use up a few more minutes of the waiting time.

Just as she reached the window the ticket clerk rolled up the shutter with a clatter and smiled out at her in surprise.

' 'Mornin', miss. Not many waitin' for me to open up this time of a mornin' Most of the commuters've got their season tickets. Day return, is it?'

'No, just a one way,' she told him. 'I'm not sure when I'll be coming back.' She was just handing over her money when a hand shot out and covered hers.

'Put your money away, Juliet. Change of plan.'

Startled, she looked up and found herself looking straight into Max's eyes. Her heart gave a lurch. 'What are you doing? I've got a train to catch. It'll be here in a minute.'

'There are other trains if you really have to go. We have to talk first.'

She couldn't look at him. 'There's nothing to talk about.'

'Oh, but there is – so much. Please, Juliet.'

The ticket clerk was looking from one to the other with increasing interest. 'You got another ten minutes, miss,' he said helpfully. He leaned forward until his nose almost touched the glass partition and whispered, 'Why not give 'im a chance, eh? Buffet'll be open by now.'

Juliet pushed the cup of coffee that Max placed in front of her away. 'I don't want anything. Why are you here? Why do you have to make it so difficult? Why can't you just let me go?'

'The answer to that is simple,' he told her softly. 'Because I love you.'

She sighed and looked at the table, feeling suddenly overwhelmed. 'You don't understand. You're making this so hard for me.'

'I do understand, Juliet. Marcus and I had a long talk last night. He came back to the flat with me. He told me everything – about his past; about your mother and what happened all those years ago. He's devastated that you're throwing your life away because of what he did.'

'He had no business to tell you.'

'Don't underestimate him. It took a hell of a lot of courage. Don't you see, Juliet? He's desperately trying to make amends – to put right what he did almost two decades ago. He was convinced that he might lose his chance of a good job because of telling me, but he did it just the same. He did it for you, Juliet, for you and me. Are you going to tell him he did it for nothing? Are you going to tell *me* that you meant it when you said you don't love me, because if that really is the truth just say so now and I'll get up and leave – never bother you again. And that's a promise.'

The hard knot in her chest and throat suddenly erupted and she choked on a sob. Tears ran down her cheeks as she fumbled in her bag for a handkerchief. Max silently handed her his.

'Come on, let's get out of here,' he said, pushing back his chair and taking her arm.

They walked to the end of the platform and he took her shoulders and turned her towards him. 'Juliet, don't you know that whatever or whoever you are, whatever you did or said, you are still the girl I love and you always will be. Nothing can possibly change that. Certainly not something that two other people did twenty years ago.'

Juliet swallowed hard. 'Your . . . your family. . . .'

He shook his head. 'What about them? They are no more interested in ancient history than I am. Why should they be? When they meet you they'll make up their own minds just as I did. We are what we are, Juliet. And you are the person I love more then life itself; the girl I want to be with for the rest of my life.'

She looked at him, her eyes huge and tear-filled. 'Are you sure – really sure?'

He threw out his arms exasperatedly. '*Sure*? Do you think I'd have dragged myself out of bed at this unearthly hour and chased you to this God-forsaken hole if I wasn't sure?'

She smiled in spite of herself. 'I suppose not.'

'You suppose not?' His voice was tender as he drew her closer. 'I still haven't heard you say it, Juliet,' he whispered. 'You still haven't taken back the worst words I've ever heard, the words that have made my life hell for the past couple of weeks.'

She hid her face against his shoulder. 'I'm sorry, Max. You'll never know what it cost me to tell you I didn't love you. I thought I was doing the right thing for you – saving you a worse heartache.'

'There couldn't *be* any worse heartache.'

'I've been miserable too because of *course* I love you – more than I can possibly tell you. I only hope . . .' The rest of her sentence was lost in his kiss.

They were still oblivious to the rest of the world when the London train drew in with a rush of wind, enveloping them in a cloud of steam. It stopped with a screech of brakes. Doors were thrown open and porters appeared from nowhere to load parcels of morning papers from the guard's van onto trolleys. A few drowsy-looking passengers alighted and made for the exit, barely noticing the embracing couple at the end of the platform. Max drew back his head to give her a rueful smile.

'I have to say you could have chosen a more romantic place for us to walk hand in hand into the sunrise,' he said.

Juliet shook her head, winding her arms around his neck. 'For me this will always be the most romantic place on earth,' she said happily. 'Platform one, Warnecliff Central Station.'✝